SNOWCASTLES
& ICETOWERS

DUNCAN McGEARY

PART ONE:

SNOWCASTLES

CHAPTER ONE

When Greylock descended the peaks of Godshome he was excited, yet strangely unafraid. The winds were cold and gusty, but he no longer cared—the harsh, pitiless message in his uncle's parting words colored his cheeks far more than the mountain winds ever could. At any other time he would have turned back, but now the words of the Tyrant still burned in his memory, and an angry, almost overwhelming resolve to prove his uncle wrong had cast out his last remaining fears of leaving the High Plateau. Exiled by his uncle, Greylock prepared to die. At times he looked over his shoulder, expecting with every glance to see the Tyrant's soldiers rushing down the steep slopes of Godshome after him. Already his knife had tasted blood for the first time, and he wiped his hands desperately to remove the sticky, drying fluid; but it clung to the cracks of his hand.

Above Greylock loomed the mighty crags of the mountain, wherein dwelt the gods themselves. Below him were the hot humid valleys, unnaturally green and warm; where, it was said, demons lived. A familiar litany came to mind almost unbidden. "Only on the High Plateau is it good and right and proper for man to live"—so taught the Gatekeepers, priests of the High Plateau.

Thus it was perverse impulse—anger at his uncle, and an even greater anger at the Gatekeepers—that sent Greylock downward; to seek not the cold bosom of the gods as was expected of him, but instead, to dare the warm clammy fingers of demons. Never before had any of his kind chosen to go down from Godshome. If ever his brethren

1

left the safety of the High Plateau, it was always upward to the sacred snows of Godshome they made their pilgrimage; never into the dreaded and unknown depths of the Underworld.

Like every child Greylock had learned the Holy Hierarchy of Tiers early in his life; drilled into him day after day by the gatekeepers. The Third Holy Tier, the lofty heights of Godshome, was the domain of the gods. The High Plateau was the Second Holy Tier of Existence, and the home of man. The First Tier of the Underworld, the Gatekeepers had taught, was the realm of demons. Greylock smiled grimly to himself. He was going where Keyholder had always said he would go, if a bit sooner than his old teacher had imagined!

Demons there may be, he thought, but it was his uncle's Steward he feared the most at this moment. When Carrell Redfrock discovered the direction his prey had escaped, there would undoubtedly be pursuit. Next in the line of succession by virtue of his office, the Steward would not rest until he was certain that the only surviving blood heir was truly dead. Greylock knew that the Steward no more believed in demons or gods than he did, but Carrell Redfrock would be relying on the cold ice of Godshome to rid him of his rival. He would not be certain of the deadliness of the Underworld's mythical denizen's.

His uncle, the Tyrant, had long ago fallen under the sway of the Steward Redfrock's intrigues. One by one, Greylock's brothers and cousins had been banished from the High Plateau, until only he survived. But his uncle had grown old, and had ignored his youngest nephew for so long that, for a short time, Greylock had hoped he could frustrate the Steward's schemes, and escape the fate the other members of the royal family had suffered. Then, one day, he too had dared to raise his voice in protest against the foolish teachings of the Gatekeepers, as had his three brothers before him. Too late, he had noticed the presence of his uncle's Steward hovering in the doorway.

Greylock could still summon the awesome scene that had passed before him that morning. He could still see the Steward Redfrock standing behind the throne, bending low, whispering the malicious rumor of his heresy into the Tyrant's ears; could still remember his uncle looking up, searching for him, at last seeing his only nephew across the crowded Court; could still feel within him the fear the Tyrant's icy gaze had created; could still hear his uncle's words ringing in his mind

"You are not of my family!" the Tyrant had roared. "You are Demon-spawn! I should have destroyed you the same day I discovered the perversion of your mother—and cast you down to the First Tier with her. Begone, Demon! I do not wish to see your kind in my Court again."

Already suffering from his final illness, the Tyrant still had enough spite and strength to rid his kingdom of the last threat from his own blood. Though the old man must have known he was dying, he had exiled the only legitimate claimant to the throne.

His uncle was hopelessly senile, Greylock realized sadly—or why would he have said such things? His mother had died at his birth—so Key- holder had told him, and the old priest had been there! Greylock could only shake his head in dismay at his uncle's foolishness. There would be months of bloodshed when the now hidden rivals emerged to fight for the title of Tyrant; and the ancient tradition of the men of the High Plateau to challenge their Tyrants would make the throne unstable for years to come. The Steward would find that not even his brutal tactics could secure his ambition without a long and bloody struggle.

Greylock knew that Carrell Redfrock would not cease in his efforts to destroy him until the throne, the wealth of the royal family, and—most especially—the Lady Silverfrost, were firmly and finally his. Once the Steward had taken Silverfrost as his wife, his power would be as secure as Greylock's had promised to be. If only Silverfrost had wed me long ago! Greylock thought. He would not have been exiled if he had married the Tyrant's only daughter, no matter what the blasphemy. But she had remained infuriatingly undecided up to the very moment of his exile.

His face flushed in anger as he recalled his leave-taking of her from the icetower of Castle-Guardian, overlooking the green garden of its Icemelt.

"Why do you not do as you are told, Greylock?" she'd asked petulantly. "Why must you always do what is forbidden? If you had not been so rebellious—if only I could have been sure of you—we would have married, and this would never have happened." She was idly pulling the red petals of a snowflower and letting them drop onto the fragrant shrubs far below. The petals made their way down through the leaves and fell lightly onto the dark earth, warmed by the volcanic activity beneath the High Plateau.

Greylock reined his impatience and tried once more to explain why he had chosen to journey to the Underworld.

"If I go upward to the Three Peaks, I shall die. I must prove that your father is wrong about the Gateway. If I can find the true course of the path, he will have to take me back. Don't you see that, Silverfrost?"

"Hurry, Greylock!" his sister, Ardra, had hissed from the door of the icetower's uppermost room, where she and Slimspear had stationed themselves nervously to watch for any sign of discovery by the Steward's soldiers.

Silverfrost turned from the open window, her light blond hair appearing truly silver as it caught the last rays of moonlight. Her face was uncharacteristically serious.

"You should trust in the gods, Greylock. Just this once, you should place your faith in them. If you did not doubt them so, Father would not have exiled you."

"You know I do not believe there is anything on the peaks of Godshome but the frozen bodies of other exiles; all of them blameless—sent there by the schemes of Carrell Redfrock. I intend to return and fight him, Silverfrost! But you must promise me that you will have nothing to do with him until I return. He is evil!"

"You know that I loathe him!" There was no mistaking the hate in her voice. By now, the first rays of sunlight were glinting off the white snows of the plateau and into the window of the icetower, already raising cold sweat from its walls.

"They are coming!" Slimspear shouted, and at the same moment Greylock heard the sounds of soldiers rushing up the icy steps notched into the tower. Four of the Steward's men burst into the tower room, bowling over the rotund shape of Slimspear, and rushed toward Greylock. The first soldier was impaled on his long royal knife, and in the stunned confusion that followed, Greylock shouted a hasty farewell to his sister and friend, thrust on his Talons, and leaped through the window, catching at the ice with the sharp claws to break his fall.

Luckily, Castle-Guardian, the snowcastle of his friend Slimspear's family, was perched on one corner of the huge glacial plateau that nestled between the Three Peaks of Godshome, looming over the tattered remnant of the trail called the Gateway. Since his route of escape was so near and unexpected, Greylock was able to leave the High Plateau without further challenge.

Suddenly, Greylock tripped over some loose rubble on the path, and almost pitched out over the steep cliff that bordered his road. Brought back to the present by this dangerous stumble, he watched his step carefully. The treacherous mountain trail was seldom used, and in places had crumbled away altogether. At its widest, the trail was no more than a few yards across, and at its most narrow there was no trail at all. Finally Greylock was forced to use his Talons—the slivers of animal horn with which the men of the High Plateau could grip the sheer and frozen sides of cliffs.

At first the sweet full air of the lower elevations had been like nectar to his spirits, adding spring to his step and a broad, brave smile to his face. Now the heat began to raise the sweat on his body, and the thicker air threatened to burst his lungs. His tread became heavy, firm, as if he could only by this solid step convince himself that he could go on. As it grew warmer—unnaturally hot, his senses told him—he kept his eyes open warily for any sign of demons.

He was by now within the layer of clouds that always carpeted the High Plateau, hiding the Underworld, and all he could see was a few feet of gray rock, glistening with moisture. He was relieved that he had not discarded his outer garments, in spite of what he considered an unbearable temperature. At any moment now the snows would begin to fall.

But the moisture he had detected never turned white, but instead began to fall as a thick, cloying rain. The wet droplets confused Greylock. Never before had he been below the snowline, and this soaking rain was more disconcerting to him than anything he had yet faced! Even in midsummer, the clouds dropped only snow or ice on the

5

High Plateau; never in memory had the temperature risen above freezing.

Suddenly—unexpectedly—he heard voices ahead. He stopped and peered fearfully into the murk. Demons! he thought, and just as quickly he was disgusted with his superstitious reaction. He didn't even believe in demons! He must control this foolishness! At these stern thoughts, the voices disappeared, confirming to Greylock that his fears were creating imaginary enemies. When he continued, he was purposefully striving to subdue his fears, and he stupidly, almost disastrously, failed to guard the trail behind him. Four soldiers, wearing the black crow insignia of the Steward, and moving with nervous and stealthy speed down the mountain path, were able to surprise him completely.

One of the soldiers could not keep from bellowing a shout of triumph at the sight of their prey, and only this warned Greylock in time. He whirled around, knife in hand just in time to deflect the first blow. He followed this parry with a stab under the extended arm of the soldier, who was pinned with a shocked look against the rock of the cliff. Then the other three soldiers were on him, and he went down heavily in a swirl of arms and legs. Greylock kicked out strongly, and connected. One of the attackers rolled over the cliff, and Greylock could hear his Talons scratch twice—and then heard the man scream as the claws failed to catch. To his dismay he saw the Steward's pet, a huge black mountain crow, fluttering onto the trail above them. The bird watched the fight from a safe distance, smoothing its feathers fastidiously. Greylock briefly wondered how much the bird understood, and for the first time he even wondered if the shiny black bird could somehow communicate with its master.

Suddenly, Greylock realized that they did not mean to kill him at all, but were seeking to capture him. Perhaps the Tyrant has changed his mind, he thought wildly. Far more likely, the Steward Redfrock wished to witness his rival's death personally, and had sent his noisome pet to oversee the capture.

Again Greylock thought he could hear voices drifting up the trail, even from beneath the heaving bodies and muffled grunts of his captors, and he cursed his mind for playing tricks on him at such a time.

He was already attributing intelligence to that bird; now he was hearing demons!

This time the soldiers also seemed to hear the sounds, and Greylock found himself struggling with men who were frozen with fear. Suddenly they released him, getting to their feet hastriyp- ready at that moment to face even the wrath of the Steward Redfrock rather than confront demons. Greylock also rose, at first wary and confused by his sudden freedom, but he quickly saw that the soldiers were not even paying attention to him. Instead they were peering fearfully into the thick fog. Even the crow had cocked its head at the unexpected sounds.

"Demons!" Greylock hissed, and the soldiers were gone, vanishing into the concealing safety of the clouds. The crow cawed once as it hopped nimbly out of the way of the retreating men, but it remained. Greylock thought with a smile that they would probably not stop running until they were safely behind the massive white walls of the snow- castles of the High Plateau. He threw a rock after them, attempting in the' same throw to hit the crow. But the crow dodged the stone, and remained poised to take off at the slightest threat from anything other than Greylock.

Greylock turned with grim determination toward the sounds. If he could not go up, then he would have to face the owners of those ghostly voices! Listening carefully, he found that the accents were strange, but except for a few words, he could understand them. There were at least two people from the sounds of the voices, an old man and a young girl. The girl was chastising her companion unmercifully.

"I shall never listen to you again, Grandfather," she was saying. "You promised me that there is Glyden on this mountain. You said it was just lying around waiting to be picked up. You swore that if we did not find any we would return home. Well, where is it?"

"There *is* Glyden, my dear," a mild voice answered. "We just have to go a little higher."

"If we keep going any higher, we shall be joining these gods of Godshome the Townsmen were speaking of. I'm not ready to join the gods, Grandfather! I will not go any higher until we have found some of this Glyden that is supposed to be so abundant."

7

"The Townsmen also spoke of Glyden, Mara. They promised me that there is a Room of Glyden near the top of this trail!"

"And you believed them?" she snorted. "Why don't they come up and get it themselves? I will never forgive myself for following you on another one of your wild chases for Glyden. It is the last time; you can be sure of that!"

"Just a little higher, Mara."

"No!"

"Well, at least you could block the wind a little, couldn't you? Are you a Wind-Witch or not? After all, I have contributed the fire."

"You would be lost without your fire-magic, Grandfather." The girl was not hiding her disgust. "I don't ever intend to so depend on my magic. The powers of the wind and fire were never meant for the trivial purposes to which you put them!" The voices continued to argue, but Greylock was satisfied at last that the owners of these two quarrelling voices could not be demons, and he was strangely certain that they would pose no threat to him. Nevertheless, to be safe he drew his knife before advancing cautiously down the trail. The crow hopped curiously after him, but he ignored it.

The clouds seemed to part reluctantly from the trail, inch by inch, until they were hovering finally about his head. The two strangers he had overheard were crouched over a small fire, set next to a crude wagon, which spanned the trail. Greylock saw a blue flame nakedly burning in the cupped palms of the man's hands, yet he could feel the fire's heat even from the distance he kept between himself and the two strangers.

Beyond this peculiar couple, Greylock was met by the sight of mile upon mile of green valleys and winding blue rivers stretching in every direction, a wondrous contrast to his white land of snowcastles. He was astounded by the colors, the growth, the free-flowing waters. So this was the Underworld that the Gatekeepers spoke of in such contempt! He would never have imagined such a beautiful vista as this!

If the effect of his sudden emergence from the clouds was astonishing to him, it was even more so to the two strangers crouched on the trail. To them it appeared as if Greylock had stepped out of the sky, a vision slowly materializing until only his head was still wreathed

8

in the white gossamer of the clouds. On his arms, appearing as a natural extension of his hands, were the sharp claws of his Talons. As he was slowly unshrouded, the young girl, with her mind still on the gods waiting for them in the mountains above, imagined the worst and screamed.

The old man's eyes widened and he stepped back in astonishment. He stumbled against the little cart he had been pushing, and it went over the side of the narrow trail. For a few seconds the old man tried to keep his balance, but then the huge crow—which Greylock had forgotten in his wonder at the Underworld's unveiling— inexplicably flew at the stranger, its claws digging at his face. The blue flame in his hands winked out as the old man protected himself, and he toppled over the cliff after the crashing cart.

Without thinking, Greylock jumped over the side of the cliff after him. He reached instinctively with his talons for cracks he could only hope were there. But his skill in climbing was such that he easily found the few holds that existed in the rock face, and solidly planted his Talons to stop his slide. Then he hurried down to where the old man clung desperately to the mountainside.

The stranger had slid twenty feet down the side of the pass before he had caught precariously at the hardy scrub brush that lined even the steepest of the slopes, wedged into every open crack in the mountainside. But the roots were dangerously shallow and the brush was slowly giving way to the old man's weight. He was in danger at any moment of sliding further down the steep slope, which ended in a sheer drop.

Greylock reached down with one arm while digging in with his Talons, and grasped the desperate man's wrist, knowing that he was probably causing the stranger pain, but hoping that the strength of his grip would also reassure him. He grabbed the man further by the back of his neck and dragged him, not gently, up to safety. Within a few minutes, the two men had crawled exhausted and covered with scratches over the lip of the trail. The old man fell into the waiting arms of the girl, glancing around him fearfully.

"Have you been hurt, Grandfather? That awful raven is gone now."

"Hush, girl!" the old man replied, as if the fall had never taken place. "Why did you scream? He is only a man, as anyone can see!"

"Grandfather!" she repeated, but this time in anger, not concern. "At least you could show gratitude to this stranger for saving your life."

"Yes, I have never seen such climbing!" Greylock shrugged away the girl's thanks, and the amazement the man expressed at his feat of climbing. How could he tell them that he had always had an affinity for the rocks and stones of the mountains. He did not deserve praise for this commonplace skill.

The two strangers and Greylock stood back now and examined each other openly. That the girl had mistaken him for a god was understandable, for Greylock was as tall and as handsome as any picture of a god she had ever seen. His black curly hair fell about his shoulders, and despite the cold, his chest, was bare. He was not heavy, but finely muscled, and he moved with quickness and grace, as they had just witnessed. The only feature that marred his aspect was a thick lock of gray hair that fell over his forehead, though he could not yet have reached his twentieth year. Right now, he was staring back with startled black eyes.

Most of this gaze was reserved for the other man. Greylock could not understand how a man this old could still be living! On the High Plateau such a man would long ago have sought the comfort of the gods before it was too late, or he was too enfeebled to reach the heights. Surely this man was on his way to Godshome now, and therefore could demand of Greylock whatever help and assistance he needed! The old man must be near death, Greylock thought, for the skin was drawn tight about his face and speckled with brown spots. Only the mass of brown hair belied for a moment Greylock's impression of great age, but then the man's severely deformed back obviously showed that he was very old.

He paid little attention to the girl during the first, brief scrutiny. That she was blond and green- eyed, and had reached an awkward age between child and woman was all he noticed. Obviously she had shot up in height recently, and she needed much more weight on her bones to be pretty.

"Who are you?" he finally demanded of them. "What are you doing down here?"

"Why are we *down* here?" the old man seemed startled by this unexpected question. "My name is Moag, a wandering conjuror of fire-magic. And this is my granddaughter, Mara, who also serves as my assistant. But I think before we answer any more questions, we should ask who *you* are, and why you are up here!"

Greylock was satisfied by their words and manner that this strange duo of conjurors were not Carrell Redfrock's spies. But then why were they here? Could they truly have journeyed from the Underworld? He was astonished to find any people on the trail at all, despite his claims of open-mindedness. Only now was his mind beginning to play with the startling idea that they had not come from the High Plateau.

"I am Prince Greylock," he said grandly. "I come from above the clouds, from a land of snow- castles and icetowers. I have been banished by my uncle, who is Tyrant of the High Plateau, and I seek the source of the Gateway." He could see from their amazed reactions that they were as surprised by his origin as he was of their existence. "Now, why have you come to the Gateway?"

The old man hesitated, but then greed got the better of his caution. "We have come in search of Glyden."

"What is Glyden?" It was one of the few words he had not understood.

"What is Glyden?" Moag exclaimed, not bothering to hide his disappointment; but the girl did not seem at all surprised.

"I *told* you there was no Glyden, Grandfather." "Hush, Granddaughter. Perhaps he has a different name for it." A crafty, hopeful look had entered the wizard's eyes. "It is a heavy, yellow metal, easily melted and malleable. Do you know of any in these mountains?"

By now Greylock was convinced that these two strangers had indeed emerged from the Underworld, where there should have been only demons. Perhaps no other citizen of the High Plateau, he thought, even Carrell Redfrock, would have been open to such an idea; but Greylock had entertained such ideas since childhood. For the first time he began to hope that there might be a future for him beyond the High

Plateau after all. But he would need these two strangers to help him. survive the Underworld, at least at first. How could he convince them to accompany him?

From the old man's description of "Glyden," Greylock was fairly certain that he knew of what metal they were speaking. He had to suppress a smile at the wizard's naked greed, as Moag waited for an answer from the man from the land of snow- castles. Obviously, this "Glyden" they spoke of had great value in the Underworld. Perhaps he could use this greed to his own advantage, Greylock thought.

"A yellow metal?" he asked, letting a naive bafflement cross his features. Then he allowed the hilt of his royal knife to be shown. "A metal such as this?"

The old magician almost leaped forward in his eagerness, but Greylock immediately shifted the knife back so that its long blade was facing forward again. Moag stopped at the sight of the gleaming steel.

"Yes, *that* is Glyden," he exclaimed uneasily. "I have promised my granddaughter that I would find her some nuggets for a ring. A worthless metal, of course, but it makes very nice trinkets. Where did you find it?"

Again Greylock had to suppress a smile at the wizard's transparent questions. "Why, Glyden is quite common on the High Plateau! As you say, it is handy for jewelry. We also use it to decorate our buildings— for roofs, and streets, and such."

Which was not quite true of course. Only the Tyrant and his family possessed Glyden, and even then it was used only for jewelry and weapons. Castle-Tyrant, the largest and most ornate of the snowcastles, had some etchings of Glyden on the inner walls, but that was all. No one knew where the metal had come from. Legends placed it in a "Room of Aurim" somewhere along the Gateway—of which the pitiful mountain trail they were now on was the lower reaches. The story Greylock had overheard the wizard tell earlier would not help the old man in his search—it was a tale which every child of the High Plateau knew and nurtured, in hopes of finding the "Room of Aurim." No trace of the metal had been found in its natural state.

Yet there was no denying the existence of the precious metal. It was far more valuable on the High Plateau than Greylock hinted; but judging from the wizard's reactions, not quite as valuable as it was in the Underworld.

The wizard Moag cleared his throat and glanced quickly at his granddaughter, who was still staring at the handsome stranger in amazement.

After leaving the last of the minor fiefdom of Trold, the wizard and his granddaughter had imagined that they were nearing the very ends of the world in their search for Glyden. The names of the lands they had passed through reflected this common belief of the Underworlders. First there had been Far Valley, with its BorderKeep nestled within. Then the endless-seeming, never-changing Twilight Dells. And finally the mountains themselves, dominated by the three spires of Godshome, their white tops barely visible from a great distance. Beyond that, no one they had questioned could say—or seemed to care. But the lure of Glyden and the many legends of its abundance had drawn the wizard halfway across the known world, and into the unknown. He would not stop now, just because of a lack of maps! So it was easy for Moag to believe a stranger's incredible story of riches, of a land where the houses were built of Glyden. After all, it was what he had come to hear.

"I thank you for your information, Greylock. We will not forget your kindness." Moag motioned for Mara to move along with an urgent wave of his hand from behind his back. "But we must be on our way. I have kept my granddaughter waiting for her ring of Glyden much too long. We'll just visit your land of snowcastles and icetowers for a little while, and perhaps pick up a few nuggets. Not enough for anyone to notice, of course." He said this in a rush, all the while trying to angle unobtrusively past Greylock.

But Greylock could not let them pass so easily, and quickly gave out the last piece of his hasty scheme. "Surely you do not mean to enter the High Plateau! They would consider you demons, of course." Recalling all the horrid legends of the Underworld, he chose the worst of them. "Did you know that they kill demons—then eat them?"

This last was a wild exaggeration, borrowed from the most horrible of stories about demons; but Greylock thought it likely that any strangers to the High Plateau would be instantly killed, on the assumption that they were demons.

"Eaten?" Moag finally managed to sputter, and for a few moments Greylock did not think his story would be believed. Then Moag fell silent, and he seemed to be weighing the risks. Glyden must be a great temptation indeed, Greylock thought, for the old man to even consider the risk of being devoured!

Suddenly, however, it was the girl who seemed to have grown suspicious. She had stood back and watched the conversation with narrowed eyes.

Now she asked, "You say Glyden is a common material where you come from, Greylock. Yet you, by your own account a prince, have a royal knife encrusted with this valueless metal."

"Yes, it is true," Greylock said with a tone of regret. "I am in disgrace in my uncle's eyes. I was fortunate to have been allowed a weapon at all." "Why are you bruised and bleeding? Have you been in a fight?" She barraged him with questions, while he tried desperately to think of an answer that would be believable.

"I must have cut myself sliding after your grandfather."

"Where did that raven come from? Was it a pet of yours?" she demanded.

"Hush, Mara! Quit pestering him!" The old man had ended his gloomy reverie, to Greylock's relief, just in time to forestall more embarrassing questions from the girl. Now he was looking at Greylock speculatively. "You say that you are the Tyrant's nephew. Would you also be the heir?" This was the kind of question Greylock had wanted. "So I would have been. But my uncle grows unfortunately senile, and banished his own heir."

"Your uncle is very old then?"

Greylock nodded.

"Well, Granddaughter," the wizard said heartily. "You must restrain your impatience for a ring of Glyden a little while longer. We must help this young man gain his rightful throne, which he has been so unfairly denied by the capricious whims of an old Tyrant. We must help each other, Prince Greylock! I have some influence in the world

14

below." Mara snorted at this, and the wizard glared at her sternly. "I shall get the help we need!"

"Do not tell me of the capricious whims of an old Tyrant!" Mara said scornfully. "And quit pretending that it is *I* who wants Glyden, Grandfather! You are not fooling anyone. If you are going to be taken in by another wild story of Glyden, then I cannot stop you!"

The girl's admonition prompted Greylock to look at her closely for the first time. Her blond hair had once again fallen into her eyes. She was constantly brushing her locks aside, he had already noticed, with a quick, impatient flick of her hand. Her eyes narrowed at every movement, and she seemed to scrutinize every word that was said. Though she was many years the younger, she seemed by her manner to be the older of the pair—that is, if age could be measured by suspicion.

Greylock sensed that the time would soon come when he would no longer be able to read the old man so well, or see through his blandishments. He guessed that if he had not overheard them on the trail, he would doubt the wizard's motivations even now. Greylock decided then that he would have to keep a close watch on the girl's suspicious but open expression instead—to keep a semblance of honesty in the new relationship.

"Well, Prince Greylock?" the wizard repeated. "Shall we be partners? All that I will ask of you is that you reward me for my help with a small measure of Glyden."

"It will not be easy, Moag," Greylock felt he should warn them of the danger they faced. He had lied enough. "It will take an army to enter the High Plateau from the Underworld. A very large army indeed if we wish to wrest Glyden from my uncle's kingdom. My people would fight what they consider 'demons' to the death."

Moag seemed eager to agree, despite the warning. "If we need an army, then we must journey to the fiefdoms of Trold! I know King Kasid personally." Again, the wizard glared warningly at Mara.

"Above all, I must command this army," Greylock continued to lay down his conditions. "The people of the High Plateau would never accept the rule of an Underworlder. No other exile has ever returned before—the snows have claimed them all—so I do not know what my reception will be. But perhaps by the time such an army has been mustered, I will have found the evidence I need to convince the Tyrant, and such a force will not be needed against the Steward. Perhaps "

"I am certain that King Kasid will help—for a price."

"Very well," Greylock said, at the same time surprised to find within himself the same cunning he had so often seen in his uncle. "Let us be partners then!" Whether or not the old wizard could actually fetch an army was doubtful, Greylock thought. But at least he would have Moag to guide him for the first part of his journey through the Underworld.

Suddenly, Greylock felt the urgency to hurry off the mountain, but without letting them know that they might be pursued. The soldiers would have returned by now, and Steward Redfrock would have been told that his enemy was still alive. At any moment now, another, more determined sortie of soldiers would be coming after him. And if the crow had gotten back sooner, and had somehow communicated what had happened, then this dawdling on the trail could be disastrous.

"I feel a storm coming," he lied, explaining that the people of the High Plateau could always feel a change in the weather. "We had better hurry off this exposed path."

Mara looked at him, suspicious of the sudden urgency in his voice, once again eyeing his bruises and obviously feeling that her grandfather was committing them to a dangerous partnership. But she followed Greylock without a word, for she too felt exposed on the high mountain trail.

Carrell Redfrock was at that moment angrily dismissing the two soldiers who had come back to report their failure. He made a mental note to find a proper punishment for them, but most of his rage had already dissipated. His Familiar, the black crow that the people of the High Plateau foolishly believed was a simple pet, had related what had happened minutes ago. Unfortunately, the Familiar had not stayed to see if Greylock was able to save the old man. But the Steward knew Greylock's climbing abilities well, and did not doubt he would succeed in retrieving the stranger.

Redfrock could not help but wonder at the coincidence that had placed two Underworlders on the Gateway at the same moment that

Prince Greylock descended. Only he knew how unlikely that was, for Greylock was wrong when he believed himself the only person of the High Plateau capable of going down from Godshome. The Steward Redfrock had made the trip several times long ago, in his search of methods to overthrow the Tyrant. He had come back with his Familiar — and the knowledge of powerful allies in the Underworld.

Redfrock berated himself for not considering the Gateway as an escape route for Prince Greylock. The youth had made his opinions well known. But the Steward had not believed Greylock would have the courage to face demons. Now, he had two reasons for making sure that his rival was dead. As long as the prince was alive he was a threat to the Steward's plans. But even more important, Greylock was now a threat to his Master.

It had been made clear to Redfrock that no one was to discover the true location of the Gateway, and for this reason the Steward had encouraged the superstitions of the mountain people. Now Greylock was very close to the truth, without realizing it. There was only one thing to do: he must send a party after Greylock. The youth must never discover the true entrance to Gateway, and the easiest way to accomplish this was to remove him from the Tiers of Existence.

He called back the two disgraced soldiers, who entered the room chastened and servile. "Gather a company of two dozen men, and go after Prince Greylock. I want him dead, and I do not want you to come back until that has been done. I do not care if you have to cross half of the Underworld — I want him dead!"

The two soldiers blanched, but immediately saluted and started to leave.

"No, wait!" he changed his mind rapidly. "I think I will have to lead this expedition myself. The Tyrant is already regretting his action. If Greylock should ever return, the Tyrant might even welcome him. I must be sure that never happens. Now go! We shall leave in the morning. One of you tell the Lady Silverfrost that I wish to have dinner with her tonight."

One of the soldiers hesitated, and the Steward demanded, "Well? What is it?"

"The Lady Silverfrost has already received your invitation, Steward. She … refuses to come." "She refuses to eat dinner with me?" Redfrock was incredulous. "I must believe that you did not ask her properly. Now go back and ask her again. Tell her it is my *wish* that she come to dinner— tonight!"

After the two soldiers had left hastily, the Steward smiled and turned, crooking a finger at the crow, which was perched on a dead trunk of a tree installed in the corner of his icetower. The Castle-Steward had the smallest of the High Plateau's Icemelts, but Redfrock did not mind. He had never cared for greenery, and he shuddered at the thought of descending into the Underworld again. He had no power over the denizens of the Underworld and he always felt vulnerable in its humid growth.

The crow jumped onto his shoulder and he began absently feeding it meaty scraps. Carrell Redfrock appeared slender and frail, and almost as old as the Tyrant—and he cultivated this image. For beneath his scarlet robes, the Steward was wiry and strong, and far from old. His carefully thinned white hair was swept back from his forehead, displaying his bushy white eyebrows and craggy features.

He maneuvered the crow to his gauntleted right hand. "Tell our friend in the BorderKeep that I am coming down from Godshome. If I do not contact him again, he should watch for a stranger with a lock of gray hair. He is to agree to everything this stranger asks. Is that understood?"

The black eyes of the crow seemed to stare back for a moment, and then the bird rose with the Steward's hand and launched itself noisily through the window of the icetower, where it was quickly lost in the night.

CHAPTER TWO

Greylock concealed from his new partners the fear he felt when the trio began to descend into the bright sunlight of the Underworld. It would not do for them to see that he was frightened of mere legends and superstition. They had already laughed heartily at his descriptions of grotesque ghouls, just as he had laughed at the horrible beings they had imagined lay in wait for them on Godshome.

Despite his own skepticism, and their reassurances, Greylock kept a wary eye open for demons, and his hands never strayed far from the Glyden hilt of his knife. He doubted, however, that any of his people would follow him this far down the mountain, even under the Steward Redfrock's dire threats. At least he was safe from that!

Greylock noticed that the wizard's covetous eyes rarely strayed from the gleaming Glyden for very long, and he even wondered briefly if he would be able to trust the old man not to club him on the head when he wasn't looking. He began to suspect that there was more than greed in Moag's looks of longing.

Little by little Greylock discarded most of his thick mountain garments, until he was left with a thin robe—and he was still sweating heavily beneath that light cloth. His new partners remained heavily bundled well into—what seemed to Greylock, at least—the hot and steaming foothills. The sharp claws of his Talons hung loosely from the hide straps tied to his wrists, to be taken up in his grip whenever the

19

trail became too rough and the Underworlders needed his help to get by the sudden gaps.

This became less and less necessary as the trail finally broadened near the bottom of the pass, and their progress speeded. He began to watch for any sign of the rubble and rusted iron that might indicate the ruins of Gateway's giant portals. He thought it unlikely that there was a gate at all—only a figurative closure from the Underworld, never opened until now. But he had doubts.

It was difficult to believe, for instance, that the narrow and treacherous trail they were now traversing, so long unused, opened near the upper reaches of the pass into a wide, magnificent roadway. It was this road, with its mammoth stones and intricate patterns, that had succeeded in raising doubt in Greylock's mind, and had kept him from discounting the ancient legends entirely. It was this remnant of the Gateway that the Gatekeepers were pledged to protect and maintain. Yet the road led nowhere, ending in the desolate snows of Godshome. Everyone knew that the Third Holy Tier contained nothing but the falling snows and howling winds of nature, and none had ever returned to tell of "gods." Greylock's mistake had been to say aloud that the passage of time had distorted the true meaning of Gateway, and it was this heresy that had finally given the Steward Redfrock the opportunity to disgrace Greylock in the eyes of the Tyrant. But if he could prove he was right, and that there was more to Gateway than this unused pathway, then his uncle would have to take him back, and allow him to wed Silverfrost.

The boundary between the mountains and the Underworld was clear, at least to Greylock. The ground seemed somehow tainted to him. It seemed as if he were stepping from a robust and cruel land to a sickly and even crueler land. Something within him, something that had never before been touched, was offended by the light loam earth, and he hesitated before he stepped onto it. The first few steps brought a violent shudder; a strange revulsion at the feel of the brown dirt beneath his feet. Greylock followed the wizard and the girl only because they appeared to be unaffected by it. Indeed, they didn't even seem to notice that this land was different, decaying.

Greylock could see layer upon layer of the emerald green valleys, and rounded foothills seemingly perched on top of each other, wreathed in swirling mists. The light appeared to grow dim, as if the sun had suddenly gone behind a cloud. Yet when Greylock glanced up, the shimmering globe of the sun still filled the sky. The heat grew even more intense, despite the darkness, and the unfamiliar itching discomfort of his sweat made him miserable. He was irritated when the other two travelers moaned their appreciation of the heat.

On a stone ledge overlooking a river that ribboned back and forth down the last of the steep slopes, Moag warned Greylock of the dangerous lands they were now entering. The wizard explained how the two had fallen on hard times in the Twilight Dells.

"I depend on the patronage of rulers and landowners," he said. "I do their bidding with my magic and they reward me with their Glyden. But in this land there are no rulers, no rich men. Each house is a stronghold for a small clan, and they jealously guard their own worthless territories, though each valley is small, poor, and infertile. I do not understand why they have not left this country long ago. This earth will yield no more!"

Old man Moag shuddered. "I have not eaten well or slept well since I entered this accursed land! We will find no armies among the Wyrrs. We must go beyond the Twilight Dells, beyond even the BorderKeep—to the glorious fiefdoms of Trold, my homeland! Let us travel as fast as we can through this country, for only death lies in its valleys."

Greylock realized that what the old man had just said explained his own uneasiness at entering this new country. But how had he known that the land was ill? It looked no different than any other land, the little he had seen of the Underworld.

Yet he did not raise this perplexing question, to his later regret, for he never suspected that it would concern him. Instead, he was much more interested in what he thought the wizard had just revealed. Greylock believed he had detected in the old man's words the real motivations for his greed—more, perhaps, than Moag may have wished. He eyed the mage's tattered garments doubtfully. "If the Kings of Trold would pay you in Glyden, then why did you not stay in Trold and earn their reward?"

"It is their Glyden, not mine," the wizard growled, his tone indicating that he did not like these prying questions. "The Glyden is never mine—it is the wages of a servant, and I do not wish to be a servant any longer."

"But if you are a magician, why do you not just summon the wealth you wish?"

"There are two things a wizard cannot conjure, and those are money and food. Nor may he conjure up anything for just himself. And he must be paid in Glyden for his services; only then is his magic released, to serve that person. Yet at the end of his service, he must give it all back! That is why the wizard is always under the domination of others; why he must always serve the rich."

So this was the reason for the wizard's single- minded obsession with Glyden! Greylock could see that the whole arrangement had obviously soured the old man, and it seemed Moag would be willing to travel anywhere and do anything to possess his own Glyden—for Glyden meant freedom.

"If only Mara and I had our own wealth!" the old man wailed. "A simple trade and we would be free. I would never have to serve another stranger again."

Mara, as usual, had the last word. "Of course, it never occurs to Grandfather that he might earn Glyden by some honest labor—say with his hands!"

Greylock soon learned that crossing this land of hills and sudden dales would not be easy. It was more a maze than a road, he thought, for they could not just cross any valley they wished, moving in a straight line that might reasonably have brought them to an end of the land. Instead they were forced to follow a winding course; halfway down one valley, only to retreat and move at right angles, and so on in an incomprehensible way, until Greylock was at last hopelessly lost, and dependent on the wizard completely to guide them out of this nightmare land.

Moag had apparently learned from bitter experience which valleys would prove friendly, or at least safe, and which were dangerous. "If I had not already traveled through this land," the old man said darkly, "it would take us a very long time to cross. But even now we must be careful. If we turn into the wrong valley we could be set upon and beaten. Or perhaps even killed. We must hurry to set our camp in a safe place, for it is in the dark hours that the Wyrrs truly have power we need fear."

So far the mage must be choosing correctly, Greylock thought, for they had yet to see any of the inhabitants of this land of constant evening, friendly or unfriendly.

"Where are they, old man? Hiding?"

"They are actually more frightened of us than we are of them," Moag explained. "Some great ill has crossed this land, setting neighbor against neighbor. Though each valley alone can afford only a poor existence, they never leave their own valleys as far as I know. I gathered from my inquiries at the BorderKeep that, just a few years ago, surviving such a trip as we are now on would have been unthinkable. But it seems that the natural human spirit is reasserting itself, and time is wearing away their fear. The Wyrrs are not as murderous as they once were, though there are still pockets "

"Why are they afraid?" Greylock asked, somehow moved by the plight of the Wyrrs.

"They do not say. I believe their crime was so dire that, whatever it was, they will never tell. Sometimes they seem to be watching, as if they are waiting for somebody. Perhaps that is why they no longer murder every stranger who steps into the Twilight Dells."

The three visitors moved carefully through valley after valley, each one seeming more silent and eerie than the last. Soon Greylock had the disquieting sense of being watched—but Moag hushed him quickly when he mentioned this.

"Put away your Talons, Prince Greylock. They look too much like a weapon. We do not want to provoke the Wyrrs."

"Are we not to fight if we are attacked?" "Perhaps not. You must let me decide. Only if our lives are in danger will you need to fight. They may just wish to taunt us."

"But how will you know?" Greylock had already decided he would fight.

"I may not!" the wizard answered cryptically and would not explain his answer. The old man's hunched back bobbed up and down in front of Greylock's eyes, forbidding any more questions.

Greylock compared what the old man had just told him to the legends in his own land about the Underworld, and was startled to see the similarities. Indeed, it did seem as if each "demon" was caged, only to strike out in murderous anger at interlopers. Despite the danger, Greylock almost wished that some of the strange natives of this land would show themselves. If what the old man had heard was true, it was no wonder that no one had emerged from the Underworld before—and that no one had dared to visit it!

Their torturous route began to seem to Greylock like one of the games of his childhood, when he and his friend Slimspear had explored the hundreds of caverns which served as a kind of highway beneath the snows of the glacier. There they had tried to lose each other by cunning turns. Now the trick was to find a path through adjacent valleys that were safe. Often the wizard would stop and frown and remain unmoving for long minutes of concentration, while Greylock would wait impatiently. Greylock began to suspect that the old man was also lost, but since he had long ago lost his own way, and had only Moag to guide him safely out of the puzzle, he said nothing.

Occasionally they could see the roofs of the Wyrrs' crude dwellings at the ends of the valleys, but Moag was careful not to wander too close to the interiors, and they remained unmolested that first day. The old wizard actually seemed to cheer up as they made camp in one of the few empty dells, near the ruins of an old shack, with its gray wood hanging over them, decaying and moldy.

Before daylight had completely left the valley, Greylock caught Mara staring at him surreptitiously with a wondering look. She turned away quickly at his scowl. For some reason, Greylock was irritated by the girl's constant scrutiny. "Well?" he demanded. "What is it now?"

To his surprise, she answered him. "Your hair "

"What about my hair? I have had this gray lock of hair since my fifth year of existence on the Second Tier." Greylock realized with some surprise that it was the first time he had had to explain his distinction since those first years, when he had gotten into fight after fight to defend his wounded honor. The other children had called him an "old man," he remembered, and had teased him with the question of how soon he would ascend to the First Tier. He wondered why it should bother him now. He had long ago proven that he was a match for any man.

"I'm sorry, Prince Greylock. I did not mean to comment, but your hair did not seem so gray when we met you on the mountain trail. It seems to have spread over your scalp. Perhaps the light of the fire is misleading."

Moag turned from his tending of the fire and looked at his partner with some interest for the first time in many miles. "Mara is right, Prince Greylock. Your hair has become more gray since we first met you. Look for yourself!"

With that invitation, the fire behind Moag's back leaped toward the tree limbs high above, and by this magical light Greylock was able to catch a reflection of himself in the wide blade and glowing red handle of his knife. He saw that the lock of gray hair that had always marked him had spread, so that most of the matt of curls which fell over his forehead had turned gray. He was dismayed by the change, for the hair on his head had not changed in color for many years.

"It appears that this land has wrought a change," Moag mused. "Perhaps there have been changes inside of you as well, Prince Greylock."

The next morning the old man led them with uncharacteristic straightforwardness and assurance, but Greylock felt a strange foreboding. He was becoming accustomed to this strange land, and somehow uncomfortably attuned to it. The old man was right, the earth was creating a change within him. Often it seemed as if he could sense the presence of Wyrrs before Moag did, and sometimes he could not restrain his impatience when the wizard dawdled, trying to decide by memory and sight whether a valley was safe to enter.

Finally, after another of his long ruminations, the old man made the wrong choice. Greylock could feel that they were approaching a dwelling that was not empty or deserted, but was filled with the odd aura of the Wyrrs. But since Moag was whistling happily, and seemed sure of his route, Greylock did not object.

Suddenly, he saw the wizard looking about him nervously, as if he had just noticed his mistake. At the same moment they were surrounded by scrawny creatures so dirty, pale, and emaciated that they appeared inhuman. What hair they still had, even the youngest of them, was silver gray.

"Demons!" Greylock yelled, even as he realized that they were human, though barely alive. Some of them indeed seemed more dead than alive. Despite the sweltering heat, they were bundled heavily in swaths of cloth that were little more than rags. Yet even through these coverings Greylock could tell that they were bone thin. These people were almost what he had envisioned demons to be like. They made no threatening movements. "I think I may have found demons after all!" he said.

"You may be right, my boy," Moag muttered under his breath balefully. "You may be right. But do not fight them. There are more in this group than I have ever seen together. I will see if I can talk to them."

The wizard stepped forward with his hands showing empty. As if this were a threatening gesture, instead of a sign of peace, the mass of Wyrrs surged toward them with a shrill roar.

Since the Wyrrs were unarmed, Greylock did not draw his weapon, but batted the first attackers away easily with his bare hands. The Wyrrs appeared so weak and ill nourished that Greylock thought he could fight his way out of the trap, if he used his knife. But the magician once again shouted for him not to resist, and he realized that in order to escape he would have to leave his new partners behind. Not admitting to himself that he had grown to like them and would never leave Mara, or even the old man, with the Wyrrs, Greylock told himself that he needed them still to regain Silverfrost and find the course of Gateway. He would trust the wizard this time, he decided. If he was wrong in his trust, it would be the last time—one way or another.

The Wyrrs saw his resolve weakening and attacked him in a mass. His sense of dignity was sorely tried at being overwhelmed by such scrawny specimens of humanity. Their blows hurt his pride even more than his body. Yet, along with his scorn, Greylock felt an inexpressible pity for these people—doomed to live forever in this sad land of twilight.

The three prisoners were led roughly toward one of the huge, primitive structures they had glimpsed earlier through the trees. Greylock realized at a closer look that the building was rather pathetically designed to withstand siege, but only to hold off foes just as weak.

The trespassers were dumped on an uneven dirt floor. The building was just one room, divided, it seemed, by the natural refuse of clan living. In the center was a fire, and smoke found exits through the many cracks in the roof and walls. The structure did not seem to give much shelter, for the hard packed earthen floor was still damp from the rains. Rubbish and badly cured hides lay in piles about the floor. Children were perched silently on the rafters, staring down on them with unnaturally bright and enlarged eyes.

The leader of the Wyrrs, grotesquely tall and thin, had still not said a word, and now the troop retreated back against the walls at his gesture. Of the three captives, they had seemed to be most interested in Greylock, several of them pinching him as if to see if his muscles and fat were real, running their dirty fingers through his gray locks wonderingly, and pulling at his longer dark hair. Greylock suffered this examination without a word, wincing as they probed the muscles of his arms and legs.

"What are they going to do to us, Moag?"

"I believe that they are going to eat us," Moag said gloomily.

"What!" Greylock didn't believe him. "No human would do that to another!"

"Why, Prince Greylock!" Mara said mockingly. "I thought that is what your own people did to strangers! You should not be surprised. At least these people could use the food."

"Of course we don't eat anyone!" Greylock did not think it was a time for humor. "I thought you were barbarians to believe that. But don't feel smug. My uncle would have killed you without another thought."

"We believed you, Prince Greylock, because we had just passed through the real danger of the Twilight Dells!"

The three prisoners glumly watched the huge central fire being stoked, its black smoke curling up through a hundred small holes in the roof. Every once in a while, in spite of himself, Greylock would mutter, "Demons!" Was he about to die discovering that his father and the Gatekeepers were right? It was too much for him to continue his stoic restraint. He would not end being someone's meal! He shuddered and vowed that he would fight his way free if he had to, even if it meant leaving the other two behind. Even with his hands tied, he was a match for these Wyrrs!

The fire's heat was now becoming uncomfortable, and Greylock imagined his gray hair singeing. Mara squirmed beside him, turning first one part of her body and then another to the exposed fire. But the wizard lay quietly on his back, the hunch at his shoulders elevating his head just enough so that he could stare gloomily into the flames near his feet.

"Why did you let them capture us?" Greylock asked him. "Why did you not let me fight them?" "Do not worry, Prince Greylock. I know a means of escape if nothing else works. But I do not wish to use that way unless I must."

"You had better hurry, Moag," Greylock urged. "Whatever route of escape you choose had best be quick!"

Finally, the magician saw that Greylock was right. The Wyrrs were obviously not going to let them go. "I was hoping I would not have to do this, but there does not seem to be any other way." He looked at Greylock as if it would hurt him woefully to say what he was about to propose. "You must be my patron, Prince Greylock—master of my services. Only then will I be able to use my magic."

"Of course, Moag," Why hadn't the wizard said something before now? "Get on with it! What must I do?"

"You must promise that you will pay me, and take care of my worldly needs as long as I am in your service, which will not be for long."

Greylock was disappointed. "But I have nothing to give you, Moag! I will share whatever I have."

"You need not give it all to me now," the wizard said impatiently. "Just promise me the payment, and it will be done."

"I so deed it," he said hastily.

"The payment must be in Glyden, Greylock!" the old man warned. "You must promise that you will give me your knife—that will be adequate." Greylock hesitated at this condition. "I will get it back?"

"As soon as you release me from your service," Moag assured him. "I have no wish to be your servant, Greylock. You will get it back."

"Then you may have the blade. Now get on with it, Moag! They're just about ready."

"Good," the wizard nodded, satisfied. While these hurried and whispered negotiations had been going on, the Wyrrs had continued to gather along the walls. Finally, all the stealthy movement had stopped, and the prisoners realized with a shock that all the bright eyes of the Wyrrs were on them, and the fire was prepared.

"Now which spell would be best?" Moag mused. "Ah, yes. A simple smoke spell should be sufficient. Keep an eye on the tall Wyrr leader who has your knife, Greylock. You must retrieve it, at all costs!"

"Hurry, old man!" Greylock hissed.

"I have already begun," the wizard said complacently.

At first Greylock could see no results from Moag's vague mumblings. As he waited and watched for something spectacular to happen, the hot fire's smoke seemed to be getting into his eyes. He saw the dim forms of the Wyrrs moving forward to lift him to the fire, and he prepared to fight them with the bulk of his body, if nothing else. When Mara coughed beside him, Greylock finally had his first inkling of what the old man meant to do. The smoke grew thicker—and the black figures of the Wyrrs never reached him. He hurriedly marked the last position of the leader of the Wyrrs, the one who held the Glyden-hilted knife.

The smoke had completely filled the interior, and he felt hands pulling at his bonds. "Quickly, get the knife and let us begone!" he heard the old man's voice say from behind him, though when he turned he could see nothing. He wondered how the wizard had managed to free himself. "You must get the knife!" the voice repeated, and then was gone.

Greylock moved quickly toward the last spot he had seen the tall Wyrr, already masked by the smoke. But it did not prove necessary to search blindly. The Wyrr stumbled into him, his reddened eyes watering and closed, coughing violently. Greylock wondered at this reaction, for the smoke seemed mild to him. Much as he wanted to punish the man, pity suddenly moved him and he merely stripped the man of the weapon and pushed him away.

Yet even this gentle rebuff was too much for the Wyrr. Greylock could hear the air forced from the man's chest when he was pushed, and felt his own hand penetrate deep into the Wyrr's stomach. As the tall man folded up and fell to the ground, Greylock was left with a squeamish feeling in his hand where it had touched the Wyrr's backbone.

"I have it, Moag!" he shouted, when he had recovered from this shock. "I have the knife!"

Then he was outside somehow, though he could not remember passing through a portal. The smoke seemed just as thick, but he could see the moon shining dully through the fog.

"Greylock!" He heard his name called, and the voice seemed to him to be coming from all sides at once.

Turning and spinning at the echoes, he dared to shout out, "Where are you?" once, hoping that he was not revealing himself to the Wyrrs in the process. His shout seemed to be quickly absorbed by the damp suffocating fog.

"Stay where you are, Greylock!" This time the wizard's voice seemed to be much closer—almost beside him, though he knew that was impossible.

Then he did feel the presence of his two partners, though he could still not see them. The girl's small hand pulled at his and he followed obediently, blindly. Suddenly, they were clear of the fog—or the old man had removed the last of its concealing mantle from them. Greylock looked back to see the fortress, and a hundred yards on all sides of it, bounded in by the clouds of smoke—yet the rest of the clear night sky was lit by the light of a full moon. Occasionally, the muffled form of a Wyrr would emerge, surrounded by his own little cloud, until the thin form would stumble inevitably back into the fog to join the others. Their cries—dismayed, frightened—drifted over to the watchers.

Yet Greylock was disappointed with the results. "So that is fire-magic? It is not so much."

"It worked, didn't it?" the mage said crossly. "Never be spectacular if something humble will work just as well, I always say. Now if you will just hand me my payment."

"You'll give it back?"

"Yes, hurry!"

Reluctantly, Greylock pulled the blade from his belt and began to hand it over to the old man.

Moag snatched it from his grasp while it was still several inches away—and Greylock was showing signs of changing his mind. "You must pay me, Prince Greylock. One does not deny the forces of magic."

The wizard stared down at the royal knife and turned it over in his hands, fondling the soft hilt of of Glyden. Then, with an ostentatious show of sacrifice, he proffered it to Greylock. "I have been paid, and now I return the payment for my freedom." He said this almost formally. "Take it, Prince Greylock! Once you take it back it will release me from the agreement, and we can be on our way. I cannot hold the smoke forever, you know."

"Release you from our bargain already?" Greylock asked, confused by the wizard's eagerness to give back the knife. "I thought you wanted Glyden. Perhaps you should hold onto it a while longer. We may have desperate need of your magic."

"I have told you—it is not my Glyden, it is yours. I do not wish to be a servant again, not when I will have to give the Glyden back when I no longer serve you."

"But what if we should need you again?" Greylock was troubled by their vulnerability in the Twilight Dells, and indeed, in the Underworld. The wizard had just shown that his magic could be most useful.

"Then I will enter your service again!" Moag was beginning to look noticeably worried.

"What if it is too late? Or what if I should lose the knife, and don't have the Glyden you require next time?"

"If you don't release me," the wizard said angrily, "then you must pay me. In Glyden! The only Glyden you have is also your only weapon. Will you give me your weapon or my freedom?" Greylock paused at this, while the old man looked on smugly at his dilemma. He

31

had not thought of that! Reluctantly, he came to the conclusion that, useful as the wizard's magic could have been, he could not trust the old man with the only weapon among them; not when it was also his heirloom, the only proof he still owned of his royal heritage. If he ever hoped to return to the High Plateau, he would need to hold onto his knife.

Mara saved him from making a painful decision. "Don't release him, Prince Greylock!" she said, and Greylock caught a rare unguarded look from the mage—a cross look that told her to be silent. Greylock snatched his hand back. "Why?"

"Let him keep the knife. Once in your service, Grandfather can do nothing to harm you. Remember you are now his master. It is as safe with him as it would be with you."

"A nice paradox!" Greylock said.

"You would not hold me against my wishes?" the old man asked in a horrified tone.

"Perhaps I will. For a little while."

"I will not serve you willingly, Prince Greylock," the wizard said furiously. "I will not forget that you have done this to me!"

"But, Moag! You tried to trick me and your trick did not work. Do I not have a right to your services for a little while? I will release you soon, I promise you. As soon as you have learned your lesson. Besides, this is best for us all, don't you see? Now we shall have the use of your magic; and since you lost your packs on the mountain, and I lost mine in the Wyrr's fortress, we shall need magic."

"I curse the day I met your grandmother," the wizard said angrily to Mara. "The women of this family have been nothing but trouble! "

"Careful, Grandfather! Remember, your magic is working now."

The wizard hastily made a sign and muttered, "Forgive me, Mara." Moag was obviously speaking to the grandmother—or perhaps the mother—but not the girl.

Greylock interrupted what he saw might turn into a long argument. "Now, Moag, as you pointed out, we had better be on our way. The smoke seems to be dissipating somewhat."

As they moved hastily from the valley, Greylock was already feeling troubled by his betrayal. But when, at the last moment, the wizard turned and crooked a finger, summoning the cloud of smoke, Greylock once again convinced himself that it was for the best. They had need of the old man's powers. He would let the wizard go as soon as they were out of danger, he told himself.

Soon they were enveloped by the harmless fog, and thus shrouded and concealed, they walked directly east, no longer caring if they encountered Wyrrs or not. None of them said a word. The old man walked stooped over as if he were examining the trail, and Greylock thought he could occasionally hear an angry grumble from the wizard, his mottled face seemingly fixed in a permanent scowl. The girl followed close behind him, seeming tiny and frail between the two men. She too had not said anything since they had left the valley of the Wyrrs, and was apparently also suffering from the guilt of her betrayal. Her frown made it clear to Greylock that she had not done it for him, but had her own reasons. Her smoke-smudged fair face and darkening blond hair seemed to fit her mood. It was obvious that she would not welcome any questions from Greylock. He was last in line, still not certain that they were safe, and feeling naked without a sword.

Once he thought he heard the sounds of fighting behind him, and several times he saw the black shape of a mountain crow flying far overhead. Such birds were common, but Greylock was becoming more and more uncomfortable with his defenselessness. Finally this vulnerability became too much to bear, and he called out for Moag to stop.

"What is it now?" the wizard said crossly.

Despite the old man's glowering countenance Greylock asked his question. "I must have a weapon, Moag. Can your fire-magic make me or summon me, a weapon?"

"I cannot make something out of nothing," the mage growled.

"What would you need?"

The wizard's impatience was becoming increasingly noticeable. Greylock doubted he would have even been answered if it were not for the fact that he was also Moag's master.

"I would need the same ingredients as would be in the weapon itself; metal for metal, stone for stone, wood for wood, and so on; though it need not be in the same proportions."

Greylock looked around at the landscape of small trees, and sharp stones, doubtfully. Then he remembered the last gift of his eldest brother, before he too had been sent away by their uncle's envy and wrath. It was a small jewel-encrusted Glyden replica of their uncle's royal sword, Thunderer—exact in every detail, but only two inches long. Greylock always carried it with him in a small homemade sheath, for the blade actually cut and was useful for little things.

"How about this?" he asked, drawing it forth from his pocket with some difficulty. "Can you do anything with this?"

Despite the wizard's obvious anxiety at having stopped in the middle of the Twilight Dells, he grabbed the little blade and examined it with gleaming eyes. "Why did you not tell me you had this?"

"Does it matter?"

"No, I suppose not." Moag seemed troubled. "You did say that this kind of metal and stone were common in your land."

The wizard turned his attention to the little sword again and nodded. "I may be able to reproduce the steel of the blade itself, but alas, the valuable stones and Glyden are beyond my power, as I have told you. Still, it is better than nothing. "You *should* be armed. Lay it down, with the sheath on it, and turn your eyes."

Greylock placed it upon a rock which was about waist high, and turned to cover his eyes. Even so, the flash that ensued raised stars before his eyes. He turned to see a new Thunderer, still glowing from the intense heat of its creation. Greylock gasped and gingerly felt the warm Glyden of the hilt. He removed the crude sheath with a caressing movement, and the new blade sparkled even in the dim light of the Twilight Dells.

"It is Thunderer! " he said, wonderingly.

The old man sat sprawled upon the path, his legs stuck out in front of him like two knobby branches of a tree—stunned and more than a little confused.

"Something went wrong with the spell!" he said. "It was as if someone took control of the spell and bent it to his own will. I have never felt such power!"

Moag got up slowly, unsteadily, and his eyes focused on the new sword. He seemed completely taken aback by the sight.

"This is not possible! I chanted a simple spell of forging, nothing more." He examined the sword as if he could find an explanation in its surface or a flaw in its work. "This is a better weapon than it should be—better than the laws of magic should have allowed. It cannot be true Glyden. It must be simulated, somehow. Still, I believe we shall be the object of every thief in the hundred fiefdoms of Trold!"

"It is real, Moag. I can feel it."

The wizard shook his head, confused and unable to accept what he was seeing. He was startled by the sword's beauty and aura of power. For the first time, he began to look upon Prince Greylock as someone other than a partner in greed—or an unwanted master. This uncommon deed had not been done for a common man!

Mara was also looking at Greylock with a different look in her bright green eyes. As he strapped on the new blade, fancying the way it slapped against his leg, he smiled gleefully at her. She smiled back shyly.

The smile changed her sullen countenance into the fair and pleasant face her green eyes and blond hair had always promised. Perhaps she finally believed that he was a prince, he thought, and it somehow pleased him to impress her. She was just a girl compared to the Lady Silverfrost—yet she seemed to have unaccountably gained weight and was more and more appealing.

As they continued, the old man walking ahead of them bent over in thought, Greylock tried to engage her in conversation.

"Why did you help me, Mara?"

"I did not do it for you! I did it for Grandfather, and for myself. I am tired of traveling from place to place, always in search of Glyden and never finding any. It is only when we serve someone that we settle down for a while. But lately Grandfather would rather starve than give in. After this, I'm afraid he will never use his magic for others. He has this dream of finding Glyden, you see." She sighed deeply. "I suppose he thinks we shall hire each other, and therefore be able to care for each other's every need for the rest of our lives."

"But I do not have a home to give you, Mara. I am as poor as you are."

35

"You *will* have a home, Prince Greylock. Someday you will have a kingdom!" Greylock wondered how she could be so certain. "It is time we found a place to stay," she continued, "and it is better that we serve a Tyrant than a poor farmer who happens to own a small trinket of Glyden. It is better to serve in luxury, after all, than serve in poverty. If we must serve, of course."

"If I ever reclaim my throne, you will be given all you ask!" Greylock vowed fervently.

She looked at him searchingly, her green eyes showing doubt and concern. "You must promise me that you will let my Grandfather go when that happens, Greylock. Let Moag finally have some Glyden of his own, with no price on it."

"Of course!"

They both fell silent at this, troubled by the trick they had played on Moag.

Several times during the rest of that long day, Greylock thought he caught a glimpse of movement behind him, but since it was still far away he assumed that the Wyrrs were stalking them from a safe distance.

The Twilight Dells seemed never changing; never fully light, never fully dark. When night fell, and they sat around a fire, it did not seem as if a full day had passed in all the time they had been traveling. Yet it seemed as if they had always been traveling. Though Moag grumbled at the loss of his cart, he seemed to be able to do most things by magic. Greylock watched the wizard light a fire in the rain with damp wood.

"Can you teach me some of this fire-magic?" he asked curiously.

"Don't bother to learn it, Greylock," Mara said in disgust. "Magic is nothing you cannot already do by hand, if you are willing to work a little."

"My granddaughter could learn," Moag said, ignoring her comment. "It is in her blood but she doesn't want to. I suspect that she already knows a great deal, however. I am almost certain she is a Wind-Witch, though she denies it. She refuses to use her wind-magic, for she confuses all magic with the admittedly flawed characters of her father and grandfather. It is such a waste of talent!"

"But what about me?" Greylock persisted. "Could I learn?"

"You would already know if you could," Moag answered simply. "For instance, I am a Fire- Wizard. I have always had power over the flames. My granddaughter, I suspect, is a Wind-Witch, as I have said. There are also Earth-Wizards, and Water-Witches, and so on. We all have some small measure of power over the other elements, but the power is usually concentrated in one of the four elements; earth, fire, wind, and water."

Greylock asked no more questions of the old man, but he wondered as he prepared for bed if Moag could be wrong. On the High Plateau magic was not known, yet there were often phenomena that were unaccounted for. In his family, for instance, there was an instinctive feel of the land. On the High Plateau, a youth would not necessarily know if he possessed power over any of the elements. He might realize that such an element responded well to his touch, but if he had not been trained, if he did not know it was possible, that power might remain undeveloped. It was not like the wizard's own family, which by his own account, had had generations of magicians.

He wondered briefly if he should tell the wizard of his revulsion to the land, now stronger than ever as he prepared to lie upon it for a night's sleep. But he knew the old man would just dismiss the vague feeling as imagination.

There was one thing the old man's magic could not provide them. They ended their second day with no more food in their bellies than had been found on the trail. In the Twilight Dells this was not much.

As the fire reached its zenith from the thawed wood, all three of them seemed to have the same thought at the same moment. Greylock saw the old man and Mara looking at him, and when he raised his eyebrow, she answered him.

"Yes, Greylock. Your hair has become more gray!"

That night Greylock had the first of his distressing dreams of Wyrrs calling to him, beseeching him for help. When he awoke in fright, he could not remember the reason for their pleas—yet the prayers directed to him had seemed proper. He shook off the nightmare as nonsense.

Yet the land of the Wyrrs undeniably disturbed him and he could not say why.

The next morning, as they prepared to leave on what the old man had promised could be the last leg of their journey through the Twilight Dells, Greylock sighted a huge column of curling black smoke hovering above the normally white mists of the dells. He was strangely certain that the dark haze was hovering over exactly the same valley from which they had escaped the day before.

Mara looked up quickly from her task of gathering the bedrolls when he pointed out the unusual sight, flicking hair from her eyes. Then she turned to Moag accusingly. "Grandfather! There was no need to punish the Wyrrs. They have suffered enough!"

"It is not my doing!" Moag seemed as puzzled by the smoke as they were. "I did not create a fire; I used a simple smoke spell. It should have been blown away by the winds long ago."

The three of them watched the smoke rise over the Twilight Dells a while longer in silence, each lost in his own thoughts. Greylock was remembering the children, with the huge eyes and bloated stomachs, and wondered if they had escaped the fire. Even the Wyrrs did not deserve to die such a horrible death.

"Perhaps, in the confusion, the fire got away from them," Mara said quietly, but Greylock did not believe it. Something must have happened to the Wyrrs after they had left, he thought. Though he did not say so, for fear of frightening the others, he kept a close watch on the trail behind them as they started on the day's journey.

Just as he feared, the sun had not long risen above the horizon before he caught a glimpse of movement behind him. He watched a little more carefully—but not, he hoped, too noticeably—and this time he was rewarded with the fleeting sight of half a dozen dark figures among the trees. They were still some distance away, but Greylock had no doubt that their own small party had been sighted as well. He did not believe the followers could be Wyrrs, for those strange people could not be seen if they did not wish to be, and they would even now be swarming down upon them.

Greylock had a sudden sick certainty that he knew who was causing the swath of destruction through the Twilight Dells. He was surprised and alarmed that any of his own people would have dared to come this far, but perhaps they had also discovered that the "demons" were not as deadly as they had been taught. The Wyrrs would not be able to stand against the soldiers of the High Plateau during the daylight, he knew, though from what the old man had said, the Wyrrs were formidable on their own land by night.

And yet, Greylock still did not say anything to the others. Instead, he took the lead from the old man, and used his new sense of the land to lead them more quickly through the winding valleys. Moag relinquished the lead without comment, not objecting even when Greylock purposely led them very close to the fortresses of the Wyrrs. But he quickly saw that he could not shake his pursuers this way, or leave them behind. As the trackers gained steadily on the trio, Greylock took the only course he hoped could frustrate the pursuers, a course that appeared equally hazardous to the three partners. If he could just provoke the Wyrrs to come out, he thought, perhaps the followers would be waylaid.

By now even Mara was looking over her shoulder, aware that they were being followed. It was she who let out the shout of surprise that alerted the others to the presence of three men in their path.

Two of the men were dressed like Greylock, though they had evidently not discarded as many layers of clothes—no doubt because they meant to return as soon as possible to their homeland. The soldiers stood on their toes, with their swords ready, should Greylock decide to rush them with the big sword that hung from his belt.

The third man stood idly, casually, between them with a grin of triumph. The man was tall and dark, and wore a single, heavy red robe. Perched on his shoulder was a black crow, the silhouette of which was stitched onto the uniforms of the soldiers.

"Well, Greylock!" the man said. "You did mean what you said, and I see that you were right. There are no such beings as demons—though some of the denizens of this loathesome land come very close!"

"Go back, Redfrock!" Greylock answered in despair. "I was banished by my uncle from the High Plateau, and I have left as I was commanded. You have no authority here!"

"Of course I have authority! I have six soldiers—while you have an old man and a girl. I am surprised that you were able to survive your trek through this horrible land. True, these beings that have pestered us are weak and unskilled opponents; but by their very numbers and persistence, they have taken the lives of fully half my men."

"So you have been burning their houses," Greylock said bitterly. He saw no way of escaping the Steward and his soldiers.

"Are you ready to go back, Prince Greylock? You have proven that there are no demons, but what of the gods? Do you not wish to investigate them as well?"

"I do not know if there are gods or not," Greylock said defiantly. "But I do know that no one can survive the snows of Godshome. You are going to have to remove me from the Three Tiers of Existence altogether, Redfrock!" With this he drew the replica of Thunderer, and the morning light caught the burnished metal in a blinding ray.

The two soldiers gasped and backed away from the sword, but Redfrock quickly recovered. "It is a fake, you fools! Did you not see Thunderer in the hands of the Tyrant?"

The soldiers hesitantly advanced on Greylock, and then moved more boldly as the other four soldiers the Steward had spoken of came from the trees behind them to join in the battle.

Greylock hoped that the wizard had been thinking of some way to use his magic while this talk had been going on; and hoped that Moag remembered that the men of the High Plateau were unaware of magic and would use his power to its most startling effect.

Then two things happened simultaneously to save the three partners. Out of the trees, on all sides of the clearing, came the Wyrrs that Greylock had sensed earlier. And from his two partners came the magic he had hoped could extricate them from the Wyrrs.

As the advancing soldiers stopped and looked at the pitiful army rushing toward them uncertainly, the ground before them exploded in flames. The fire was whipped to a deadly height by a sudden mysterious morning gale, and the partners began to retreat. The wind would not have kept away the soldiers of the High Plateau for long, but the Wyrrs were unable to stand before it and rolled away like the dried stalks of a bush.

The Wyrrs turned their fury on the men of the High Plateau, who sliced through them with their swords as if they were merely practicing the art of war, instead of waging it. But the Wyrrs kept coming, climbing over the bodies of their brothers, and the last sight Greylock had before they left the valley was of the Steward Redfrock, standing in the middle of the little circle of his men, shouting orders while they were being overwhelmed by the vast numbers of Wyrrs. The black crow hovered over the fight, cawing.

Greylock doubted that the entire company of soldiers would be destroyed, yet he was not worried any longer of pursuit, for he did not believe the Steward would try to follow him. If half of Redfrock's company had already been killed in the Twilight Dells, Redfrock would be thinking that he would need an equal number to make it back to the mountains; even then, it would be close. Besides, the Steward would now have the mysterious fire and sudden wind to think about.

But Greylock was not at all content with just escaping alive from the encounter. Steward Redfrock now knew that his opponent was alive—and would undoubtedly be waiting for Greylock if he returned to the High Plateau. A surprise attack would be much harder now, if not impossible.

Mara and her grandfather were breathing hard at the pace he was setting, but he did not slow down until he was well away from the Wyrrs, and the sun was almost gone. They had not yet asked him about the strangers who had attacked them; apparently there was no need to explain who they were.

"Thank you for using your wind-magic, Mara," he said, when he at last slowed the pace. "I know how you hate to use it."

"I did not use my wind-magic!" she said, and Greylock was unable to tell if she spoke the truth. "I do not know where that wind came from." Moag could not hold back a smile. "It was just a coincidence, Mara?"

"Yes!" Her tone would brook no more questions, and she said nothing more as they set camp for the night.

Again Greylock had a dream of the Wyrrs, and when he awoke in the morning, more of his hair had turned gray.

CHAPTER THREE

Greylock was able to detect that they were leaving the Twilight Dells by the same mysterious sense which had" made him notice the sickness of the land. Bad patches of ground still existed, and the terrain looked no different, but already he could feel some changes in the earth. Parts of this land felt fertile and rich.

"Where are we now?" he was finally moved to ask.

Moag seemed a little surprised by the question, and frowned as if he were about to ask how his partner could have known. To Greylock's relief, he did not pose the question. He knew he could ask the old man what it meant to have this feeling of the land, but for some reason he wished to keep it to himself; to reveal it when it was least expected. Besides, he guessed that the wizard suspected some kind of power in his new master, but had not quite admitted to himself that it could be beyond his own .knowledge.

"We are leaving the Twilight Dells," Moag said finally—as Greylock had thought he would. "Soon we will be on the borders of Far Valley, and at its center is the BorderKeep. The ruler is an officious man whose army is unfortunately mighty. He once tried to enlist me in his service. He even forced me to wield my fire-magic for him. Me! I would never serve such a fool willingly, you can be sure of that."

"Old man," Greylock said. "I believe you dislike more people than I like."

"Nevertheless, we will avoid the BorderKeep, I think," the wizard said forbiddingly. "The Lord High Mayor may be dangerous, if only because he commands a people far more worthy than he. I do not understand why they have not thrown him out long ago. But people like being dictated to, I always say. We must journey beyond Far Valley, to the first of the fiefdoms of Trold, to get the kind of help we need."

Small and unimportant Far Valley may have been to the worldly-wise wizard, but to Greylock it was a fascinating glimpse of how the people of the Underworld lived; unaware of their luxury, ignorant of poverty.

On the High Plateau, only the Tyrant and his family lived so well. The very lack of food and warmth helped the citizens accept the cruel religion of the Gatekeepers, which said that any person who could no longer produce for the benefit of all—especially for the benefit of the royal family—should seek the "comfort of the gods." All but the most hopeful of the elderly and the sick knew that this meant death, but the sleep on the snows was a better end than some other fates the Tyrant and Steward could subject them to. It was not to the Tyrant's advantage to increase the food supply, or improve the life of his people. As long as the harsh religion of the Gatekeepers kept the people of the High Plateau in his thrall, the Tyrant would never question the priests—even if it meant the exile of his nephew. Greylock was determined to change this state of affairs.

But here, at the border of a huge green valley, stretching as far as the eye could see, even the lowest commoner lived well. Greylock expected to find a contented, even smug people living here, but the old man explained that, even in this seeming paradise, there were grumbles against the Lord High Mayor. Greylock was surprised that the lavish bounty he was seeing seemed to make no difference in their dissatisfaction with life, and mentioned this to Moag.

"Don't be a fool," the wizard said. "If ever you are Tyrant, you must remember to keep your people always scrambling for sustenance. Don't make the mistake of many lesser men, and give them comfort and hope. For if they have food and a warm place to sleep, they will begin to demand something more—such as liberty and power. And these things are much harder for a ruler to give his subjects. Many rulers I have advised, but none could accept this."

"Truly, you have grown cynical in your wanderings, old man," Greylock said lightly. "Does a king rule for himself, or for the benefit of his people? Why else should he be king if he does not mean to help his own kind?"

"You have yet to learn from *your* travels, Prince Greylock," Moag snapped. "You may believe that when you become Tyrant you will improve the lives of your people, and for a short time you may even try that impossible task. If you are lucky, you will fail miserably. Only then, if your people haven't already thrown you out for upsetting things, will you begin the true role of Tyrant—to tell your people what they must do. It will not matter if you are right or wrong, or how much you enrich yourself; they will accept it as long as you rule with an iron fist."

"That would be an irresponsible use of power! I will wield my power to help my people, not harm them! One man—even if he be Tyrant—can never be more important than all his subjects."

"Every man is prey to the temptations of power. Once you have it, Prince Greylock, you will use it. Is not my own subjugation proof of my argument?"

Greylock was struck silent at this. The wizard had touched a sensitive nerve. Why *had* he held the wizard against his will—when it was also against all the principles he had just so glibly proposed? The wizard continued his argument, knowing he had scored a point.

"The ruler who is willing to sacrifice his own welfare for the people is rare; for being the lord of a country makes life all the sweeter, and harder to give up."

"Do not listen to him," Mara said in disdain. "If he were such a good advisor, then why are we destitute and pledged to a prince without a kingdom? Wizards are no wiser than anyone else, Prince Greylock, though they would like you to think so. Why else do you suppose my grandfather cultivates his every wrinkle? He hopes that an appearance of great age will bring respect. His greatest grudge is that his hair will not turn white. Instead, his back stoops until he is bent over—which of course brings laughter, not respect."

44

"Quiet, Granddaughter! I will not take much more of this insolence!" Moag muttered this with sinister overtones, but the girl just hurrumphed and shook her head.

The wizard spoke on confidentially to Greylock, while Mara continued to make scornful noises behind them. "My granddaughter entered my life too late to see the influence I could wield if I wished to. But there are more important things than being rich. I'd rather be poor and free, than serve another. Only by trickery will I serve now!"

As they began descending the short slope to the lush floor of the valley, and over well-tended fields, the girl and the old man began to argue again. This time Greylock let them debate and did not try to soothe tempers. He had learned that the two wrangled endlessly, but without rancor or grudges. Despite her harsh words, Mara's hands would often rest companionably on her grandfather's hunchback.

Instead, Greylock's eyes were drawn to the small town they were approaching. It was set in the middle of the checkerboard fields, and was without defenses. Except for the broad main avenue, it was without perceivable order or planning. Apparently these people had little to fear from their neighbors, Greylock thought, for the town gave more a sense of openness than the militarism that the old man had implied. It was further proof that the Wyrrs were somehow chained and isolated in their poor valleys, when such a rich land lay undisturbed so nearby.

They passed through an orchard of apple trees whose bare limbs were covered by a light green moss, which seemed to glow unnaturally in the afternoon's light. There was green grass, and trees and hedges grew between the thatched roof houses; a natural and appealing landscape that had been so domesticated over the years that the trunks of the trees were worn with familiar touches, and the grass was well-trodden with paths meandering from doorstep to doorstep. All this he saw from a distance, for the wizard would go no closer.

Greylock compared this peaceful scene with his homeland, where even the poorest commoner had to struggle to maintain a secure snowcastle, and where slamming doors were likely to greet the sound of even a friend's approach. There, grudges and vendettas were the overriding concerns of the royal family, and most of the citizens. What must it be like to live in such a peaceful land? Could the wizard be right, and the people have turned their attention to conquest and anarchy? He doubted it, for the town was too quiet and serene to contain such a threat. The military name of BorderKeep was misleading, he thought.

Yet Greylock was soon to learn the meaning of the old wizard's warning. As they tried to detour around this seemingly serene village, a troop of soldiers rushed from the peaceful houses, bristling with armor and weapons.

Greylock stared at them in astonishment, and had to withhold his first impulse to laugh. He didn't know whether to be impressed or to ridicule the costume nature of their uniforms. Bright blue, with silver and gold trimmings, the plump Keepsmen looked sweaty and uncomfortable under the thick layers of brocade. They frowned determinedly at his grin, so Greylock decided it best not to laugh. These men were dressed almost as magnificently as his uncle, adorned in his royal robes! The people of the High Plateau surely did not lack an appreciation of pomp.

Greylock guessed that he could fight his way free, but again he knew he would have to leave the other two behind. He was beginning to wonder if he would not be better off alone. So far, the old man's magic had only saved them from his own miscalculations.

Greylock hesitated at the commands from the soldiers to surrender, but when they tried to take his replica of Thunderer, he rebelled.

He drew the sword with a flourish, and the Keepsmen jumped back in alarm, eyeing the long blade uneasily. Greylock was left standing alone within a circle of a dozen nervous men, turning immediately at the sound of any movement to face the threat. The stalemate looked as though it would not be broken soon, and Greylock hoped that his two companions were mumbling their spells for an escape from this trap.

But Moag and Mara were outside the circle, held immobile by five or six soldiers who were carefully guarding their prisoners, obviously relieved to be out of the fray. The wizard and his granddaughter showed no sign of concocting the magic in their grasp to help in an escape. Greylock realized that he would have to kill several of these ridiculous soldiers, and leave his two partners behind, if he wished to gain his own freedom.

He lowered his blade a little at this thought, and at the same moment most of the soldiers attacked, for they saw that Greylock had no intention of defending himself. Greylock let himself be stripped of Thunderer and dragged before the Lord High Mayor's Palace.

Greylock guessed it was the Lord High Mayor's Palace, because it was the only building in the BorderKeep with the same pretensions of luxury as the uniforms. The other huts were simple and rustic, as befitted a farming people. But this residence was complimented by gables and arches, obviously tacked on over the original structure. The same man who had commissioned the ridiculous uniforms of his guards must have also had this built, Greylock thought. Over the large doors hung a huge Glyden seal of the Lord High Mayor's office, and Greylock noticed that the wizard Moag's eyes immediately filled with yearning.

"Do not tell him anything," the wizard hissed urgently as they were brought toward the grinning Mayor, seated on the top step of his splendid home.

The master of the Palace was surprisingly sedate, however. Taller and leaner than his fellow Keepsmen, the man obviously had an appreciation for style in his own clothing and manner that was not apparent in his subjects and his house. In contrast to the soldiers, he was dressed simply in a green robe and was unarmed.

Perched on the shoulders of the Lord High Mayor, Greylock was dismayed to observe a large white rat. The beady black eyes of the animal stared back at Greylock almost intelligently, until they closed briefly in a satisfied blink. The rat was burrowed comfortably under the long red hair of his master. Greylock shuddered, for on the High Plateau the rat was a competitor for the limited grain, and bounties were set for their bodies. He had never heard of one becoming a pet.

"It is his Familiar," Moag whispered. "If there is one act of magic I would take back if I could, it would be the giving of intelligence to that noisome animal." He sighed. "But there seemed to be no other way of being released, and it seemed a simple price at the time. The rat is much more evil than I had expected. Do not be confused as to who the real ruler of this town is, Prince Greylock."

"You served him?"

"Yes, but only because he trapped me," Moag looked at Greylock with accusing eyes. "Do not make the mistake of believing that these foolish pretensions of the Lord High Mayor are all there is to the man. I call him a fool, but he is much more. He is a very evil man."

"Why do you need fear him, Moag? These guards of his do not appear very formidable."

"These are just Mayor Tarelton's personal bodyguards and servants, and as I said, only fools would serve him," the wizard said, dismissing their escort. "The citizens of the BorderKeep are the real power here, if they would just wake up and throw off the yoke of the Lord High Mayor. But they do not realize that they are being used for evil."

The Keepspeople were slowly coming out of their houses and trickling in from the fields to watch the unusual parade. One of the farmers especially caught Greylock's attention. The man was sweaty and his clothes were stained from a long day's work in the fields, but he shouldered his way to the front of the crowd without a protest from others, and watched the proceedings intently. What Greylock noticed first was the farmer's size. He was as tall as Greylock, and as dark — darker when the tanned skin was considered — but he was twice as broad as Greylock. Yet the visitor to the BorderKeep could see the intelligence in the man's eyes as he felt himself scrutinized calmly. The old wizard was right in his estimation of the Town's potential, if this was a specimen typical of the men of the BorderKeep. With a sword in that bulky arm, and with training, the man would be an awesome opponent.

"Step forward, my friends," the Lord High Mayor said amiably in a high voice, bringing Greylock's attention back to what was facing him. "I apologize for my overly efficient guards. I understand there was almost a fight! For this you must forgive me. There was no need to greet you with weapons!" He turned his eyes to Greylock, obviously meaning to display most of his charm toward him. "I am Lord High Mayor Tarelton, and this is the BorderKeep."

When the man turned his attention to Moag, he could not hide his dislike. "Welcome back, old man! Have you come back for more Glyden? You did not stay long enough last time to be paid properly. I would be very happy to employ you again, if you wish. Our last association was most profitable, though it ended badly. Still, I am willing to forgive you."

"I would never serve you again, Tarelton!" the magician said bluntly.

The Lord High Mayor winced, and a brief cloud of disappointment crossed his face. At the end of his speech, he also nodded once to Mara—as if he knew that it was through the girl he had his best chance of reaching the wizard. When she turned away stonily, the Lord High Mayor flushed in anger.

Greylock, who was feeling relieved at their welcome shift from prisoners to guests, interjected hastily. "Moag means that he cannot serve you, Lord High Mayor. I have employed him for the time being, for a minor service—which unfortunately will take some time."

"I see!" Mayor Tarelton could not contain his anger. "Who, if I may also be blunt, are you?" The rat seemed to be nuzzling his master's ear, and even from several yards away, Greylock could hear the snuffling sound. Then he realized with some horror that the animal was communicating with the Mayor!

"My name is Greylock," he said finally.

"Where do you come from, Greylock?" A moment of puzzlement showed in the man's otherwise assured voice. "I have never seen you before and I do not think you could be one of the Wyrrs, despite your gray hair. None are so bold, or so healthy as you. If you have come from the east, it would have been reported to me that you had crossed the borders. Therefore, you must have come from the west, and the mountains—the land of the gods." He smiled. "Tell me then, are you a god?"

"I come from the west." Let him think what he will, Greylock thought.

The smile quickly fell from the Lord High Mayor's face. "Perhaps if you do not wish to answer my questions, you would rather stay a night in our prison. At least, until we find that you are not a spy or saboteur! How are we to know if you do not answer our questions?"

"Lord High Mayor Tarelton!" It was the big man whom Greylock had noticed earlier who spoke up to save him. "Why don't you let them be? Do we want the world to think that the BorderKeep is inhospitable to its visitors?"

To Greylock's surprise, the Lord High Mayor addressed the farmer with respect. "Do you now wish to join in my administration of the BorderKeep—as I have offered to you so many times, yeoman Harkkor?"

The big man lowered his eyes and growled, "You know I want nothing to do with it, Tarelton."

Greylock could see the Mayor's relief that he had not been challenged, nor his proposal accepted. Couldn't anyone else see that? The man's anger seemed to have left him at the interruption. The Lord High Mayor looked down upon the bejeweled sword of Thunderer on his lap, fingering it appreciatively. Then, with obvious reluctance, he extended it hilt first to Greylock.

The man from the High Plateau, who had learned much about the value of Glyden since he had left, now reflected cynically that the Mayor must have decided that there was more Glyden and jewels where the sword had come from. Now all of Tarelton's words and efforts would no doubt be directed toward finding out exactly where that was.

"Yes, well no matter where you are from or who you are, you are welcome to the BorderKeep, Greylock." The Lord High Mayor seemed to have regained his charm—and all his cunning. "My guards will show you to your rooms, where you will find food. Sleep tonight in peace and we can talk on the morrow."

Greylock noticed several things during that first audience with the Lord High Mayor. First of all, the people of the BorderKeep did not appear to like Tarelton. There was more fear than respect in their glances. Secondly, that they had looked at him hopefully when they heard that he had come from the mountains. And last, that the yeomen farmers and wives did not know their own strengths. They could have easily overthrown the Lord High Mayor, and defeated his little army. Greylock could only wonder why they had not already done so.

Throughout the audience, the man the Lord High Mayor had called Harkkor had watched him with intently questioning eyes. Obviously the big man was the leader of the opposition in the BorderKeep, for Greylock had seen that the looks of respect the Mayor had failed to get were directed instead at the big farmer. Harkkor may not know it, Greylock thought, but he already possessed the support he would need to take Tarleton's place. Again, he wondered why this had not already happened.

The answer, he thought, somehow lay in the Familiar. It was the second time he had seen an evil and ambitious man with an unusual pet. Now that he had come to the Underworld, and had seen magic at work, Greylock was becoming certain that the black crow of the Steward was more than a pet.

The three prisoners—or guests, Greylock still wasn't sure which— were taken inside to a large comfortable room, furnished, Greylock guessed from Moag's mumbles, by the old magician's over- luxurious imagination. As the guards in their blue uniforms left them, the wizard muttered at his handiwork.

"I overdid the uniforms, I guess."

"Ghastly," Greylock agreed. "No other army will ever take them seriously again. A suitable revenge, I'd say."

"You think so?" The old man brightened at this idea; but then he continued cursing the Lord High Mayor bitterly.

"I do not understand your hate, Moag," Greylock said at last, for he was enjoying the sudden comfort of the room. "This Mayor Tarelton does not appear to be a very evil man. In fact, I was thinking of asking him for the help we need."

"No! I will not ask that man for help again. I do not trust him. Not for all the Glyden of your kingdom, Prince Greylock!"

"Why not, old man?" Greylock was puzzled by the wizard's vehement rejection. "He has enough soldiers, he is close, and unless I am mistaken, he will be more than willing to help us—for a price. But will not the King of Trold also have a price? As for his faults, I can see that he is greedy. But will we find a better man among the fiefdoms of

Trold? As for trusting him, remember he will have to trust me as well, and I know the High Plateau far better than he ever will. He will need me, whereas he will know that I can get the help I need from anywhere."

"I will not serve under him, or with him either!" the wizard said stubbornly. "He is evil, I tell you!" He stomped over to reflect bitterly on the Glyden seal hanging just below the window. He refused to answer Greylock's questions, no matter how much he pleaded with him. Finally, Greylock looked at Mara helplessly, and she explained her grandfather's anger.

"You do not know the customs of wizards, Prince Greylock. In the eastern lands, no ruler would dare force a wizard to serve against his will. There is said to be a mortal curse on such an action. But the Lord High Mayor does not know our customs or does not care, and he dared to betray my grandfather—forcing him to serve on pain of death. And he did not even pay in Glyden!

Moag is bitter that the forces of magic have not destroyed the Lord High Mayor, and have even allowed him to flourish."

"Perhaps such curses take time."

"So I have told him. I have assured him that Mayor Tarelton will someday pay with a horrible fate, but he still doubts the justice of the gods." "Am I in danger of this curse?"

"He entered your service willingly, Prince Greylock, though he may not stay in your service by his own will." She looked at him sharply. "Do not break your promise to me to free him on the High Plateau, or you will have *my* curse! "

Suddenly, Moag's enraged voice boomed across the room. "Quiet, you fools! That accursed Familiar listens to our every word."

Greylock and Mara looked up to where the mage pointed and saw the rat, half hidden in the folds of a tapestry, watching with coal black eyes. At that moment, the base of a brass candleholder crashed only inches above the fat creature, creating a new small hole in the wall. The startled rat disappeared into the convenient gap.

"Next time I won't miss," Moag said grimly from behind them. Then the old man moaned and sank into one of the overstuffed chairs, burying his face in his hands.

"We are doomed!" he wailed. "It will tell its master everything. Lord High Mayor Tarelton will never let us go now." He looked up with reddened eyes and glared at them. "You utter fools! Your loose tongues have condemned us. How could you have been so stupid? Did you not realize that everything we say in the Lord High Mayor's Palace will be overheard?"

Greylock did not have any pity for the old man's troubles this time. Moag's single-minded goal of finding Glyden was beginning to annoy him. If he wanted Glyden so much, why would he not work for it? By honest labor, if he refused to use his magic! Why would he not cooperate and compromise, like anyone else? No wonder the wizard had searched so long without results!

Moag continued his string of recriminations, and Greylock felt himself becoming angry at the name-calling. Finally he marched over to the wizard's chair and loomed over the old man, meaning to teach him a lesson. His shadow fell over the suddenly frightened and wizened wizard, who ceased to speak and melted back into the cushions as far as his huge back would allow him to go. Greylock grabbed him by his shoulders and lifted him bodily from the chair.

"You forget your place, Moag! I am the master and you are the servant. We are not partners any longer, and you had best learn that! I am a prince, and therefore meant by the gods to rule. You are a wizard, and therefore meant to serve. Do not ever call me 'fool' or any other name again!"

Then Greylock's anger had passed as quickly as it had come, and he let go of the old man and looked about him once more in a startled way. Mara was staring at him with shocked eyes. The old wizard was surprisingly frightened and subdued by the berating. Greylock realized that he had let his anger turn to rage, even as he was talking — just as he had so often seen his uncle do — and for which his uncle had always expressed sorrow later. Greylock had not known that he possessed such a temper, perhaps because he had never been frustrated and thwarted before, nor talked to in such a way.

"Greylock!" Mara said finally. "It is only Moag's way! He does not mean anything by it. I doubt he even knows he is rude!"

"Forgive me, Moag," Greylock said, almost sheepishly. "My uncle sent me away to die under the spell of just such an anger. And thus did I provoke him."

"Do not apologize to me!" the wizard said bitterly. "I am only a servant!"

Despite all of Greylock's apologies, the easy camaraderie that had marked their partnership before disappeared, to be replaced by a stiff and formal master-and-servant relationship. From that moment onward, Greylock could see the resentment in the wizard grow. Trying to make amends, he said, "If it will make you feel safe, I will not have anything to do with the Lord High Mayor." But the old man was not mollified.

That night Greylock had his most vivid dream of the Wyrrs, though he had hoped that once out of the Twilight Dells they would go away. It seemed to him that the Wyrrs were right there, in BorderKeep, scratching at the second-story windows of the Palace and looking at him with wide, pleading eyes. He woke from the eerie dream breathing heavily and sweating, and it took him several minutes to realize that there was indeed a sound at the window; a sort of *ping*, as if the window were assailed by a hailstorm. Getting from the soft bed, he drew on his clothes and picked up Thunderer before he made his way to the window.

Not knowing what to expect, he stared down on the moonlit town square. Finally he saw the shadow of a huge man standing under a tree, waving for him to come down. From the size and shape of the man, Greylock recognized yeoman Harkkor.

The Palace, for all its ostentatious show, afforded Greylock with few places for his feet, but it proved no real obstacle to his climbing skill, even without his Talons. He could see the admiring look in the yeoman's eyes as he dropped silently the last few feet to the ground. But the farmer hushed him when he gave a whispered greeting, and led Greylock away from the building's walls.

"The Mayor is going to offer you the use of his army, in return for what he believes to be your vast riches," the yeoman whispered. "After that, he no doubt will try to betray you, but I do not know this for a fact. My people—the common folk of BorderKeep—would like for you

54

to accept his offer. We know that it is a great deal to ask, to bring such a viper into your land, but we ask it of you nonetheless."

"But why?"

"Little can be done against the Lord High Mayor while he is still within the BorderKeep." Greylock could hear contempt in the man's tone. "His spies are everywhere. If they cannot gain entrance, his rat Familiar will find a way. No discussion can occur in the BorderKeep between more than a few honest men without his hearing'of it, and every word that was said being reported. It is our hope that away from BorderKeep—with, or without your help, for we have no right to ask you—Tarelton can at last be overthrown."

"Will you be joining our expedition, yeoman Harkkor?"

The big man smiled. "Yes, though it may raise suspicions, for I have never joined the Lord High Mayor in his conquests, I have decided to come along this time."

"Then I will do as you ask. I would not trust the Lord High Mayor without someone like you in his army to turn to if need be. But I am not sure that it is necessary for you to go to such lengths. Mayor Tarelton is afraid of you already. He knows that the people of BorderKeep would follow you if you asked them."

"Perhaps, but I must be sure for their sake. Now, I must go. The longer we tarry here, the more chance of us being discovered. Tell no one of our conversation. Be assured that you will have allies within the Lord High Mayor's army." The farmer began to move away.

"Wait!" Greylock knew his voice had almost become audible to those within the Palace, and he dropped his voice. "I must tell Moag!" he hissed. "I told the old man I would never join the Mayor. He already believes that I have betrayed him once, and I could not do this without saying why." "No!" Yeoman Harkkor was adamant. "The wizard's hate is too noticeable. It must remain in his eyes, or the Lord High Mayor will know something is wrong."

Reluctantly, Greylock let the man go, and climbed silently back up the Palace walls. He had no more dreams of the Wyrrs, but his sleep was not peaceful.

The next morning, as yeoman Harkkor had predicted, the guards came to fetch Greylock for an audience with the Lord High Mayor. The gloomy wizard and Mara were to be left behind, with the not-very-believable explanation that the Lord High Mayor wished to talk privately with his old friends later.

"Don't go, Greylock," Moag pleaded, his hate of the Mayor coming through again.

"He already knows everything, Moag. I may as well hear what he has to say." Greylock fingered the hilt of Thunderer, reassured by its feel, and even more so by the ludicrous appearance of the soldiers of the Palace.

"Don't listen to him, Greylock!" Moag called out after him as he followed the guards from the room. "You will regret it!"

Apparently, Moag had not had a chance to work his magic on the dining room. The two servants, dressed in a garish red, were the only glaring luxuries in a room made up entirely of wood. Greylock guessed that, despite the splendor of the Lord High Mayor's Palace and the rich uniforms of his soldiers, the Mayor was in reality quite poor, and that the wizard Moag had been the only good thing to happen to him for some time. Only the seal of Glyden above the doors of the Palace showed that there might be a wealth of metal and gems in the BorderKeep, and Greylock suspected that the Mayor had stripped his people to come up with a melting of that much of the precious metal.

Greylock had already dismissed most of the wizard's objections to the Lord High Mayor, and he intended to enlist him as an ally as the yeoman had asked. Still, he waited for the other man to make the proposal, as he was sure he would. The greed that had shown in the Mayor's face each time Greylock allowed him a view of the hilt of Thunderer was laughably obvious.

"Come in, Prince Greylock," the Lord High Mayor welcomed him—by a title he should not have even known. "We serve ourselves, mostly. Let us eat before we talk. I know the wizard Moag could not supply food for your long journey, so you are no doubt still hungry."

Greylock was ravenous, for he had chosen to rest rather than eat the night before. The servants stood back from a table laden with a bounteous measure of simple but filling food, and watched with amused eyes as Greylock eagerly began heaping the food onto a plate. The last bowl was full of leafy lettuce, and as he started to scoop it up, he saw something moving in the greenery. Jumping back with an astonished shout, he barely avoided upsetting his plate, and that of the Lord High Mayor's. The head of the Familiar, seemingly puzzled by Greylock's reaction, emerged to peer over the lip of the bowl.

"I am disappointed in you, Prince Greylock." Mayor Tarelton appeared more amused than disappointed, his guest saw. "My rat is really quite tame and harmless, and very useful." The hint about the rat's usefulness made Greylock conscious that the other man was leading up to his proposal.

"In the land I come from, rats are neither tame nor harmless, and certainly not useful."

"Is it true you come from the west? From the mountains?"

Greylock looked at the rat significantly. It was now eating contentedly from the plate of his master. Greylock had suddenly lost his appetite and picked at the food in a desultory fashion, wondering if the rat always had the run of the table.

The Lord High Mayor answered the look with a smile. "Yes, if what you were telling the magician was the truth, then I also know the truth. I know that you had intended to ask me for help, if it hadn't been for that interfering old wizard. By the way, I would advise you to get from Moag what you can, and then let him go as soon as possible. That is what I did. I happen to know that you and he are not friendly. Frankly, I am not surprised, he is a very ungrateful man."

"We had not yet decided to ask you." "Nevertheless, I accept your proposal. No! I insist. You must allow me to provide you with the military assistance you need to conquer your High Plateau."

So there it was, Greylock thought. Just as the old man had said — they had no choice. Yet Greylock was not dissatisfied with the offer. He was not willing to make another long journey just to quell the old man's fears, even if they could somehow manage to escape. He was tired of the heat and the humidity of the Underworld, and wanted to return to his homeland before every hair on his head had turned gray. He had learned little of Gateway in the Underworld — he would have to return to the High Plateau to find the answer. And finally, Greylock felt a sympathy for the cause of the conspiritors.

Still, the venture was not even to be considered, unless he was allowed to lead it. For this he must remain alive and free. The treacherous Lord High Mayor must be made aware of this.

"We can only succeed if the Steward is removed from our path—and I intend to kill him," he said. "I do not want to harm my uncle. When I show him how wrong he was about the Underworld, he will have to take me back."

"Why must we convince the Tyrant, if we must conquer the High Plateau anyway? He will have to proclaim you his successor."

"There is nothing to be gained by merely conquering the High Plateau," Greylock answered. "The people must be able to accept their sovereign, and they would never accept an Underworlder. So you need me, Lord High Mayor; not just to help you find and conquer my land, but afterwards as well. You will be well paid for your help—in Glyden."

"But of course! It is the Glyden I want, as you have already so astutely pointed out to Moag. There is one other matter, though, that I feel I must bring up with you. Must you have the wizard and his granddaughter along? The old man seems to have a grudge against me, and might do something hasty. That would ruin all of our plans. We do not need him, for my army is sufficient, I assure you."

"Moag is in my service. Why do you object to him?"

"He believes that I forced him to serve me, but I never once threatened him. It is all in his mind. He has an irrational hate of me, as you have seen."

Perhaps the Mayor had not threatened Moag, Greylock thought—perhaps not in so many words. But he had already seen how the Lord High Mayor could hint with vague and sinister overtones.

Apparently, Mayor Tarelton did not believe that he could restrain the magician from casting his spells. It might prove useful in keeping his new ally in line later, Greylock thought, if he continued to believe this. There was no sense in telling him that no prince of the High Plateau would abandon a friend.

"Moag may be very useful in this adventure," he said simply. "Be assured that I will try my best to keep him from using his powers in any way that could be harmful to you."

Lord High Mayor Tarelton did not seem comforted by this statement, but they shook hands over the arrangement. Both of them inwardly vowed not to trust the other. The Mayor may have his Familiar, Greylock thought, but I have the wizard.

———

But the Lord High Mayor possessed more than just his own Familiar as a source of information. That night, the Steward Redfrock's crow made three trips over the same terrain it had taken Greylock three full days, and many adventures, to cover. As soon as Tarelton had returned to his own room after dinner, the gist of the conversation was relayed from the Lord High Mayor to his own Familiar, and then from the rat to the Steward's Familiar. In this way, the crow learned that the Mayor had followed Redfrock's instructions exactly, and it set off toward Godshome.

It flew high over the Twilight Dells, for the land of the Wyrrs disturbed it as much as it had disturbed Greylock, proving perhaps that the Wyrrs were neither good or evil, but had their own secrets. When it had reached the High Plateau, it circled the snowy plain twice in confusion, for it could not sense the presence of its master anywhere on the surface. At last it gave in to the inevitable, and landed near the entrance of one of the many caves that riddled the lava beneath the snows, and which served as convenient passageways for the people of the High Plateau to travel from snow- castle to snowcastle.

To the men working on the new and unnatural passageway that the Steward had ordered built, it was disconcerting to see the big black bird hopping down a passage so far below the earth and away from its natural habitat. Yet, with its coal black eyes, and inky feathers, it appeared horribly at home in the dark.

"Ah, there you are!" the Steward greeted his Familiar as it scratched around the last turn in the new cave, finding its master overseeing the finishing touches of his handiwork. It flew to the Steward's shoulder, the tips of its wings actually brushing the narrow sides of the passage.

"Greylock means to bring an army, does he?" the Steward said when it had reported. "Tell the Lord High Mayor that he has done well, and that he has only one thing he must remember. Tell him that when the time comes for a choice, Prince Greylock must chose the left-hand course. That is all he must do. Convince Greylock to take the left passage."

The Familiar jumped from his master's shoulder almost delicately. Then with awesome dignity it left the subterranean caverns for the night skies, and arrived at the Lord High Mayor's Palace just as dawn was breaking. The bemused Tarelton received his instructions while Greylock slept, little suspecting that the long arm of the Steward Redfrock had already touched him in BorderKeep.

CHAPTER FOUR

Greylock watched from the first of the foothills, its top sprinkled with the first snows of winter, as the army of the Underworld set off for Godshome a few weeks later. From the hilltop, the soldiers appeared as a line of white shapes, glinting off the rays of the morning sun. He had insisted that the bright colored uniforms be discarded.

"My homeland is a land of snow," he argued. "We do not wish to be targets any more than we have to. Our only chance of success is to surprise the Steward. If your guards approach in those uniforms, we will be seen from miles away!"

When yeoman Harkkor had agreed with Greylock, the Lord High Mayor had no choice but to

reluctantly comply, though in protest he had refused to give up his own bright green robe. By now the magnificent uniforms had been replaced by a hastily assembled hodgepodge of white clothing. The Lord High Mayor with his red hair and brilliant robe stood out in this company—as perhaps he wished.

Greylock was beginning to have other doubts as well. It was obvious that the men of Far Valley ate well, but except for the yeomen, without working very hard to take off their fatty weight. Many in the army were huffing and panting long before the first slopes of the mountains had been reached. Their weapons now seemed in many cases more ornamental than deadly, their determined faces only ludicrous. Greylock was irritable this morning, for he had had another frightening—and inexplicable—dream of Wyrrs calling to him, the night before.

Luckily, yeoman Harkkor had persuaded many of his fellow farmers to come along, and this sturdy component of the army, with their wickedly sharp scythes, reassured Greylock that his expedition was not a foolish venture. When the Lord High Mayor had found it impossible to talk the yeomen out of joining his army, as was their right, he had begun to defer to Yeoman Harkkor, apparently hoping in this way to placate the farmers.

Moag had come along as well, grumbling— though never to Greylock's face. He had begged Greylock to reconsider the alliance with the Lord High Mayor, insisting that he could whisk them away with the help of his magic.

"You will regret this, Prince Greylock!" he warned again. "You have made a compact with a demon!"

"Oh, come now, Moag." The temptation to tell the old man about his talk with Harkkor was strong, but he remembered the farmer's warning about spies. "You can always whisk us away later. Mayor Tarelton is just a very greedy man."

"He is more than just greedy! There *are* 'demons,' you know," the wizard said cryptically. "Just because you have not found them yet does not mean they do not exist. Evil spirits are all about, and I summoned one by mistake when I created that Familiar."

Mara had fallen silent since Greylock's outburst of three weeks before, and he wondered if he had frightened her with his temper. So it was that he found himself marching alone, at the head of the long column.

They soon entered the Twilight Dells, and Greylock reflected on the accuracy of the name. Though it was only a little past noon as they entered the first narrow glen, and though the sky was cloudless, a pall seemed to have descended over the light and the company. Greylock felt the same revulsion to the land that he had experienced before.

Though none of the people known as Wyrrs revealed themselves to the armed body of soldiers, the Keepsmen looked about them nervously. Apparently, Moag had not bothered to ask the men of the BorderKeep the reason why the Twilight Dells were out of bounds. It seemed evident they knew the secret. Greylock approached the Lord High Mayor, concealing a shudder at the sight of the ever-present rat Familiar.

"Why are your people afraid, Mayor Tarelton?"

"It is superstition," the Lord High Mayor said with a great display of scorn; but it was apparent from his darting eyes that he too was frightened. "No matter how educated my people become, they still cling to their fears. Legends of this poor land tell of a deed so dreadful that the Wyrrs are forever haunted by it, and the land cursed."

"What was this great evil?" Greylock asked. He was a little encouraged by the Lord High Mayor's bold posturing. Sometimes such a show could even take the place of courage, which he doubted the Mayor had much of, but would need.

"No one knows. It is long forgotten, or perhaps it was so terrible that the Wyrrs will keep it to themselves until the time of their extinction as a race. The story I heard as a baby on my nurse's lap was that the Wyrrs had betrayed the gods of Godshome, and are condemned to stay in the Twilight Dells until the gods call on them once more for help. But you should know more of this than I, shouldn't you?"

Greylock had no answer. The story sounded very much like the catastrophic closure of Gateway, and the casting-down of the demons. Again there was the uncanny resemblance to the teachings of the Gatekeepers—but distorted, and made more human. He had not thought of the Wyrrs since he had first passed through their valleys, except in his dreams. Now, however, their plight came back to him with such a force that he knew he would never forget them again. He did not know why he should be concerned with the Wyrrs, but their situation was something that he knew would never leave him in peace. Somehow he would have to discover the answer to the Wyrr's curse.

Greylock was not too concerned about an attack, for from what he had seen of the inhabitants of the dells he doubted that they would confront such a large body of armed men. He was surprised therefore to glimpse a host of men filling all of the next valley. Yet these were not the pale, weak humans whom he had seen before, but tall and strong men and women, with dark hair and strong faces. In fact, he thought suddenly, they looked like citizens of the High Plateau!

As the company halted hesitantly at the narrow opening of the valley, many of the Keepsmen looked at him, comparing his tall, dark frame with what they were seeing. Greylock, with his gray hair, was the flawed one compared to these handsome people. But he did not notice these glances, for he was intent on the manner and dress of the strangers. For a few seconds he was certain that he was seeing his own brethren, men of the High Plateau. He began to walk forward eagerly to greet them. Smiles grew on the faces of the strangers at the sight of him.

"Stop!" Moag's voice tugged at Greylock, but the spell was too strong for him and he quickened his step. Suddenly, the old man's hunched, stooped body moved into view with unusual speed, blocking his progress toward the strange assemblage. "Do not go further, Prince Greylock!"

The wizard led Greylock back, dazed and resisting, to the clustered group of Keepsmen, and drew a line in the dust before him. Greylock began to step over it, paying little notice to the action, and drawn once more by the spell of the strangers. His foot would not descend on the far side of the line in the dirt, no matter how much force he used to press it down.

Suddenly, the vision of the others seemed to waver, and the strong, beautiful faces turned into the gaunt white skulls of the Wyrrs. Greylock turned his face from the sight in dismay.

Moag had continued drawing his line and muttering, until he had gone twice around the company of men, gathered at his urging into a tight mass. One by one, the others gasped in dismay as the sight before their eyes changed drastically. When the Wyrrs saw the looks turn to disgust, their own smiles—now grotesque parodies— dropped completely, and the eerie gathering rushed toward the smaller body of men murderously.

At the line in the dust they too were repelled, while the old man muttered furiously under his breath to maintain the spell. The Wyrrs stood only a few terrifying steps away, unable to reach their victims and roaring with a deafening frustration. The afternoon wore on, and the wizard collapsed to the ground muttering his spell with determination that blocked out everything else.

Finally, as night began to fall slowly, the thousands of Wyrrs seemed to lose interest in their siege around the awkwardly gathered company, and began drifting away in small groups. The roar of their cries slowly died down. At last, they were gone and the only sign of their presence was the trampled earth of the empty valley.

Mara and Greylock helped the old wizard up, and for a few moments he was dazed. "I could not have held them back much longer," he sighed finally in relief. "My earth-magic is not strong, and the Wyrrs are at their most powerful by night." "There were thousands of them!" Greylock said in shock. "I thought you said they hated each other, Moag, and would murder each other outside their own little clans, their own valleys."

"We must have stumbled on one of their ceremonies," the wizard answered solemnly. "It is only when they are gathered together in such numbers that they can summon the power to call back their old appearances. I suspect they cannot often stand this reminder of their past, and it is for this reason they avoid each other."

"What has happened to them?" Greylock was beginning to understand more than he wanted. "Can we not help them?" Despite his own vows of disbelief, the Wyrrs were coming uncomfortably close to the ancient legends of an Underworld of pain and punishment. They were his people, he knew now. The ancestors of the Wyrrs were his ancestors as well.

"You do not wish to know what they did. Help? There is no help for them, though they have their own foolish belief that one day a god will descend from Godshome and lift their curse."

Greylock looked at the wizard curiously. He had been wrong apparently to believe that the old man was unaware of the secrets of the valley. How much else did Moag know and not reveal? There would come a time when he would pry that knowledge from the wizard, he vowed.

The invading army continued toward the Three Peaks of Godshome in the morning, this time not bothering to journey by the circular route of the peaceful valleys, but in a straight line, daring the

Wyrrs to try to stop them. Now the Keepsmen were confident and boisterous, but Greylock was still bothered by the confrontation. The army's revelries seemed somehow profane to him, though he should have been encouraged by them. He wondered if they would be so brave if Moag had not already shown that he could repell the Wyrrs with his magic. He noticed the yeoman Harkkor and his followers also seemed to be saddened by the encounter.

Something continued to nag at his memory, something that the Gatekeepers had taught him in his youth—of demons' curses and a prophecy of their Deliverance. Greylock had made his choice not to believe early, though he had once dreamed he could catch that lost word which, could a man but find it, would make him the master of his fate. But he had abandoned the teachings of the Gatekeepers, and thus had never read the sacred books very carefully.

He did not expect to see the ghosts of the Twilight Dells again, but tried to forget them and concentrate on his coming triumph over his uncle. As camp was set for the night, he wandered away from the others and began climbing one of the knolls, to try to restore his confidence.

The spell of the Wyrrs once again fell over him, and he recognized the landscape of his dreams, though he knew he was awake. The ground before him grew even darker, and his view of the white peaks of Godshome from the knoll was hindered by a blurry vision. He marched toward them, somehow sensing that, though the path was becoming unnatural, it was not he who was in danger. Behind, he could feel the presence of others following him, but it was as if they weren't there, and he paid no attention to their worried shouts. The dark trail seemed to slant upward under his feet, though only seconds before it had stretched before him, flat and well lit by the light of a full moon.

He was not surprised this time when out of this dark, the figure of a man emerged, followed by an old woman. The man, who could have been Grey- lock's twin or perhaps a younger brother, had well-structured dark features. But even under the spell of the Wyrrs, the old woman appeared ancient and ravaged. Greylock was mildly surprised to find a woman that old among the people of the Twilight Dells.

The man raised his hand in greeting, and Greylock stopped and also signed a greeting. The man—or apparition—seemed to be trying to say something to him, but Greylock, as in his dreams, could understand nothing but the urgent need of the stranger. Everything sounded much harsher, yet somehow removed—like someone scratching the glass on the far side of a windowpane.

"He says that the people of the valleys welcome the Deliverer," Mara suddenly said from beside him, and he noticed her presence for the first time, as if she had just stepped into the light. Whatever the meaning of this meeting, it was apparent to Greylock that in some way Mara was to play a role.

"He begs forgiveness for their attacks, but they did not recognize you when you passed before," she translated. "He begs to know when you will return to lead them to their freedom."

Greylock shook his head in puzzlement. "I am not returning! I have nothing to do with his people. I am not this Deliverer he speaks of with such reverence."

Now the old woman stepped forward and started to speak. Her voice was no more than a croak, but Greylock could understand the horrible words without translation.

"You must help the Wyrrs, my son, for your father was one of them. The greatest of their kind since they were so long ago imprisoned. For him I was banished from the High Plateau. Now you must help them."

Greylock was shocked, disbelieving—but he found himself answering. "I will return to help you, when I can. Soon!"

The ghostly figures seemed satisfied with this answer, and disappeared back into the murk. Then suddenly the bright moonlight was back again, and the Lord High Mayor was there, pestering him with questions. Mara and the old wizard were there as well, staring at him with concerned faces. Two of Tarelton's guards had followed, and had drawn their weapons.

"We followed you out here, and found you with the two Wyrrs. What were they saying to you?" "Wyrrs?" The vision still seemed unreal to Greylock, and he still was haunted by the image of the woman calling him son.

"You stood there staring at them, Greylock, for several minutes," the Lord High Mayor said in confusion. "Then the old woman spoke to you in a language I did not understand. I could barely keep my men from murdering the Wyrrs in their fear."

Greylock looked about him in a daze. It was apparent from their looks that only the old wizard, and his granddaughter, had seen what he had seen. Only the two with magic running through their veins, he thought, had seen the noble figure of the valley man and a dignified old woman, and not the pathetic visages of Wyrrs. What did it mean?

Only a short while before, he had been interested only in conquering his own homeland, and regaining his right to the throne. He had been in the easy company of the greedy Mayor and the covetous wizard. Now, whether he liked it or not, he was bound to seek the counsel of the Gatekeepers, the teachers against whom he had rebelled and who long ago had given up on their royal student. Perhaps the price would be too high, but Greylock knew he would have to pay it.

There was one other consequence of his meeting with the Wyrrs. As they strolled back into the light of the campfires, he heard Mara gasp.

"Greylock! Your hair has turned completely gray!"

He stared at her in shock, until the wizard summoned a burnished steel shield. "It is true, Prince Greylock. Look for yourself."

The stranger in the mirror of the shield looked like an old man, with young and stunned black eyes. The change was complete.

The next morning found Greylock still feeling the effects of his mysterious meeting of the day before, but he decided he must conceal this from Mayor Tarelton and appear to be concerned only with gaining his rightful throne again. Once more visions of the Lady Silverfrost, and of himself sitting upon the throne of the Tyrant, filled his head. The Lord High Mayor divined the direction of Greylock's thoughts and was reassured.

For a little while, Mayor Tarelton thought, the prince had talked of sacrifices and doing his duty. Now he was back to talking about Glyden, a much safer and more alluring subject. The Mayor was relieved, for the Steward Redfrock's instructions had been clear—to lead Prince Greylock into the trap that was being prepared for him.

It was the cold air of the foothills and sight of snow on the higher elevations that helped restore Greylock's confidence—and the increasing distance from the Twilight Dells. While the others bundled up in extra clothing, Greylock shed some of his, admonishing himself for having fallen into the soft ways of the Underworlders. In spite of this confidence, he concealed the jeweled replica of Thunderer in an ordinary sheath. There would be a proper time to reveal it, he thought.

With his long, eager strides up the twisting mountain trail, he soon grew impatient with the out-of-shape soldiers of the BorderKeep. He wished he could just continue with yeoman Harkkor and his followers, but the farmers had scrupulously avoided calling attention to themselves, and would only acknowledge their agreement with subtle signs. He was also becoming concerned that he had seen no indication of the Steward's sentries. Greylock had expected the Gateway to be rigidly guarded and was beginning to wonder if they were not marching into a trap.

"We must hurry!" he said at last. "If my people choose a successor to my uncle before I return, then we will have to fight a long and bloody war." "I'm sorry, Prince Greylock," the Lord High Mayor said. "My men are not used to these heights. You must give them a chance to rest." Moag snorted. "I told you we should have gone on to Trold. King Kasid would have given us a real army, not this fat and lazy bunch of villagers." "You are a nuisance with all your grumbling, old man," Tarelton retorted angrily.

"Perhaps it will not matter," Greylock quickly intervened. "I must reconnoiter the High Plateau anyway. If we are very lucky, my uncle will still be alive and the succession will not yet have been decided. Rest your men here, Lord High Mayor and proceed—cautiously—in the morning. I will meet you on the trail."

"What if you don't come back?"

"Then I would suggest you turn back, Mayor Tarelton." Greylock smiled grimly. "Our only chance of success is to surprise them. They will never expect anyone to come from the Underworld. They will be fighting among themselves as usual. But if I am captured, there will be no victory for you: if I am dead, they will never accept you as a ruler." Greylock hoped that what he had just said was true, and that the Steward Redfrock had given up watching for him.

"Maybe you had better not go, Prince Greylock," Mayor Tarelton looked worried, and Greylock thought that at least he was taking his ally seriously. He did not realize that the Mayor's instructions were to guide the prince, and that could not be done if he were out of sight.

"Someone must scout ahead, and only I know the way," Greylock said impatiently. "Don't worry! I'll be back in the morning. Come along, Moag. Let us see if anything has changed in my absence. You can finally get a look at our Glyden."

He turned to move up the trail when he heard Mara's soft voice object. "I am coming, too."

"You stay," Greylock answered, more annoyed that she would refute his orders than for any real objections to her coming along.

"You are not my master, Greylock," she said angrily. "I go where Grandfather goes. It has always been so."

"Hold her here for at least an hour," he told yeoman Harkkor, who complied by lifting her with one arm, still struggling, and waving them on their way with the other.

Looking back, Greylock was satisfied to see that his army blended in with the mountain snows, except for the green robe and red hair of the Lord High Mayor, which stood out clearly. He would have to convince the Mayor to give up at least the green robe, he thought, if not his red hair. The two of them quickly left the others behind.

Even so, as they rounded the first turn in the trail, hundreds of yards away, they found Mara standing before them frowning determinedly with her arms crossed.

"How … ?" Greylock managed to sputter. "Where did you come from?"

"Well, well!" Moag chuckled, and Greylock turned in astonishment at the happy sound. "Prince Greylock, you have succeeded in making her do what I have been pleading with her, and cajoling her, to do for years. She has used her magic! And without the orders from a master! Her motivation must have been very strong indeed for her to do that. And I do not think it is because she wants to be with her grandfather," he finished, looking at Greylock in appreciation.

Greylock was bewildered further to see a red flush rise in Mara's cheeks. He remembered his earlier promise to himself to look for the truth in her face. But he did not like the truth he was seeing in her face right now. She couldn't be in love with him! She was still a child! And he was promised to the Lady Silverfrost.

But even as he raised his objection to himself, he saw that in their few weeks together she had swiftly grown out of that awkward phase he had first noticed. She was almost a woman! Her bright green eyes suddenly showed a maturity that had not been there before. Her long blond hair no longer had the downy softness of childhood, but the healthy glow of a woman. And her habit of flicking the hair from her eyes was no longer annoying, but alluring. Her slim figure had filled out in a few short weeks. Not knowing what to say in the embarrassed silence, he turned abruptly and brushed by her without further word.

As they ascended into the cloud layer, the two Underworlders grew short of breath and slowed down. Greylock was forced to adjust his long, eager steps to their timid ones. Finally, even he was forced to don his last, heavy robe as the snowflakes began to obscure everything but the next few steps. Greylock found the staff he had cached on the way down, leaving it in the remote hope that he would be able to return. He wished he could have saved his Talons as well. Now the staff proved useful in probing the snow-covered trail. Several times the snowpack fell away into space at the staff's touch, and the three stared down into a sky of whirling snowflakes. Greylock helped the two frightened Underworlders around these spaces as best he could.

Finally, Greylock motioned for them to remain silent and motionless, and inched forward to study something only he could see. He brushed away some of the light powder snow, and then smiled to himself and motioned the others forward.

"We must hurry from here if we are to see anything of the High Plateau before dark."

"How are we to see anything in this blizzard?" Moag said miserably. "I can't even see the trail anymore!"

Both Underworlders were dismayed by Greylock's sudden spurt of speed from this point onward, fearing to see him fall away into the air, but they grew silent when they saw a broad, even road stretching upward before them.

Greylock smiled proudly. "This is the Gateway. From here on, every road in my uncle's kingdom is paved in stone. And some, as I have told you, in Glyden." I may as well keep up the deception of a Glyden-rich kingdom a while longer, he thought. Even Moag would have to be satisfied when he saw the treasury of the Tyrant.

But for once the wizard was not thinking of Glyden. Instead, he was stooped over even more than usual, examining their broad and magnificent roadway.

"Did your people build this?" he asked wonderingly. "This is a feat of engineering beyond any but the richest of the Kings of Trold!"

"These roads have been here for as long as anyone can remember," Greylock explained. "We have a story that we are simply the Gatekeepers of this road, which we call Gateway in our legends. We are the protectors of Godshome. This has never made much sense to me, for what is there to protect? Could an entire country, an entire people, be only Gatekeepers for others, whom we have never seen? Where are the gods we are meant to protect? Or the demons we are supposed to protect them from? Before I went down into your Underworld, I did not believe any of these stories. Now … I am not so sure. It seems to me that there must be a reason for these legends, a reason not even the Gatekeepers, our priests, know."

When they crossed the first bare patches of the road, where the mountain winds had never allowed the snows to build, the deception of a road paved in Glyden was shown up. Instead, the road was made of huge stones, placed in a mosaic that left no gap larger than the sharp edge of a sword.

The stones had not been carved, but by an almost unimaginable patience had been laid naturally side-by-side until they had fitted snugly. Moag was fascinated by the ancient road, and did not complain about the lack of Glyden, if indeed he noticed it.

At one point both Underworlders stopped and let out startled shouts. They had suddenly walked over a patch of the Gateway, which radiated a surprising but welcome heat.

"What is the source of this warmth?" Moag asked in amazement.

"It comes out of the mountain," Greylock explained quickly. The two Underworlders were lingering in the comforting heat, despite his urgings to hurry. "Sometimes it comes out of cracks in the earth, sometimes out of the earth itself. Many parts of the High Plateau are fertile enough to grow food because of this warmth, and it is around these warm spots, which we call Icemelts, that we build our snowcastles."

"But what causes the heat?" Moag insisted. As a magician he was not satisfied with this answer, and as a Fire-Wizard the fire in the earth fascinated him.

"We do not know where it comes from. Only that it comes from deep within Godshome. Sometimes the very earth is melted and boils out of the cracks in the mountain." A cloud passed over Greylock's face. "When that happens there is much destruction. Many times we have had to rebuild. The Gatekeepers tell us that the whole of the High Plateau was created from this firestone. But they also say that the evil spirits—demons —brew the firestone, so I never believed them. Now … I am not so sure."

It was the second time, he realized, that he had admitted to himself that he might be reverting to the religion of his youth—to the time when he had been fascinated by the Gatekeepers' arcane answers to the mysterious origins of firestone.

Moag and Mara were finally willing to move on, though they continued to linger at each warm spot they came upon. Greylock warned them that staying in the heat only made the inevitable cold worse, but they were unable to resist the seductive pull of the warmth. Greylock began to wonder if he would not have the same trouble with the whole army of Underworlders when he led them this way.

The road began to widen and the slope to level, and Greylock once again moved forward cautiously. At last they sighted the first of the dwellings Greylock had called snowcastles, perched on the very edge of the High Plateau. The plateau dropped off steeply on the side that was exposed to the sky. The Three Peaks of Godshome bound upon the other sides.

But the two Underworlders could not see the peaks in the mild blizzard, and their eyes were drawn to the dwelling, which indeed resembled a huge castle made out of snow. The walls were thick and imposing, towering over the path and out into the empty spaces of the mountain cliffs. Narrow windows had been carved into the sides of the walls, and a tower had been built at one corner. The ice of the tower gleamed blue even in the dim light of the storm. Barely visible within were stone buildings, the true living quarters of the inhabitants. The snowcastle seemed designed to afford a view on all, and access to none.

Greylock pointed proudly. "There lies Castle- Guardian, home of my friend, Mordref, whom I call Slimspear. Only he and my sister, Ardra, know how I left the High Plateau—that I went down instead of up, as was expected of me. He warned me not to go down, told me that I would run into demons. Unlike me, Slimspear is very religious. I cannot wait to tell him how wrong he was!"

There was one narrow door to the snowcastle, at the top of a long flight of icy steps. The white walls converged on both sides of the door, making whoever was on the steps an easy target.

"You had better stay below," Greylock warned. "It may take a few minutes for me to convince Slimspear that it is really me, and not a demon."

He bounded up the stairs, handling the slippery steps with an accustomed ease. At the top, he paused and knocked softly at the heavy wooden door set in the ice. At the last moment, he pulled the hood of his mountain cloak over his gray mane of hair. A small slit opened in one of the panels almost immediately and a frightened voice emerged. "Go away, demon!"

"Slimspear! Open up! It is I, Greylock. Hurry, let me in before someone else sees that I have come back."

"You do not fool me, demon. You could not be Greylock. The Gatekeepers say that only demons, and he who shall be their Deliverer, may return from below. Therefore, though you have taken the face and voice of my friend Greylock, you are a demon."

"Would a demon know the name Slimspear, or that you have always been in love with my sister, Ardra, but were afraid to tell her? Or have you told others since I left?"

The panel snapped shut abruptly, and Greylock wondered if he had frightened his oldest friend away. Then the massive door opened timidly, grinding slowly, and the pale plump face of Mordref could be seen.

"Is it really you, Greylock?"

"Of course it's me!" Greylock grabbed his friend by the shoulders and looked him in the eyes intently for several seconds. "Do you really have any doubt?" he said quietly.

Relief flooded Slimspear's face and he threw open the door. As he hugged the returned prince, Greylock motioned to the hidden Underworlders abruptly from behind his back. They hurried up the stairs, trying desperately to maintain their footing and their speed, the sight of the warm interior summoning them. Then they were through the open door.

Slimspear followed them through the windswept inner courtyard and into the small, cozy rooms within the stone walls at the end of the long outer corridors, staring at the two visitors in shock. All the color had drained from his face. The owner of the snowcastle belied by his appearance his name. He was anything but slim, and had received his nickname from Greylock by once vowing that he would someday be as slim as a spear. Now he looked as if he would never eat again.

"What is it, Slimspear?" Greylock exclaimed, concerned by the intensity of his friend's reaction.

"I have failed!"

"What do you mean, Slimspear?"

"For generations beyond counting, my family has held Castle-Guardian, pledged to protect the High Plateau from demons. Now I have let two—no, three, for you must be one, too—into my country!" Greylock had removed his hood, revealing his silver hair. "Demons! I have failed the Tyrant, and my people."

"Nonsense, Slimspear," Greylock coaxed, as only friends can. "I have been to the Underworld. It is not full of demons. It is not anything like what the Gatekeepers say. ..." Greylock realized suddenly that nothing he was saying was penetrating his friend's daze. Desperately he said, "Cheer up, Slimspear. How do you know I am not this Deliverer the Gatekeepers are always talking about?" Though Greylock had tried to conceal his real wonderings behind this joke, Mordref saw through it, and glimpsed his concern.

"Of course! You are the Deliverer. You must be! I should have known."

The three spies relaxed at last, and fell into the soft chairs. They were safe until morning.

Later, Slimspear took his friend aside and broke the news of the Lady Silverfrost's coming marriage to the Steward Redfrock.

"I must speak to her!" he exclaimed. "Does she believe me dead?"

"No, Greylock," Slimspear said sadly. "You must not talk to her. You do not realize all that has happened since you left. The Steward's power has increased, and Silverfrost has given in to him. She is his completely now."

"I don't believe you!" Greylock denied what he was hearing. "She hates Carrell Redfrock!" "Silverfrost was never what you thought she was, Greylock. She has a weak will and is not worthy of you. It is time you realized that."

"Let us see what she says when I am Tyrant!" Greylock said, knowing she would come to him then—and not sure if he would take her.

CHAPTER FIVE

B y early the following morning, the blizzard had passed and the skies were clear and blue. The two visitors from the Underworld, and the returning prince, stared at Godshome in awe from the Castle-Guardian's icetower. The three even peaks zigzagged across the horizon in white, crisp lines. The High Plateau stretched flat and even toward the mountain, in an almost perfect triangle. Other, smaller snowcastles dotted the plain, and two large snowcastles, with what looked to be a small village between them, sat on a huge Icemelt. Greylock identified the larger of the snowcastles as Castle-Tyrant, his uncle's home; and the slightly smaller snowcastle as Castle-Steward. Around each of the snowcastles that were visible, was the disconcerting sight of green trees and brush, where the pockets of warmth called Icemelts sprouted from the snows.

Late into the night Greylock had discussed the matters of the realm with Slimspear. Little had changed, except that the Tyrant had grown more ill and even more oppressive, and that some of the rivals to his throne were coming out into the open in the jockeying for power. Chief among them was Greylock's enemy, Carrell Redfrock. It was a dangerous gambit, Greylock thought, while the Tyrant was still alive. Apparently, no one expected any of the sons or nephews to return, which was no surprise to Greylock.

Greylock reluctantly ended their awestruck reverie of Godshome. "We must hurry down and meet the others before anyone else is up and around."

The three spies slipped down the upper portions of the Gateway, almost running until they reached the rough, lower trails. Even then they made better time than they had on the way up, for Greylock had borrowed a pair of Talons from Slimspear. They met the men of the BorderKeep far down the mountain, stymied at the base of the first of the broken stretches. This was not as much progress as Greylock had hoped, but he restrained his impatience. It did not matter as long as they arrived while there was still daylight. He did not want to be caught with these men on Godshome at night; especially since their coming was to be a surprise.

As soon as they had gained entrance to his uncle's snowcastle, he thought, victory was assured. The night before, Greylock had gone to the cellars of Castle-Guardian and made sure that the secret lava tube passage to Castle-Tyrant remained clear and unguarded. Greylock's unknown entrance would make even the Tyrant's own personal chambers vulnerable to the Underworld army, he believed.

Greylock hurried the men along the last stretch of road to Slimspear's snowcastle, past the Icemelts on the trail, glad that there was not any kind of storm. Even with the clear trails and good weather, they had been lucky not to lose any men to the mountain. Luckily they were not visible from the High Plateau at any point along the Gateway. The walls of the mountain's cliffs stretched up out of sight on one side, and an observer would have had to be well out over the edge of the plateau to see them. Only the protected portals of Castle-Guardian faced away from the plateau and toward the road, as was its function, and since its master believed Greylock to be the Deliverer himself, they were unobserved by enemy eyes.

Once the army was safely crowded within Castle-Guardian, Greylock left them in the courtyard and rushed up the icetower to survey the white plain of the plateau. Only at the sight of the calm, untroubled snows was he satisfied that they had not been seen. He wound down the stairs to where his followers waited, but instead of stopping, he continued on down the flight of stairs past them. He motioned for them to follow him, down into the darkened depths of the snowcastle. Giving each other anxious looks, the men of BorderKeep followed hesitantly.

The cellar must have been dug into the rock of the High Plateau itself, the wizard Moag thought. It was an impressive feat, and he thought it even more impressive when he realized that the base of the plateau was almost all lava stone, aside from the few inches of topsoil carefully accumulated in the few Icemelts. But the tunnels that lay concealed behind the huge kegs of ice water were natural; long spiraling lava tubes that worked their way down into the bowels of the mountain. Moag suspected that if they continued to take only the downward turns, they would reach the point where the earth melted, and firestone was created.

Greylock apparently did not intend to take this downward course, but instead led across the plateau diagonally to the Tyrant's snowcastle, through the well-traveled caves of his youth; and down a few he believed only he knew the way through.

Greylock gave every tenth man a torch and ushered the stilled and frightened company of soldiers into the yawning black cavern. When they hesitated again, he rushed forward to take the lead and was gratified to find yeoman Harkkor following. Greylock had never become lost in the caverns, though some of his childhood friends had not had such an easy time of it. He had always seemed to know where he was beneath the mountain, and where to turn next. Slimspear had never become so comfortable, and this time remained behind to keep a watch on their rear.

The air was cool and stuffy, yet the close atmosphere actually seemed to give the Underworlders a strange sense of warm safety after the blizzards they had endured. But as they descended deeper into the bewilderingly complex route of tunnels, the air became noticeably warmer, and the soldiers noticeably less comfortable with the warmth. They breathed easier when the path seemed to ascend once more, but then it dipped downward again at an alarming angle. Greylock did not answer their increasingly worried questions, and ignored their fear. They were safe, but he doubted he would ever be able to convince them of that.

Only the lava dust that covered the floor felt moist and cool. Sometimes the tunnel constricted suddenly and the way was blocked. Then they had to dig their way through, crawling through the narrow openings. Leading the troop with his hand extended over his head, Greylock called out the sudden dives and obstructions of the rough craggy roof. Since he was by far the tallest of the company, and yeoman Harkkor the broadest, no one should have cracked their heads. But occasionally one of the soldiers of the BorderKeep would cease to pay attention for a moment and would walk into the rock, creating a scalp wound that bled profusely, and which had to be bandaged. Before long, he noticed that the nervous troop was walking bent over in a stoop that rivaled Moag's.

Sometimes a crack in the roof would reveal daylight from above. The snow curved inward over these holes, dark blue and dripping steadily at their bases; pure white, with the sun shining through, on the top few inches. They could see from these glimpses how deep the snow was, but more importantly to Greylock, he guided them by these occasional markers of light. Sunlight streamed down into the dark caves, lighting the tunnels for hundreds of feet both ways. Sometimes, after traveling for long minutes in the dark, it was a shock to come across these spots of light and realize that it was still day outside.

As children, Greylock and Slimspear had defied their parents, as generations of children of the High Plateau had, and explored the endless caverns, until they knew every path to each other's castles, as well underground as they did above.

Still, the familiar paths sometimes seemed to shift on them if they were away from them for long—and Greylock had not been below for years.

The first change he noticed was a turn to the left that should have been to the right, and then a turn that should not have been there at all, and finally a long descent that did not appear as if it would ever end. At the bottom of this pit he was confronted by an unfamiliar fork in the path.

As Greylock hesitated, Moag noticed his puzzlement and distress and hurried over to him. "What is wrong, Greylock?" he asked in a low voice, not wanting the others to know they were lost, for he knew they would panic.

"This shouldn't be here! I have never seen this fork before, though it is on a level I am sure I have fully explored."

"Well, the choice is simple enough. One goes left and up; and one goes right, and down!"

"So it seems. But for how far?"

"Well, hurry up and choose, Greylock. Your army is getting nervous."

By now, the Lord High Mayor had realized something was wrong, and demanded to be told.

"My Familiar can find out which is the right one," he volunteered when it had been explained that they needed to go upward for some distance to reach Castle-Tyrant. Greylock could hear the claws of the rat as it scrambled down the Mayor's tall frame and disappeared into the dark. It was back within a few minutes.

"The right hand tunnel goes only downward," he announced when the rat was once more on his shoulder. "The left tunnel is the one we want," he said with certainty in his voice.

"Sometimes a tunnel will go downward for quite a distance before it angles up again," Greylock said doubtfully. "I think I will explore it a little further, just for the feel of it." He did not see the Mayor's face go pale as he darted into the same passage the rat had investigated.

This choice quickly began to angle further downward, as the rat had reported, and Greylock just as quickly changed his mind. He backtracked and found the others, who met him with nervous muttering, as well as a relieved look from the Mayor. But Greylock refused to show them any worry, and they continued to follow him, though very near to panic. The cave on the left seemed to be going in the proper direction, and he was still not suspicious; confident he could find his way out no matter what. Eventually, he reasoned, he would have to come across something he recognized.

The second tunnel also began to drop slightly, but took longer to reveal its course. The overweight and out-of-shape soldiers were exhausted by now from this continual up and down movement, and when Greylock saw the yeomen also were sweating, but uncomplaining, he decided to give them rest before they were actually into the coming fight.

As the soldiers collapsed gratefully onto the dusty floor, breathing heavily and staring at each other in commiseration, Greylock took this time to slip away into the dark. Running back down the pitch black tunnel, with only a small torch for light, he backtracked for some distance to see if he could discover where he might have gone wrong. The troop's path was easily discernable by the turmoil they had created in the lava dust. The churned up tracks would be seen for many years to come, he thought, if no one happened along to disturb them. Yet, suddenly, these tracks came up against a solid rock wall! Greylock dropped to his knees and searched desperately for a seam at the base of the wall. They were in a trap!

It seemed impossible to Greylock that the old caves could have been tampered with. Secret passages and mysterious doors that closed after you had passed were the stuff of legends. But now he recognized where he had passed the old, well- traveled corridor—that was now blocked off and disguised by a false wall. There was no budging the stone slab.

There was only one person who could have engineered this—the Steward. Very well, Greylock thought, even Carrell Redfrock could not seal off all the caves. They would explore every tunnel; explore as long as they still lived. Above all, he must not let the others know of their danger!

"I remember now!" he announced loudly when he rejoined the others, though he doubted that he had fooled the magician and his granddaughter. "This was the right way all along. Now, it may get a little rough from here on out, but we are almost there. Stay together and keep an eye on me."

The passage actually started upward for a short way and Greylock had a sudden, wild hope that he might have somehow outmaneuvered the Steward. Then an almost impossibly steep slope dashed his hopes. Joining hands, they started to inch their way down. Greylock was encouraged to see side passages begin to appear. He declined to turn into any of them—guessing that the Steward would expect him to take these invitingly convenient exits.

Down they went into the mountain until the walls began to glow with an eerily red glow, and became too hot to touch. The men began to remove their outer garments, careful not to accidentally brush their hands against the steaming rock. Their surface discipline was finally beginning to crack, and Greylock began to hear muttered curses and threats behind his back. As these became louder, Greylock was made aware of yeoman Harkkor's stolid presence as he jostled him, smiling encouragingly. But the soldiers depended on him, now more than ever, to lead them out again, so he was safe. As long as they still think I can lead them out, he thought.

By now Greylock was sure that he had gone further into the mountain than even Steward Redfrock could have predicted and allowed for. He at last began considering a turn away from the approaching heat, though all the side tunnels also appeared to descend. But suddenly they emerged on a natural balcony, high in the side of a vast deep cavern.

The pit was brimming with molten lava. They watched in awe as a huge globule of firestone sprang violently from the shimmering pool and seemed to hang before their eyes, larger than the perch on which they stood and radiating an intense heat, before it dropped slowly, majestically back into the pool. At several points along the sides of the cliff below them, rivers of bright firestone flowed from lava falls into the bright lake. This was the source of the High Plateau's heat, Greylock thought, the source of its Icemelts, and its life.

At first they were too stunned to move, but within a few seconds the intense heat had driven them back, covering their faces with their hands and the folds of their cloaks. They did not cease their retreat until they had gone around the first of the abrupt turns. The steaming walls now seemed relatively cool, and they leaned against them, catching their breath and feeling as if their lungs had been seared.

Without a word, the subdued soldiers followed Greylock into one of the side passages. All of them seemed to have become unnaturally sensitive to the hellish pit and knew instantly when they were nearing it again. For a while, it seemed as if every choice led back to it again, but because of their new awareness of temperature they began making slow progress toward the cooler portions of the underground network.

Eventually the maze started to lead upward at last, and Greylock excitedly recognized a few marks on the walls. He suddenly knew where the path was leading—and it was where he wanted to go. He led quickly from that point.

———

The huge cavern beneath Castle-Tyrant was the most public and familiar of all the lava tubes. Lying near the village, many celebrations had taken place within it over the years, safe from the cruel mountain blizzards. Natural skylights spotted the enormous roof and the cavern was well lit—almost blinding to the men entering suddenly from the dark caverns below. Blackened stumps and half-burned logs marked where bonfires had been lit to give some warmth, and potholes lined the walls where children had dug into the soft dirt.

No celebrations or festivals had been allowed for some time, apparently not since the Tyrant had first fallen ill. Litter spotted the eroding footprints in the dust, and crude ladders and ropes hung forlornly from the roof. This traditional gathering spot had always been untended and natural, but now Greylock had to wrinkle his nose distastefully at the smell of garbage. The ancient pit had become a refuse heap, a dumping place for all the trash and slop of the High Plateau. Even the wind whistling through the gaping holes in the roof could not take away the awful odor.

Straight ahead of them were the beckoning broad stairs carved into the walls, leading to the entrance of Castle-Tyrant. The army rushed toward them, anxious to confront a human enemy at last—and Greylock was at their head, eager to fling his escape at the Steward Redfrock. His feet had barely touched the first step when a roaring wind flowed down the stairs, throwing Greylock violently backward onto the earth. The torch was plucked from his hand and snuffed out.

The torches in the hands of the others sputtered only briefly in defiance of the gale before they, too, winked out. For a few more stunned seconds, the daylight continued to stream down the holes in the roof, the muffled glow catching the disturbed particles of dust briefly in its light. Then platforms of rock slammed down over the holes with a frightening thud, knocking huge fragments from the roof down upon the terrified Keepsmen.

A ghostly voice filled the chamber, and Greylock could recognize the strained rasp of his uncle's throat. The voice must have been magnified by echo chambers somewhere in the staircase, he thought. All of the men of the BorderKeep could hear the frightening words of that whispery voice.

"Now, I have you, demons! Did you think you could surprise me; that I would not have every entrance to my kingdom thoroughly guarded? Or did you believe I would be fooled by the guise of my nephew? Stay where you are, demons, and rot! There is no escape from this prison!"

Greylock realized that his uncle's trap had succeeded where the Steward Redfrock's had not.

CHAPTER SIX

Greylock learned quickly the fickleness of his allies, to his dismay. It did not take more than a few seconds of total darkness for the men of the BorderKeep to panic. Most of them had never before been plunged into a world where they could make no light to fill the darkness without the flames being blown out by another of the magical gusts of wind.

When he had finally had enough of the Keepsmen's wails and of the Lord High Mayor's recriminations, Greylock called out in his quick temper for Moag. His voice was drowned out twice before he angrily bellowed above the furor. The startled soldiers ceased pleading to their gods for a few shocked moments, as if they expected him to reassure them that there was a way out. Then it was past, and the first of the Underworlders began to shout again, with the others quickly following his example. But not before Moag was able to feel his way over to Greylock, his bony strong fingers searching for a calm and unmoving figure among the frightened soldiers, and knowing instantly when he had found Greylock.

"You must get us out of here, wizard!" Greylock demanded desperately, knowing that he was being unreasonable.

"There is little I can do, Prince Greylock," the old man answered. "Did you know that your uncle has the power? A strong earth-magic, I believe. We are sealed in by the physical, and we are sealed in by the magical, as well."

"I was a fool to challenge my uncle." Greylock finally allowed his doubts to emerge. "He has beaten me every step of the way; just as he has always outwitted the Steward Redfrock and every other opponent. If only I could speak with him, and tell him what the Underworld is really like! " "No, you were not a fool. You just picked the wrong army, Greylock. We should have gone to Trold. Then we wouldn't have had to skulk underground."

"At least you could give us some light, old man!" Greylock said angrily to the old man's carping.

"You realize that a fire will use up air?"

"If we do not have light, we shall never escape anyway! We may live longer in the dark, but the end will be just as certain."

Moag did not answer* and Greylock could hear the sounds of the wizard bending over and his hands scurrying along the ground. Then he saw the light of the unnatural blue flame of magic nestled in a small pile of rubbish that the old man had apparently collected. Then the flame caught, and Greylock blinked at a clean white light that was not blown out but grew—until at last the shapes of the Keepsmen were illuminated and their shadows were sent swiftly climbing the walls.

Before Greylock had a chance to stop them, the soldiers had spread this one fire with joyful cries to a dozen other fires lit about the chamber. Those men who weren't clustered around these reassuring flames, glorying in the light, were off gathering bits o-f burnable trash.

Luckily, Greylock thought, the fires did not seem to be giving off much smoke and he reasoned that putting out some of the fires would cause more smoke, and more complaining, than could be endured. Besides, he hoped, there had to be *some* air entering the chamber through the porous lava stone.

The Lord High Mayor had come to join Greylock and the wizard by the original fire. The rat sat unconcernedly on the Mayor's shoulder, and Greylock thought with a shudder that the Familiar could live indefinitely in the cave, feeding off the trash. Soon there would be even fresher food for it. Greylock doubted the animal would decline the temptation of dining on his former master. Greylock could not see that the thoughts of the Lord High Mayor were running in much the same vein, as Tarelton wondered if he had been betrayed and abandoned.

It was Lord High Mayor Tarelton who first noticed that Mara was missing.

At first, Greylock was not really worried by the absence. After all, where could she go? he thought. He remembered seeing her just before the torches had gone out, therefore she had to be in the chamber somewhere. But soon his search became frantic when she did not turn up, no matter how hard they looked, and his shouts echoed off the roof and walls. She had vanished into thin air.

When the Underworlders had first entered the cavern below the Castle-Tyrant, Mara's eyes had been caught by the unmistakable gleam of Glyden flashing near one of the walls. Thinking vaguely of how nice it would be to present her grandfather with a gift of Glyden, and remembering Greylock's tales of its plentitude on the High Plateau, she was drawn toward one of the children's excavations along the wall. This hole was quite deep, and just wide enough for a young boy — or a small woman. At the bottom flashed the gilded object, but she could still not see what it was.

While the others were absorbed in the sights of the cave, and just beginning their dash toward the stairs, she jumped in idly, knowing that she was being foolish and hoping that the loose earth would not cave in on her. When the child's tunnel ended after only a few yards, and she found nothing, she shrugged at her foolishness and began to back out, hoping that the others had not left her behind in her brief sojourn.

But backing out did not prove as easy as entering had been, and she felt herself squeezed by the roof, whereas on her way in she had not felt it at all. Soon she was sure that her inward passage had dropped enough earth from the roof to obstruct her exit. Half cursing her stupidity in searching for Glyden, when if she had waited as she-had always told her grandfather to do she would have gotten all the Glyden she wanted, and half in panic, she struggled to turn around. This proved too much for the roof, which had never been meant to contain an adult, and it collapsed behind her, filling the hole with dust and drawing from her a coughing fit, which threatened to bring down the rest of the tunnel at any moment.

Trying desperately to maintain her presence of mind, Mara began calling out; at first for her grandfather, and then in more panic, for Greylock, and finally with frightened shrieks, for help from anyone who could hear her. But no sounds penetrated her tomb, except for one loud thud that again threatened to bring down the wall of the tunnel. After a moment she thought she could hear a ghostly laughter, but then decided she must have imagined it. She did not realize that the others had also just been sealed within a deadly trap.

The tears began to streak down through her dust-covered cheeks and the dirt collected at the corners of her lips. Her blond hair fell over her face, but she did not flick it aside for it did not matter — she could see nothing. Not for several minutes did she think of using her magic. She had so stubbornly refused to summon any help from magic in the past that the habit had never become part of her thinking. Even now she was reluctant to use it. She tried to remember the spell she had used once before, with astonishing results, up on the mountain pass. Her eyes closed and she summoned the hated and unwanted power, but though she could feel it just beyond her grasp, she discovered as her grandfather already had above her, that she was constrained by a power greater than hers.

Left with only one recourse, she began carefully, then more frantically, to dig upward. She shoveled the earth behind her harder and faster as the seconds passed, but the air she was breathing was the same air, she realized, that had been trapped with her long minutes ago. She was breathing it in great gasps now, but this did not seem to relieve the ache in her lungs. Soon she was no longer paying any attention to the direction she was digging, but just grabbing handfuls of the earth, the dirt that came away easiest, and it fell about her like rain.

It seemed ironic to her that, as a Witch of the Winds, she had always stubbornly refused to use her power over this element; now despite her willingness at last to use her magic, she was about to die of suffocation!

Suddenly, she realized to her horror that she had ceased to go upward at all, but had settled for following the soft earth almost directly forward. Her second shock was that when she proceeded to correct this direction she was met by solid rock. She fell back into the hole sobbing in frustration, ready at that moment to give up. She clawed futilely and pathetically at the wall, the dirt now causing pain under her fingernails, and to her astonishment, her hand suddenly went through the earth and encountered air on the other side!

For a few minutes, she did not bother to enlarge the hole, but settled for breathing deeply the wisps of fresh air it tantalizingly provided. Then she pulled at the earth with renewed vigor and it came away easily, enlarging the hole to her satisfaction. She called out twice, but when no answer came back, she realized that she must have emerged into another of the endless caves. But at that moment life seemed good, if only because it provided cool, sweet air—never mind that it was just as dark as before and that she had no idea where she was.

She soon realized that it was not quite as pitch black as she first thought. There seemed to be a pinpoint of light that could barely be perceived by the eye, visible perhaps only because there was no other light to compete with it. If she glanced away from the dot of light for even a moment, she could believe that she had imagined it. But it stayed there, unmoving, to be appreciated if she stared at it long enough, and she decided it was real.

She crawled out of her own little cave, which had almost been her grave, and walked cautiously toward the prick of light, her hands extended blindly. From the echoing sound of her footsteps, she realized that she was in another giant enclosure, at least as big as the one she had just left, and as she neared she saw that the light was high up on its wall, a square doorway of light that barely illuminated a flight of narrow steps. Unafraid, she mounted the staircase and passed through the shimmering portal. ^

On the other side was a simple stone platform, flanked by two other staircases leading down a few steps until they were blocked by massive wooden doors; and one staircase that led up out of sight, lit by torches. She skipped down to one of the doors and tugged, then pushed at it. As she had suspected, it would not budge. With determination in her young face, she marched up the long flight of stairs.

At the top of the long straight stairway, another of the huge doors confronted her. Behind it she could barely hear a great bustle, the clanking of pots and pans, the shouts and laughter of women. This door was unlocked, and daring to push it open a crack, Mara saw what she immediately assumed to be many serving women, moving about a steaming kitchen with good- natured and agile speed, despite their bulk. One by one, giant trays of food were lifted with grunts and carried from the room on their shoulders, until at last it was empty, of both food and servants. It certainly did not seem as if they were concerned about the fighting, she thought wonderingly. Where were the others!

Cautiously, but licking her lips hungrily, Mara stepped into the room. A few scraps of meat had been left on a long wooden slab, a huge block of wood that served as both a table and a cutting board. Dozens of knives were stuck negligently into its scoured and stained surface. Not knowing that she was stealing the food of the Steward's Familiar, she grabbed at the food and ate it hungrily. Then she began to explore the snowcastle. At the last moment, she plucked a knife from its stubborn hold in the wood.

On the other side of the wide swinging doors through which the serving women had exited, Mara heard the loud noises of dining and triumphant laughter. But to the right, she spied a narrow staircase that seemed to follow the path she had taken to the kitchen, and she darted over to it, almost as to an old friend.

Many doors and landings led off these stairs, but she went on to the top, not knowing what else to do and thinking vaguely that she would find a vantage point there that would afford a view. At the top, though, there was only a narrow and dark door without a landing. Reaching up from a few steps below the door, she opened and peered in.

It was a sparse room; a small room with no windows. Only a huge stone bed filled one end of the room, and the rest was bare stone. But what she noticed most was the cold. It felt like icicles were being thrust into her hands and face.

Yet, despite the freezing temperature, an old, old man was lying on the hard frame of the bed, asleep with his mouth open, and very near death. Suddenly, the ancient red-lidded eyes in an almost blue face opened, and black eyes pierced her even more than the frigid cold of the room. Only when those eyes changed suddenly into a deceptive merriment did she recognize his features. This old man had to be Greylock's uncle, the Tyrant of the High Plateau!

"Come in, demon girl," his voice cracked. "I am not so ill that I imagine you, nor am I so ill that I cannot defend myself against any demon. It does not matter anyway, for I have already entered the Deathroom, and once here I may not leave. Come in, and sit by me on my deathbed. Tell me of Greylock. Why has he returned?"

The old man's twinkling eyes did not fool Mara. She had heard too many stories of the hard life on the High Plateau, and of the cruel leader who had ruled it for so long. Shivering, she sat on the very end of the bed, on the edge, ready to flee at any moment. "He has come to take his rightful place as your heir. And to tell you that you have been wrong about the Underworld and the Gateway."

"He has come to take my place!" The Tyrant would have roared, had his voice been able, but the strain in his face was just as effective. Then the old man laughed strangely. "I hope he does take my place—better him than that treacherous Steward. But he must win by fighting for it, as I did. First he must kill the Steward Redfrock, for I am already dead. He will not find that easy."

Mara was confused by the sick man's sudden shifts of mood. The Tyrant is mad! she thought with a sudden insight. She fingered the carving knife concealed under the folds of her cloak.

"Tell my nephew, if he lives, that I am proud of him. I thought none of my heirs would challenge me. They all accepted exile and death meekly. Perhaps the time has come at last when the Gateway can be opened again."

"I will tell him."

Now the black eyes were changing again, and the face was filling with the rage that was the curse of the royal family.

"Demon!" he hissed, as if he had just noticed her, as perhaps one part of him had. "How did you escape my trap? Guards! Guards! Bring me Thunderer, that I may destroy this creature."

Mara dropped the kitchen knife clattering onto the stone floor, and fled from the room.

"I thought you said you could not use your magic to escape!" Greylock was angrily accusing the wizard in the cave below Castle-Tyrant.

"I can't!" Moag answered in a defensive and bewildered voice. "If I can't use my power, at your command, neither can she—not alone. Her natural power may be greater than mine, and I have often suspected just that, but that power is still untrained."

The Lord High Mayor had followed the two in their frantic search, at first bemused but not really concerned. Now he was beginning to have second thoughts about the Steward's intentions. He whispered into his Familiar's ear, and the rat left his master's shoulder for the second time, using his claws to scramble down his master's chest and dropping the last few feet to the floor of the chamber. Then it disappeared into the rubbish and the shadows.

As the others continued to search and argue fruitlessly, Mayor Tarelton made himself comfortable in the soft dust near the fire and waited for his Familiar to return. The rat came back eventually licking its snout, having apparently dined while it was gone, and scurried up to its comfortable perch on the shoulder of its master. As the rat reported what it had found in its own search, the Lord High Mayor casually rose to his feet and went looking for Greylock and the wizard. He found them out in the dark, still arguing heatedly.

"I know where she is—or where she was last," he said, interrupting their worried discussion.

"What do you mean?" Greylock asked, fearing the worst.

Moag only stared at the Mayor in shock, his face growing suddenly pale. He put both of his hands over his face and grew very still. The other two stopped curiously, and watched silently, knowing that this was not a reaction to the news, but something deeper and internal. Then the old man seemed to recover, as if he had reassured himself somehow about Mara's fate.

"She is alive, yet she is not here," he announced.

"How could that be ..."Greylock began, but the wizard shushed him.

"Show us where she disappeared," he commanded the Mayor.

By fits and starts, for the Mayor continually had to stop and listen to the Familiar's instructions, he led them toward one of the cavern walls. The light was dim here, but all could see the caved-in remains of a child's excavation to which he pointed, a few yards from the blank wall. Now it was Greylock's turn to grow pale. He dropped into the shallow hole and began digging in panic at the freshly caved-in earth.

"She is alive, I tell you," Moag said calmly above him. "Yet she is not with us here in this cave."

Greylock ceased his digging and stared at the wizard. "What do you mean? What are you two talking about?"

"She has found a way out, Greylock," Moag appeared to be confused. "Yet not by magic." "How can that be?" Even as he said this, Greylock quickly realized the only possibility.

Now the Lord High Mayor joined in the hopeful speculation. "Perhaps this tunnel leads to another cave and she was able to dig her way out!" he said excitedly.

"If she has done that, by herself, then together we can dig another tunnel!"

Many of the men who had followed them, willing to help in the search, seized at this hope and began digging. But others seemed to have already given up and sat together in lackadaisical bunches, seemingly grateful just for the next breath. The fires were flickering and sputtering, and though more rubbish was being thrown onto them, the flames were a pathetic remnant of the roaring fires of a few minutes before. Even as Greylock watched the dwindling energy of his men, the first of the fires went out, and then another. Black smoke spiraled upward to meet the unyielding rock of the cave roof, and then filled the chamber with an acrid, choking fog. Increasingly, they could not even see the smoke they were choking on.

Greylock saw that it would be a race between suffocation and escape. He directed his men along the line of the old tunnel, thinking that it would be easier digging. But huge stones, impossible to budge, constantly confronted them. They could never tell when a rock was first uncovered whether it was only a few inches across and could be moved, or whether it would turn out to be frustratingly deep in its grip on the earth. They wasted a good deal of precious time and energy on these hopelessly mired stones, until finally Greylock ordered them to dig around them, even if it appeared to be a roundabout way of reaching the wall.

At last they were under the original wall, and perhaps close to freedom. Yet, so near to their goal, the Keepsmen began to slow down considerably. Greylock saw to his frustration that progress was coming to a standstill, and he himself had dropped into an exhausted crouch, as if standing were too much of an effort, and he was breathing so heavily that he could hear himself. He could not ask the Keepsmen to do more, he thought, for they were as aware of the danger of inaction as he was. They were so close! Yet it was obvious they were going to lose their race with the rapidly dwindling supply of air.

The last of the fires winked out, and Greylock heard the wizard mutter, "How I wish I had my granddaughter's power over the wind!"

Then no one said a word, for to speak would have been too much of an effort.

Mara fled down the stairs from the Deathroom, her feet flying over three steps at a time, and she felt as if she were falling into a deep, great well. Every stone in the wall seemed to leap up past her, brightly lit. But she was still in control when she reached the junction of the kitchen again.

At the bottom of these steps, Mara was suddenly confronted by one of the inhabitants of the snowcastle. A young girl, with dark hair and eyes, and a plump cheerful face stared back, as Mara's eyes darted about desperately for an escape. As far as she could see, this girl was her single obstacle; but the old Tyrant's enraged voice was still drifting down the halls, and guards could happen along at any moment. She brushed by the strange girl, who grabbed ineffectually at her arm.

"No, wait!" the other girl cried. "I am Greylock's sister!"

"Ardra?" Mara stopped and turned, immediately seeing the resemblance to Greylock in this plump girl.

"Is it true? Is Greylock with those others?"

"Do you know where he is?" Mara asked anxiously.

"The Tyrant has trapped them below. Follow me! I know where they are, but I do not know how we can free them!"

Ardra took the steps as quickly as Mara had done. Their pursuers would not dare to follow, Mara thought. They would undoubtedly be constrained by their own bulky armor and by the steepness of the stairs. They would need to take each step carefully, one at a time. But it still would not leave them with much time to free Greylock and her grandfather, if what Ardra had hinted was true.

Ardra led her back to that same landing she had entered from the darkness of the caves. To the right was the door that led back to the chamber she had just emerged from—so she knew they were not there. And the left-hand door led away from the direction she had known the others to be last.

Only the door directly ahead of them could be hiding the captives, she thought, and Ardra confirmed this suspicion by pointing at the giant barrier.

"But it is locked! I have already tried to open it!"

Ardra could only shrug helplessly. She looked back up the stairs in alarm at the sound of armor.

Mara began to examine the huge oaken door, with its braces of hardened leather and bolts of brass, for some way to opening it; first with her hands, and then with her mind. Her senses quickly told her that she would never be able to force the door open physically, and the same barrier that had confronted her magical powers before was still intact, and actually seemed concentrated at this very door. But it was a simple, if very strong, trap spell, designed only to keep men within its grip, not to keep others out. On this side of the door she was no longer constrained by the spell, and it would not be a hindrance to her powers.

She knew her grandfather could have opened the door with a minimum of fuss and with great finesse. If he had been there, the portal would no doubt have simply popped open at his command. But she did not have the time and the patience to work with such care. She summoned the raw power she had always known she possessed and directed it at the wooden barrier.

The door exploded with killing force, sending deadly shards down both sides of the passage. But the very force of her magic wind continued to protect Ardra and her from the fragments, sending them glancing off them in mid-air and burying the splinters in the walls and floors.

It was dark and quiet beyond, and the air smelled stale and sickly. Mara sent fresh air from the halls behind her whistling down into the black hole beyond the door. Then, and only then, did they dare enter.

Behind the two girls, though still far above, came the clattering of weapons as the snowcastle's guards realized where Mara was at last and what she had done, and hurried to stop her before she had freed her companions. But it took much longer, as she had hoped it would, for the soldiers in their bulky armor to negotiate the narrow steps. They did not dare take them at the speed with which Ardra and she had escaped. Indeed, if she was not mistaken, some of the racket she had heard was the sound of one of them who didn't make it falling. She hoped that the careless soldier would bring others down in his fall. To help them along, she sent the wind whistling down the narrow twisting corridor once more.

The steep stairs continued from the landing down into darkness, but the walls gradually fell away on both sides, and she realized from the echo of their steps that she was once again within a vast cavern. But where were the skylights? Even more important, where were Greylock and Moag? She was certain, even without Ardra's assurance, that this was the same cave in which she had left the others.

Timidly at first, then realizing that it made no difference if anyone heard her, she shouted as loud as she could and Ardra's hesitant voice was added to hers. Their cries seemed to shock the atmosphere of the tomb, as if only whispers were meant to be spoken here, and how dare they break the ancient silence! But presently Mara thought she could hear a muffled answer from somewhere within the cavern, from the far side—and then she was sure that she heard several weak shouts.

Once beyond the light of the door, she tripped and fell once or twice in her hurry to reach the others, and Ardra helped her up. Summoning the blue flame that she had seen her father call forth so many times, and which was a physical manifestation of her magical powers, Mara cupped it in the palm of her hands. It did not glow as strongly as she would have wished and she realized with a fright that she had just about exhausted her magical powers this day, as well as her body's resources. She had wasted too much of it on the opening of the door, she realized, and now she was feeling a fatigue that was completely unfamiliar to her. Before, her problem had always been the other way around. Sometimes, for instance, she had felt she would burst with the malignant and destructive force of magic if she did not expend some of the awful power within her—a power she had been granted, but had neither asked for nor wanted. And now she had to admit to herself that she had experienced a kind of satisfaction in at last doing what her grandfather had always insisted she was capable of, but which she had stubbornly resisted.

Before they had explored half of the cave, the muffled cries of amazement and joy they had heard after the bursting of the door grew stronger.

Then Greylock stumbled into Mara's blue light.

He appeared dazed and at first did not even seem to recognize her. She left her blue flame hanging in mid-air and reached for his shoulders, shaking him violently.

"Greylock, you must prepare! The Tyrant's guards are coming, this minute! What is wrong with you?"

"Mara? Ardra?" Slowly, the truth of his unexpected freedom—and his new danger—filled his awareness. By now other men were gathering around the dangling blue flame, like moths in the light of a torch.

"Quickly!" he shouted at last. "We must escape before they seal us in again! "

More than anything else could have, this threat seemed to alert the dazed soldiers of their danger, Revived suddenly, they bounded toward the beckoning square of light that was their only escape route— just as the light was blocked by the figure of a warrior. The guards had reached the landing just as the Underworld army surged toward it.

The battle that followed was a bloody struggle that horrified Greylock. All his plans of conquest had depended on surprise—but they had been the ones who were surprised. Only the lucky escape of Mara had saved them from being sealed forever in a tomb beneath the Castle-Tyrant. Now evenly matched and determined armies confronted each other on the small stone landing under the snowcastle.

In this strange battle, only a few men could fight at the same time, while the others watched the life and death struggle in dread, and waited to take the place of the fallen. Only the presence of the yeomen of the BorderKeep such as Harkkor saved the Underworld army from being annihilated, for only they could withstand the assault for long. There were no survivors on that awful battleground. All who entered were slain. Only the length of time they managed to stay alive changed.

There was no danger now of the door being replaced, for it was shattered completely by the magic wind, and the Underworld army would never allow the other army to seal them in again, unless each and every soldier of the Underworld army was dead or dying. But Greylock could almost imagine that the narrow corridor would be impassable from the fallen men, for the bodies piled up between the legs of the fighters. The walls, and steps for many yards around, were red with their blood.

At last Greylock ordered a tentative retreat, ready to rush forward again if the snowcastle's army tried to seal them in again. As he hoped, the Tyrant's men followed them into the chamber. This was the kind of battle he liked, where skill could save a soldier, and only his own mistakes would cost him his life. He guessed that the Tyrant's guards also preferred this kind of death to the nightmarish slaughter on the landing.

Moag had cast his blue light high into the cave and let it grow, with the help of his granddaughter, until it illuminated every corner of the vast cave. It seemed that neither army would surrender or retreat in this twilight battle, and that one or the other would be destroyed to the last man. A few of the men Greylock faced appeared surprised at the sight of him, and their eyes would open slightly, and their guard would drop. Greylock did not wish to take advantage of these sudden doubts, but nevertheless dispatched them without mercy. Others seemed to fight with renewed vigor at the moment of recognition, believing that it was a demon with whom they dueled.

But the battle's inevitable end could be seen early. Unless something could save the army of Underworlders, they were doomed. Though the forces had seemed evenly matched at the first, Greylock quickly realized that his uncle could call on all the royal snowcastles, and all the common snowcastles that owed him allegiance, for reinforcements. Despite the Lord High Mayor's claims of the prowess of his soldiers and the indulgences he had lavished on them, they were not equal, man for man, to the soldiers of the High Plateau, trained by years of blood-feuding. The yeoman farmers, though sturdy and determined, lacked the training of constant battle that seasons an army. If only he could get close to his uncle, Greylock thought. He would not try to convince the old man this time. No feeling—not pity, or loyalty—nothing would stay his hand!

Always before the old Tyrant had appeared at every battlefield, summoning his strength to enjoy one more glimpse of carnage. No doubt if the man could still wield a sword, he would have done that, too. His uncle must be very ill indeed, Greylock thought, not to be here now exhorting his men to further bloodshed in his royal name.

The Steward's staff descended three times, its iron base striking the hard rock of the steps with a screeching, piercing sound that rose above the sounds of battle. The men of both armies looked up, astonished that this strange old man, with a black crow on his shoulder, staring out into space and waiting silently for the fighting to subside, would dare to stop their war. Wondering how long the Steward had been standing there, hoping for the death of his rival, before he had become impatient enough to signal for silence, Greylock —without taking his eyes off the royal Steward —waved for his men to cease fighting. When the men of the Underworld lowered their arms, the soldiers of the High Plateau ceased their strife as well.

Like an ancient teacher who no longer cared if any of his pupils was still there to hear him, the Steward Redfrock waited until there was absolute silence and attention before he spoke. Then he boomed with an astonishing force for a man so slender and frail, until Greylock remembered that such official announcements had been his duty, as the Tyrant's messenger and advisor, for many years.

"The Tyrant is dead!"

This brought a murmur from the assembly, and a few cheers from the men of the BorderKeep, and Greylock frowned at them as the Steward intoned.

"The throne of the Tyrant is now open! The Gatekeepers wish to speak with the one who claims to be the nephew of the Tyrant Ironclasp, the demon known as Greylock. The Gatekeepers call upon him to end this bloodshed until the manner of succession is decided — peacefully."

Greylock hesitated at this seemingly generous offer. He knew that as long as he was considered a demon he would have less chance with the Gatekeepers than he would by fighting. But the men of the High Plateau would fight just as fervently for the Gatekeepers as they had for the old Tyrant, until the new Tyrant was named, and the ending would be the same — the elimination of the Underworld army. They were within the Gatekeepers' grasp, and under their brief mercy. Greylock knew the Gatekeepers to be no kinder to their enemies than the old Tyrant had been. If there was one Council Greylock would prefer to avoid in deciding the question, it was his old teachers, and old foes, the priests of the Gateway.

Both armies parted for him expectantly and * curiously, which decided him. He could not allow the killing to go on in his name, as he had once accused his uncle of doing. He must face the Gatekeepers and somehow convince them of his identity. It would not be easy, for no one knew better than he how dogmatic they could be.

He sheathed his replica of Thunderer and let himself be escorted by Carrell Redfrock, who turned with a sweep of his scarlet robes and led the way up the stairs with an imperial hauteur worthy of the Tyrant Ironclasp himself. The men behind them in the cavern followed them, reluctantly mingling with each other at the narrow portals of the staircase into the snowcastle.

Greylock was not fooled by Redfrock's seeming lack of concern over who was to be Tyrant. The old soldier would like everyone to believe that he cared only that the precious protocol be fulfilled; but Greylock knew that Carrell Redfrock was still his greatest rival and barrier to his uncle's throne, even after the succession was decided one way or the other.

Once the Gatekeepers named a Tyrant, he would then become a fair target for the intrigues and feuds of the Court and the Castle-Tyrant that characterized the royal family. Greylock's uncle had been unusual in the longevity of his reign, and unusual in his repressiveness and brutality, eliminating those most likely to threaten his rule—his own family.

At the top of the staircase, the Steward turned left toward the room where Mara had heard the sounds of dining earlier. Beyond was a room large enough to accommodate many of the soldiers of both armies, and the double stone thrones at one end of the room showed that it was the castle's Court. Waiting grimly before an enormous fireplace opposite the cold thrones were a dozen of the brown-robed and white-haired priests of the Gateway. They were old only because they allowed themselves the kind of age that they denied to everyone else but the Tyrant and the Steward. Greylock suspected that there were practical as well as religious reasons for the harsh and unforgiving penalties of the Gatekeepers. The population never seemed to rise above—never was allowed to rise above—the numbers that had existed when the society had first become stable hundreds of years ago. Greylock also suspected that this was the reason so many sought to become Gatekeepers or Tyrant or Steward; the peaceful seeking priesthood, the more warlike seeking the throne, and the cunning seeking the Stewardship. Yet all went without complaint when their time came to seek the cold comfort of the gods.

Most of the Gatekeepers were staring unhappily into the flames of the huge fire, stoked to an almost unbearable temperature, when the Steward announced Greylock, and a few of them did not look up even then. Greylock followed their gaze and saw the lump of molten Glyden deep within, with jewels lying like blackened cinders around it. Only the blade of Thunderer had endured the intense heat of the flames. It was hard for Greylock to believe that anyone would have subjected the ancient weapon and badge of office to the hot coals. Only the Steward could have done that with such impunity, and then only at the Tyrant's command! Ironclasp could not have been in his right mind, Greylock thought, to have allowed such a thing—or perhaps he had allowed Carrell Redfrock to convince him, for it was the Steward who had the most to gain from the destruction of the family heirloom.

It was Keyholder, the most venerable of the Gatekeepers, and Greylock's teacher, who addressed him first.

102

"Welcome, Greylock. Come forward so that we may see you."

Encouraged that his old teacher had not used the word demon, Greylock came forward awkwardly until he was close enough for the old priest to reach out a scrawny arm and grab him. The bright birdlike eyes searched Greylock's face intently before letting go the painful grip.

"You appear to be Prince Greylock ...1 do not believe that a demon would look such as you. But you must understand, my boy, that we must be sure. There is no test we can go by. This has never happened before! Only Thunderer could have decided, for no demon could have possessed or even held onto the sacred blade. But your uncle has burned it! How do we decide?"

Though he had wielded the copy of Thunderer during the battle, Greylock had since sheathed the blade, and until now had forgotten it. Apparently, the sight of Thunderer in his hands had not yet been reported to the Gatekeepers. Hesitating for only a moment, and wondering if he was not perhaps making his situation worse, he drew the replica from its crude sheathe.

The Gatekeepers gasped when Greylock had removed entirely the makeshift gray covering from Thunderer.

"Demon!" he heard one of them hiss, just as he had feared. "You do not fool us!"

"It is impossible!" Redfrock objected. "A fake! I saw the Tyrant throw the blade into the fire myself!"

"Did you, Carrell Redfrock?" Greylock said, knowing it would make no difference in the outcome. "Mara saw my uncle on his deathbed. Did he leave the Deathroom to destroy Thunderer?" Without knowing it, he had scored a point, for all the Gatekeepers knew how unlikely it was that the old Tyrant would leave the Deathroom once entering it, for they knew him to be a devout man in his last days.

"Let me see it," Keyholder demanded. "Let me have it!"

Almost reluctantly, Greylock handed it over. The old priest would surely see that it was an elaborate, if magical, fake, and then he would denounce Greylock as a demon.

"I do not understand it!" Keyholder exclaimed. Greylock had never seen his old teacher's composure break before, even in the face of his most obnoxious student's most serious provocations. Now he was obviously bewildered and mystified. "This is Thunderer! The real Thunderer! I recognize the markings."

This announcement instantly changed the atmosphere in the room, and Greylock could almost feel the threat of violence that had surrounded him lift. He realized with a surging relief that the people of the High Plateau were not aware of the kind of magic the wizard Moag had employed to create this blade.

Yet that did not explain to him the startling similarities between the real and the fake. Or was it fake? How could the markings have been reproduced? Respectful glances were being cast in his direction as one by one the other Gatekeepers examined the blade and verified Keyholder's identification. Then came the words Greylock had never thought he would hear spoken, but had fought so hard to hear.

"We have decided that you are truly the person we knew as Greylock," Keyholder announced. "You possess the proper identification of your office. The sword you bear is Thunderer—a sign of your acceptance by the gods. You are the true successor to the throne! You are the Tyrant of the High Plateau."

Keyholder came forward—smiling, Greylock was astounded to see—and led him to one of the stone thrones. Greylock seated himself uneasily and wondered what he should say to the audience, as they eyed him curiously.

"My first command as Tyrant is..." The Steward Redfrock must have guessed what that command would be, for he moved with a suddenness that surprised even his Familiar, perched on his shoulder. As Redfrock moved toward the wall, only a few feet away, the black crow was unwittingly launched into the air to circle above the surprised audience in the Court chamber, cawing loudly in distress. The Steward must have positioned himself carefully when he had first entered the Court, for after a few quick hand movements behind a tapestry, the wall slid aside and he slipped through. Before anyone could react, the wall had already slid shut again, leaving the tapestry billowing in the brief gust of its passage. The soldiers following were met by a solid stone wall, which would not move aside no matter how often or in what sequence the Steward's hand movements were duplicated.

"It does not matter," a troubled Greylock said at last. "Redfrock has had the time and power to make all the changes he may have wished in this snowcastle. You will not catch him now. Therefore I declare him to be banished from this kingdom, on threat of death if he should be found or if he returns."

"What of his Familiar?" one of the soldiers, who a few minutes ago had been fighting him, asked. The crow was still flying about the room in a panic.

"Let it go. The Familiar will know what kind of master it has now."

As the doors were opened, and the bird chased from the room, Greylock turned to his allies from the BorderKeep. The Lord High Mayor looked stunned by the events, he noticed, but Harkkor was smiling broadly.

"I congratulate you, Tyrant Greylock!" the yeoman said. "You have accomplished what you set out to do."

"But not all of what I wanted to prove, Harkkor. Nor has your own problem of leadership been resolved. You realize, of course, that we were betrayed?"

The smile on Harkkor's face had disappeared, and the big man turned on the Lord High Mayor, who cringed at the sudden threat and retreated to the same wall through which the Steward had escaped, as if it would miraculously slide apart for him as well. But the unyielding stone stopped his retreat abruptly.

"So the left hand tunnel was the right course, Tarelton?" Harkkor said as he advanced. "You were very sure of it, and now we know why. I thought that when this time came, I would kill you gladly and without another thought. But now I foresee a better fate for you."

The yeoman reached out with a gauntleted hand and snatched the Familiar from the Lord High Mayor's shoulder. No matter how it struggled and bit, the rat could not get free, and Harkkor stuffed it into a heavy leather water bag, and sealed it tightly.

"You are no longer the Lord High Mayor, Tarelton. Your title will be simply Mayor of BorderKeep from now on, as it was before you. And you will no longer rule us—you will serve us, night and day. You will be watched, always, as we were watched, and never will you know freedom from prying eyes or our commands."

Tarelton looked relieved at this judgment, but an admiring Greylock thought that the Mayor would soon rue his reprieve, if he knew anything about the people of the BorderKeep.

There was one final matter for him to face, he thought. While the matter of his succession had been decided, he had heard the entrance of the Lady Silverfrost behind him. Now he turned to see both Silverfrost and Mara smiling at him. His heard ached at the Lady Silverfrost's beauty, and at the thought of how much he had once loved her—and desired her still. As he had feared, Mara appeared plain and skinny beside her great beauty, but he smiled as he saw the suspicious lines curl between her eyebrows as she glanced from Silverfrost to him, and back.

"Come, Mara! Sit beside me, as I promised."

An imperial and haughty Lady Silverfrost, who had always expected to be the consort of the next Tyrant—no matter who the Tyrant was—swept from the room.

As the reign of the Tyrant Greylock began, he was already suspecting that he would have more trouble from her; more than from Steward Redfrock, Mayor Tarelton, and all his other enemies put together.

PART TWO:

ICETOWERS

CHAPTER ONE

The dim light of the desk lamp slowly revealed the pale ghostly face of the demon. At first, only the tortured, emaciated head of the Wyrr appeared before him, its thin lips forming soundless words. Danger! It seemed to be saying. Danger!

A sense of evil permeated the bedroom, and Greylock realized that this dream was different from the others. He was awake, his eyes were wide open, but this seemed to have no effect on the clarity of the vision. Always before the demons had appeared in the guise of beauty, pleading for him to return to the Twilight Dells. They called him their Deliverer, and begged with an overpowering intensity for him to save them.

"Beware Godshome!" the demon said, though Grey lock heard no word. He seemed to understand what the demon wanted of him. "The mountain awakes!"

This was the entire message of the Wyrr, but it repeated the thought over and over again, until Greylock knew that his eyes had closed and he was truly asleep.

He could not resist the intensity of their need! It mattered not that he denied being the Deliverer; the dreams came without bidding, night after night.

Something passed before the lamp, briefly darkening the glowing face and breaking the spell. Greylock woke with the warning "The mountain awakes!" still echoing in his mind. His bed was drenched with sweat.

But his relief at wakening was quickly replaced by alarm.

A broad, gleaming blade hung suspended over him, its tip pointing downward only inches from his exposed chest. Greylock rolled violently off the bed to the floor.

The assassin's blade grazed his shoulder as it descended with the powerful force of unseen arms and gravity, passing through the bedding and fixing itself into the wooden frame. Unable to see who his attacker was, Greylock lunged to where Thunderer hung by its hilt from the wall. But before he could reach the royal sword he heard the grunt of the assassin as the other blade was pulled from the bed with a dull squeak.

Greylock turned instinctively, without drawing Thunderer from its bejeweled sheath, and caught the assassin's second blow on its glittering side. The other blade shattered a ruby and sliced through the yellow glyden, striking the steel of Thunderer.

The assassin backed off, still too dark and fleeting a figure to identify. The shadow apparently expected Greylock to draw Thunderer, and seemed willing to let him do so while he caught his own breath. But Greylock pursued the retreating assassin without drawing the sword and struck at the side of the man's head. The attacker collapsed limply.

By the time the guards had responded to the clashing swords, Greylock had already rolled the man over and held the lamp to his face.

It was another faceless assassin, one among many, a young man that the Tyrant did not know well, but was sure he had seen among the gatherings of the royal families.

As the guards dragged the unconscious youth away, Greylock rubbed his shoulder and reflected ruefully that if the assassin had chosen a knife for that first plunge instead of a sword, or if the bed had been against the wall instead of standing free, the assassination attempt would have been successful.

Slimspear would be enraged when he learned of the attack, Greylock thought. The steward would replace the guards, and punish the young man. But the attacks would continue for as long as he was

Tyrant. He himself had once held the same ambitions. A Tyrant was fit to rule only so long as he could defend himself from those who thought themselves smarter and stronger—and luckier. How much longer would his luck last?

The Tyrant realized that it was hopeless to try to go back to sleep, and was surprised to see that morning was breaking. Stopping only to put on his sword, he began climbing to the topmost guardroom of his icetower to survey his realm.

It was a warm morning, and as he sat on the very edge of the balcony, he could almost believe that the snows were melting at last, that the glacier was drawing back to the summit of Godshome, never to return. In its place would be a fertile land, he thought, a warm land, a land finally capable of feeding all his people.

The vigilance of the guards patrolling the white ramps of the snowcastle testified that the hoped-for thaw had not occurred, and that not all his people were content with his rule.

The Tyrant gazed toward Godshome reproachfully, but the mountain was, as usual, indifferent to his anger. "Beware of Godshome!" the demon had said, and somehow the Tyrant was not surprised.

He had climbed the icetower's lonely turret quite often lately, to stare at the mountain and to rebuke the gods who were said to dwell within. But they had never answered his curses. Surrounded on three sides by the looming mountain peaks, it seemed to him that sometimes his domain was clutched between the threatening claws of an awesome creature of cold and ice, an evil, heartless creature that would one day leap and ravage the High Plateau.

His land was now suffering from the latest challenge by the mountain. For a while the unpredictable snows had almost succeeded in destroying the icemelts, those precious oases of volcanic warmth that sustained the snowcastles, dotting the ice with startling patches of greenery. An unusually heavy snowfall, followed by a strange warming of the lava rock, had begun pushing the glacier downward.

Just the day before he had inspected the network of caverns which ran beneath the plateau. He had felt for himself the warm air, coming from somewhere deep within the mountain.

For centuries the icemelts had thawed the glacier as fast as the snows could encroach. Islands of sanctuary had been created, and the ponderous glaciers had been gently parted on their downward journey. Each snow- castle was surrounded by an icemelt, keeping the massive ice from tearing the icetowers from their moorings.

Now, suddenly, the mountain was threatening to upset this ancient equilibrium. Was this what the demon had meant?

He leaned further out over the parapet, looking for his own marker of the glacier's progress. The turret was round and bare, with casements on four sides separated by narrow pillars of stone. Now he grasped one of the supports with his right hand and searched for the lava rock that had long ago been caught at the base of Godshome to be carried inexorably downward in its grip.

He sighted the black boulder at last, and was shocked by how far it had traveled since he had last seen it. As a small child he had first noticed the stone from this very balcony; later he had begun to align it with the corners of Castle Tyrant. The boulder had taken many years to move halfway down one wall. In the last few weeks, however, it had covered the rest of the distance.

His eyes lifted to the ugly black smoke, which spiraled over the snowcastles. He could see the flames created by the magic of Moag flickering over the snows. If they survived this crisis, Greylock thought, it would be with the help of the fire wizard.

The floor of the icetower suddenly began to tremble, shocking him from his daydreams. Then the room swayed violently to one side, and he lost his grip on the stone pillar. As he started to slide toward the edge of the parapet, he saw to his horror that there was nothing to keep him from being pitched onto the hard- packed ice far below.

He clawed desperately at the sweating ice of the tower, but his numbed fingers slipped off the surface futilely and into space.

A beefy hand caught him firmly at the base of his neck as he reached the edge, and held him motionless in its powerful grasp. The mountain continued to sway for a few moments, then, as though frustrated in its attempt to kill him, grew still.

Greylock quickly rolled backward onto the cold floor of the guardroom-.

"You should not be up here alone, Tyrant!" he heard a familiar voice say above him. "Must I watch over you every minute?"

Greylock looked up to see the plump and disapproving face of Steward Slimspear. "Oh?" he said, smiling. "And where were you last night?"

The steward's face flushed, and Greylock was instantly sorry that he had teased his old friend. It appeared that Slimspear had heard about the assassination attempt.

"I beg your forgiveness, my lord!" the steward cried. "The guards have been replaced and will be punished. No one should be able to reach you without being challenged!"

"It was just a boy, Slimspear," the Tyrant said lightly. "I was never in any real danger." Despite his tone, Greylock was shaken by the narrowness of his two escapes. If it had not been for the Warning of the Wyrr...

Another slight tremor ran through the icetower, and he glanced down at the guards far below to see if they had noticed the trembling. They continued to patrol, unperturbed. Such tremors were not unusual on Godshome, though a large, destructive earthquake had not visited the plateau for many years.

But Greylock did not trust the mountain to stay so quiet. All was not well within the mountain. His instincts for the forces working beneath the ground had grown much sharper of late. Once this sense had manifested itself in the simple skills of mountain climbing, and an uncanny ability to find his way. Now the very earth seemed to speak to him. The Gatekeepers told many stories of past destructions, he thought, of the mountain opening up with ash and fire. And now there was the warning of the Wyrrs.

He uneasily turned from the sight and saw that Slimspear was still standing back diffidently, rigid and formal despite having just saved Greylock's life. The severe posture was slightly ludicrous to the Tyrant, who knew from experience just how lazy and carefree Slimspear really was. The pudgy shape of the steward's waist, and the cheerful lines in his round face, testified to this lack of discipline. In any other man, Greylock would have disapproved. But in Slimspear he forgave the indulgence.

He himself was still slim and vigorous, unlike the lords of the other snowcastles, who, like Slimspear, usually let themselves go to pot. The Tyrant had tried to make himself an example to the other nobles of the High Plateau by sharing with servants and nobles alike what little food came from the icemelts of Castle Tyrant, but a massive girth had long meant status and he had been unable to change them. It was the slender ones, the hungry ones, he thought, that he had to look out for.

His long hair, once black with a single gray lock, was now nearly all gray, cut square away from his face. Despite the gray mane, he moved with a speed and grace that came only with youth, and his dark eyes were bright. As was the custom with the people of the High Plateau, he dressed lightly despite the cold, and his simple tunic revealed a lithe, but finely muscled body. The royal sword Thunderer never left his side, for he was Tyrant only so long as he possessed the talisman.

Right now he was wishing that he had not appointed Slimspear to the office of steward, though he knew that there had been no other choice at the time. He had looked among the new subjects to find that there was no one else he could trust. He had immediately installed Slimspear, the one man he could still trust, as steward in place of the missing Carrell Redfrock, the man he most distrusted.

The Tyrant frowned at the thought of Carrell Redfrock. The guards had never found the old steward after his escape from the throne room, when Greylock had revealed the sword Thunderer. Long after he had been proclaimed Tyrant of the High Plateau, the feeling persisted in Greylock that the crafty traitor was still hiding somewhere on the mountain.

Slimspear was continuing to stand at attention, and Greylock realized sheepishly that the steward was waiting for permission to speak. He sighed at the formality.

"Was there something you wanted to tell me, Slimspear?"

"Mayor Tarelton has just arrived from Bordertown, Tyrant," the steward announced. "He wishes to speak to you again—immediately." Slimspear mimicked this last word with a withering tone of contempt.

Greylock frowned at this news. The once mighty lord high mayor of Border Keep was now the lowly mayor of Bordertown, a servant to the townspeople, watched always and reviled. Despite his lowered rank, the mayor remained irritatingly arrogant.

Steward Slimspear received the instructions he seemed to be expecting.

"Tell Mayor Tarelton that I will see him tomorrow, at my regular audience."

After all, he thought, the mayor was not officially his servant, though the yeomen had made it clear that Tarelton was to take orders from him as well. The revenge of the humble farmers on the mayor for his once dictatorial rule was subtle, but potent.

"Wait," he said, as Slimspear turned to leave. "On second thought, I will see him. Have him come to my chambers for breakfast."

Slimspear looked as though he was about to object, then he nodded and left the guardroom.

Greylock turned to look at Godshome. The sun was suddenly caught behind the middle peak, and it grew dark in the guardroom. At the same moment, a shudder ran through the tower.

For a few seconds Greylock thought the shudder was his own, but then realized that another quake was rumbling through Godshome. He left the turret abruptly, for the room had begun to freeze suddenly in the absence of sunlight. As he followed the winding steps down into Castle Tyrant, he tried to justify to himself giving the mayor a private audience. He realized that he dreaded another morning alone, spent staring into the giant fireplace of the throne room, fearing the mountain.

Mayor Tarelton was not happy. The mayor was never very satisfied with the state of affairs, but occasionally Greylock had been able to ignore the intensity of his complaints. Not on this morning. It seemed, from what the mayor was saying, that the people of the High Plateau were doing everything in their power to obstruct the men of Bordertown in their attempts to create trade between the two domains. And it seemed as well that it was the Tyrant's entire fault, though the mayor was careful never to say so in so many words.

"Your people must show more cooperation, Tyrant Greylock," the mayor insisted again. "We are forced to pry every bit of trade from them."

"I cannot reverse the centuries of isolation overnight," Greylock repeated. "You must remember that, Mayor Tarelton."

"My people tell me that they are meeting resistance at every stage," the mayor said in his high voice. "Can you not at least direct your people to help us? It is to the advantage of both our countries. You need our food, our clothing, all the things you never had before to make your lives comfortable."

"And you need our glyden?" Greylock finished for him.

The mayor did not appear to be amused. Again, Greylock wondered what kept Tarelton working so hard when it was for the benefit of others. He seemed driven, not just by his own people, but by something deeper and hidden. Once the Tyrant had thought the punishment for the mayor to be merited. Now he could only feel sorry for the man.

The lord high mayor had become a pitiful figure in the last year. Once the tall red-haired man had been bedecked in the finest robes and jewels. Now he was reduced to a single, worn green robe, which he was obviously not finding warm enough on the High Plateau. Tarelton had always been thin; now he appeared scrawny and unhealthy.

As always, the familiar was on Tarelton's shoulder, a rat, peeking out hungrily from under the tangled red hair of his master. At first the familiar had been taken from Tarelton, but the mayor had become so agitated that the farmers had kindly, perhaps foolishly, allowed him to keep his pet.

It was this animal that kept Greylock from trusting the man, even now. It reminded him too much of the black crow of Steward Redfrock, which had always seemed to be hovering over tragedy.

Tarelton and his familiar were both closely" watched, of course. Even in the presence of the Tyrant, the mayor had one of the sturdy farmers at his back not as a servant, but as a guard. Greylock smiled at the young man, but did not recognize him.

"I will instruct my people again, Tarelton," he said. "But it will take some time for my people to adjust."

"Some of my men—not I, of course—I instantly reprimand them— feel that the resistance is coming from the top. They feel that one or two leaders are responsible for the slowdown, and if they were to be removed ..."

"Oh?" The one word was cold, the end of the discussion. The Tyrant wondered how much of a threat had been in the mayor's words.

Greylock did not blame his people for refusing to deal with the Underworlders, though he encouraged them to trade. It was becoming difficult to remain friendly with the men of Bordertown, who were accustomed to sharp trading with the fiefdoms of Trold. The people of the High Plateau, on the other hand, had never had anything with which to trade, and Greylock was hearing more and more complaints of his people being cheated. This he knew was the real source of the High Plateau's resistance, not the reluctance of its leaders.

The Underworlders seemed to be interested only in gaining more of the precious metal glyden, something that Greylock had first noticed in the wizard Moag, but which he had come to learn was common to them all. He had rewarded the men of Border town well after they had helped him gain the throne. In his first flush of gratitude he had thrown open the royal treasury. Even Mayor Tarelton, who had proven to be a reluctant and treacherous ally—and though Greylock could not prove it, in league with Carrell Redfrock— had been given some of the glyden. There had seemed enough for all.

But now the Underworlders seemed to believe that there was no end to the treasure. Though some of the townsmen remained honest, such as the yeoman Harrkor, they tended to stay on their farms and let the mayor, guarded by one of their number, conduct the business.

Throughout the meal, the rat familiar had peered hungrily at the food. Greylock refused to have it feed at the table when he was eating. The animal had grown as scrawny as its master over the last year, now that it did not have the pick of the food, and its fur seemed to have ruffled a bit with age, both of which only seemed to add to the evil in its long face.

Now it darted down its master's chest and lunged for a scrap of meat. Greylock struck out at it, but the rat proved too quick and retreated with its prize to its nest under Tarelton's red hair.

Losing his appetite, Greylock pushed away from the table and approached the fireplace. The throne room was occupied by two bare thrones, a low crude table, and an enormous fireplace with logs half as long as the room. He moodily warmed his hands.

Finally, Greylock turned and asked the question that had prompted him to ask the mayor to the throne room in the first place.

"How is the construction of the mountain road going?"

"Slowly," the mayor said, frowning. "As I say, your people do not seem enthusiastic."

"Any difficulty with the Wyrrs?"

"None. I had thought we would have to fight our way over each and every inch of the Twilight Dells, but there has not yet been a battle, not even a skirmish! They just stand there, back from the road, and watch the work. Sometimes I could swear there are smiles on their faces. On Wyrr faces!"

Rather than this being good news, Greylock found himself falling into an even deeper gloom. Every night he would dream the same disturbing dream of the ghostly Wyrrs. The same beautiful demon who had confronted him on his journey to the Underworld would come to him again, and though Greylock could not hear or understand what the Wyrr was saying, he knew what the demon wanted.

Behind the Wyrr sometimes stood the old woman who had called him her son, pleading with him to come back. Again and again they would chant the word *Deliverer*, and in the morning, when he woke, the word would still be ringing in his mind.

Last night had been the first break in that pattern. Now Greylock feared that the dreams would afflict him during his waking hours as well. He could not forget the pitiful people known as Wyrrs. Dwelling in the hilly country between Bordertown and the High Plateau, the Wyrrs had once been a deadly barrier between the two lands. Yet when Greylock had descended into the Underworld, the first of his kind to face the legends of demons in many generations, they had proclaimed him as their Deliverer.

Greylock had promised to one day return and free them from their curse, and now he felt the weight of that unfulfilled prophecy.

There was nothing he could do for them, he thought angrily. The Twilight Dells were barren and infertile. This he had sensed with his affinity to the earth. But he did not know how to make the land good.

118

He did not know how to cut the invisible bonds that kept them tied to a dead land. He was not their Deliverer!

Tarelton abruptly brought his attention back to business, and Greylock was thankful for the interruption.

"We need more guards for the Vault of Glyden, Tyrant Greylock."

"To protect it from your people or mine?"

"It is from others that we have the most to fear," Tarelton answered gloomily, seeing no humor in the question.

It was an old complaint. Tarelton could not conceal his anxiety at the thought that any of that precious metal might escape the clutches of Bordertown. If things continued as they were, Greylock thought, the vault would be emptied into the coffers of the Underworld entirely.

Greylock almost wished that the Room of Aurim, as the Gatekeepers called it, had never been found. The treasure made the High Plateau a tempting prize to any would-be conqueror, he knew, whereas before none of the Underworld monarchs had shown any interest in the newly revealed country of ice and snow.

Only a few months before, workmen on the cold, windswept slopes of Godshome had punctured the side of the mountain, revealing a new unsuspected network of tunnels. At the bottom of the maze of handcarved corridors had been found the Room of Aurim, told of in the ancient books of the Gatekeepers.

It was ironic to Greylock that the mythical vault had been found after all. He had used the greed of the Underworlders by promising them shares of the glyden, but he had never really believed that the treasure existed.

Now, Tarelton could no-longer benefit from the find; Greylock himself had little use for glyden; and even the traveling fire wizard Moag seemed to no longer care for the metal.

The vault was not actually constructed of glyden, but was lined with heavy bars of the metal, coming from a single vein along one wall. By a feat of engineering that still astounded Greylock, the light of the sun somehow found a way through the twisting caves to strike the glyden. The brilliant square of light emerging from the excavations had been seen as far away as Bordertown.

But it was not the glyden itself that most interested Greylock. Inside the mountain the workmen had found elaborate carvings and stone placements that reminded the Tyrant of the lower reaches of the Gateway. But these mosaics were unharmed by the cold and the winds, and still showed the intricate patterned beauty of the day they were made.

"I will put more guards at the entrance," he said at last. "But the only true defense is to keep the discovery a secret."

The mayor snorted, but said nothing more.

Tarelton obviously did not believe that secrecy was possible, Greylock reflected, and he could not help but agree.

The rest of the meal was spent in discussing minor details in the construction of the new road, and in matters of trade. When the mayor left, Greylock continued to stare gloomily into the fire.

A distant rumble brought him to his feet. The walls of the throne room seemed to sway for a few moments, then settle. The Tyrant realized in dismay that the glacier had jogged the snowcastle from its foundations.

Without thinking, Greylock headed for the steps to the icetower. As he ascended to the guardroom again he wondered which force would destroy his realm first: the assault by the mountain, the treachery of Redfrock, or the greed of the Underworlders.

CHAPTER TWO

Greylock shaded his eyes, trying desperately to find his marker of the glacier's progress, but the light was too bright to endure for more than a few seconds. Lofty towers of ice and graceful snowcastles dotted the snows, but today even these structures were all but washed from view by the intense light springing off the snows. The light could seem to find no escape, and turned everything but the largest of the dwellings to white. Only the gray rock of Godshome, so high that no man had ever climbed it, interrupted the glare.

Though the sun gave an illusion of warmth, Greylock knew this was misleading. The bitter chill of the High Plateau was locked forever within the crystals of ice. The cold would emerge with renewed sting the moment the sun left the sky.

A year had passed since his ascension to the throne of the High Plateau, but it seemed to him that he had done little to alleviate the poverty and hunger of his people. Within the magnificent structures of the snowcastles the common people of the High Plateau were still starving.

The Tyrant simply could not understand it. He had vigorously implemented the ideas and reforms he had garnered from his visit to the Underworld, ideas and reforms that should have made the High Plateau a paradise. Yet little had changed. There was always the snow to be reckoned with, the cold, unyielding snow. The snow never ceased to fall.

Greylock could barely see the flames created by the fire-wizardry of Moag through the glare. He could not help but wince at the vast stores of precious wood which were being consumed by the costly battle with Godshome. Hours of labor were being squandered, he thought, chopping away at the invading glacier, inch by inch. It was time and energy and material he had hoped to spend growing more food for his people. But this goal, like so many others he had once envisioned, would have to wait yet another year.

Only the reopening of the Gateway was proceeding as planned, he thought, and even the clearing of that mountain roadway was creating more problems than it was solving.

He heard Slimspear enter the guardroom behind him, and turned to find the steward standing at attention. Once again, Greylock wished he had chosen someone else as steward. The appointment of Slimspear, while filling his need for an ally, had changed their old easy relationship. The new steward took his position and duties very seriously.

"What is it, Slimspear?" he asked, tiredly.

"The wizard Moag wishes to see you again, my lord." The steward seemed reluctant to say even this much.

Greylock smiled to himself. Slimspear obviously did not like the way the wizard was pestering them. The steward had no understanding of the bond that kept the wizard obedient to the Tyrant, but at the same time resentful of every order. He did not know that this bond had been bought by the precious metal glyden, which released the fire-wizardry of Moag only in the service of the Tyrant.

"Is Mara with him?" Greylock asked, and he could not keep the eagerness from his voice—or his disappointment at Slimspear's answer.

"No, my lord. He is alone again and angry."

"I see," Greylock said, turning back unhappily toward the mountain. Things had not turned out the way he had hoped with the wizard and his granddaughter. When he had refused to free the wizard after gaining the throne, as he had promised, Mara had chosen to stand by her grandfather. She had been just a girl when he had first seen her in the Underworld, skinny and awkward. But she had become a graceful and thoughtful woman during their travels. And as she had become more and more beautiful, and Greylock more and more in love with her, she had become distant and aloof. Sometimes the Tyrant wished that the three of them could have remained partners in a fruitless quest for glyden, without cares or responsibilities.

"I have no wish to see anyone today, Slimspear," he said at last. "Tell Moag that I will grant him a private audience in the morning."

Slimspear nodded, and slipped from the room silently.

The Tyrant already knew what the old man would ask of him, and he wanted more time to prepare for the storm that was sure to follow when that request was denied. But he could not let Moag go now! He needed the wizard's powers more than ever.

Someone entered the guardroom behind him unannounced, and Greylock turned quickly, instinctively grasping the hilt of Thunderer. The royal sword was already half drawn before he recognized the bent shape of the wizard.

"Why did you refuse to see me, Greylock?" the wizard demanded, without preamble. "Are you avoiding me?"

A storm was indeed brewing on the thick brows of the wizard. He marched noisily into the room, hunched over, ignoring the naked blade of Thunderer. Unlike the citizens of the High Plateau, the old man was not ashamed to bundle up in thick swathes of clothing, though all the robes could not hide the wizard's severely deformed back. His face and arms were mottled with brown spots of age, though his thick hair was dark.

Right now, his mood was like the first sharp gusts of a gale.

"I did not know you have been asking for me," Greylock said placatingly, quickly sheathing the sword. "Slimspear is sometimes too protective of my time."

As if to accent his words, the steward suddenly appeared at the door, his face flushed and angry, with three armed guards at his back.

"I am sorry, Tyrant!" he cried. "The old man must have slipped by me!"

"I'm all right, Slimspear," Greylock said hastily. The guards looked ready to strike Moag at any moment. "Leave us. I will speak to him."

The steward glared at the wizard, then reluctantly motioned the guards away. But Greylock could see that Slimspear would not be far off.

The Tyrant could not blame Slimspear for being so protective. Over the past year, the attempts on his life had been almost too numerous to count. It was one of the traditions that Greylock wished he could change, this never-ending challenge to his rule. It was wearing him down, and diverting him from the jobs that needed to be done.

Perhaps if he was harsh enough, and if he managed to survive another year, the number of assassination attempts would fall off. But right now, he could not complain against the tradition without seeming weak. The temptations to be brutal and harsh in achieving his goals, as the Tyrant Ironclasp had been, were almost irresistible. It was only now that he was Tyrant himself that Greylock understood the frustrations that his uncle had faced, and the strains that had finally driven him mad.

Greylock wondered briefly why he did not treat the wizard the way he would have treated any other trespasser. The Tyrant Ironclasp would never have stood for such questioning of his commands!

The Tyrant had to admit that he felt guilty for still holding Moag against his will.

"What is it you wish to ask me, Moag?" he said tiredly. He hoped he was wrong and that the wizard had come to him with a request he could fulfill.

"You know what I want!" the wizard snapped. "I want my freedom!"

"Not yet, Moag," Greylock answered, simply.

"When, Greylock?" the wizard demanded. "When you bought my services you promised it was just so we could escape the Wyrrs. Then it was to fight Red- frock and gain your rightful throne. That is long past, and yet you still hold me."

"I do not keep you here by force."

This statement only seemed to make Moag angrier. "You know as well as I do that by the laws of wizards I am as securely bound to you as I would be in chains!"

"Wait a little longer, Moag!" Greylock pleaded.

"How much longer?" The wizard had heard it before. He did not believe him. "When I accepted your knife of glyden I did not expect to have to serve you forever, otherwise I would have made conditions to our contract, despite the dangers of the moment."

"Have I not paid you well enough?" Greylock asked. "Have I not given you more glyden than you could have ever hoped for? Where else could you receive such treasures? I do not understand your complaints, old man."

"You can have your glyden back! I was wrong to desire it so much."

"Without glyden you will lose your powers, Moag," Greylock said, knowing this to be his strongest argument.

"I want my freedom!" The wizard was adamant.

Greylock finally looked away, knowing that he would not convince the old man, but knowing also that he would not release him.

"I am sorry, Moag. I realize that I am being unfair to you, but I need you and your magic. Try to understand. Enemies surround me, and not all of them are human or natural.

Greylock wondered briefly if the old man would understand his fears of Godshome, or the visions of the Wyrrs crying for help, or his certainty that the High Plateau was about to be invaded by the armies of the Underworld, but he decided that these arguments would not sway the wizard either.

"I need everyone who is loyal to me close by," he finally chose to say, simply. "Even if they are only loyal to me because they must be. Just stay with me one more year, Moag! 1 will reward you with more glyden than you have dreamed of!"

"Glyden is of no use to me now," the wizard said defiantly, glaring at Greylock.

The Tyrant turned unhappily toward Godshome, still shrouded by the brilliant sun. But he was not watching the spectacular brightness of the sun.

"I am sorry, Moag. I do not wish your anger, but I need you." His voice trailed off lamely. What more could he tell the old man? That he did not trust the mountain? That he was afraid of the Wyrrs?

"You are not fooling anyone, Greylock," the wizard said. "It is obvious to everyone that it is not me you want to keep here. It is Mara you want! But as long as you hold me, Tyrant, you will not have her!"

Without another word, the wizard turned and left the icetower. Greylock turned to watch the light, knowing that the old man had been right.

Without Mara, Greylock found that he did not really care if his land prospered or fell to the Underworlders. Without Mara, it did not seem to matter. And yet, she refused to even see him.

Every night, as he passed the chambers he had given to Mara and her grandfather, he resisted the temptation to turn towards them. But on this night, he gave into the desire, telling himself that he was only checking to see that they were well guarded, that he would not actually try to see them.

He felt foolish as he passed by their doors, and he examined the guards who came to a surprised attention. The Tyrant continued to pretend to himself that as master of the snowcastle it was up to him to check all the rooms and to make sure that they were safe and secure.

Half hoping, half dreading that one of the doors would open, he explored the corridor to its end. The hall remained quiet and empty, and he continued on with a vague sense of relief and disappointment.

He stopped briefly at the portal of the garden, hoping to see the slender blond girl standing among the red snowflowers. The garden was immaculately kept, though Greylock had never seen the keeper; carefully groomed, though no one ever saw or appreciated the effort. The Tyrant never had the inclination to visit the garden. It was a pavilion created especially for him, but so immaculate that he had never dared disturb it.

Slimspear was waiting for him at the doors of the throne room, and anxiously inquired if he was ready for his meal.

"No," Greylock decided suddenly. "I am not hungry. Let the servants go to bed. I will serve myself something later."

He looked at Slimspear sharply. "Why don't you return to Castle Steward? You don't see enough of my sister. Ardra deserves better."

"Yes, my lord." The steward began to leave dutifully. Once Slimspear would have stopped to ask what was bothering him, Greylock reflected, sadly.

Unknown to him, these emotions were indeed battling within Slimspear, fighting with his duty as steward.

"Greylock?"

The Tyrant turned to look at his friend in astonishment. Slimspear had not used the familiar name since the day he had become steward.

"I observed the girl Mara going up to the deathroom," the steward said, hesitatingly. "I wonder if it is safe for her to be alone up there? If anyone should see her…"

"I see," Greylock said, appreciating his friend's tact and his hint. "I am sure that she will be fine. None of our people would dare go up there. Still, perhaps, I had better go check."

Greylock found her in the dusty abandoned room, crying. He could still smell death in the room. The stone frame was still covered by ancient and decaying blankets, and took up fully half the room. Though it was a mild night outside the snowcastle, inside the deathroom it was frigid. The bare stones of the room seemed designed to catch the coldest of the winds that blew over the snowy plateau.

As a child, before he had known its meaning, Greylock had been delighted to find the apparently unused hideaway. His uncle had found him playing there and had whipped him harshly. Later, he had learned what the tomb was for, and he had not returned since. Only now did it occur to Greylock to wonder what his uncle had been doing up here himself that day. Apparently the room held a fascination for others as well.

Mara tried to cover her tears, but Greylock was not fooled.

"You will freeze up here, Mara!" he cried, and he was surprised by the tenderness in his own voice. Surely she could hear his concern!

"Leave me alone, Greylock!" she said. "I came up here because I thought I would be alone!"

"This room is important to me," he answered, softly. "I will come here when it is my time to die. But no one is supposed to be here until that happens."

Greylock tried to look into her face, but her long, unruly hair fell in the way again as she bent to hide her tears. He had a pretty good picture of her face at that moment anyway. He knew that the serious green eyes would be reddened, and that her brows would be knit in a suspicious frown. Her pale skin would be flushed, her mouth set. Compared to the Lady Silverfrost, she would not appear beautiful, but he had chosen her, knowing that it would make an enemy of Silverfrost. Right now, all he could see was her thin shoulders and pale hair. She was shivering.

"This room is used often, from what I have heard." She sniffed loudly, trying to regain her composure.

"It is our tradition to challenge our leaders, Mara," he said, calmly. "It has kept our leaders, and therefore our people, strong."

"This is a deathroom!" she hissed. "A room constructed for death, so that your frozen corpse can be gaped at by all the citizens!"

Greylock was stunned by the hate in her voice.

"Have you been praying for my death, Mara?" he asked.

Her reaction was all he could have wanted. She grew pale, and looked unwillingly into his eyes.

"No! Never that!" She seemed about to come towards him, then said hopelessly. "Why won't you let my grandfather go?"

He remained silent, and she rose to leave the room.

He stepped in front of her hastily, blocking her exit, holding her briefly in his arms. For a few moments she did not resist, and even relaxed at his touch. But when he lifted her chin to look at her face, she pulled away.

"Let go of me, Greylock," she said dully.

"If Moag is freed, will you stay?"

"I don't know, Greylock. He is an old man. He needs me now more than he ever did."

"I need you, Mara!" he pleaded. "Both of you!"

She tried to pass by him again, but he held her back firmly.

"Please, Mara! My land is threatened. The Wyrrs are calling to me. And the mountain always threatens."

"Will you let my grandfather go?" she repeated.

"This is not something for which I will bargain!" he shouted, angry at her obstinate refusal to listen to him. "I will keep Moag here for as long as I wish. I will not be blackmailed by your love, Mara!"

"And I will not abandon my grandfather!" she answered, just as fiercely.

"I see," he said stiffly. He did not want to go through another wrenching night of knowing that she was under the same roof, but knowing he could not visit her. "Perhaps it would be best if you moved from Castle Tyrant. Slimspear will have moved from Castle Guardian by now."

"I think Moag would like that very much," she said coldly. "And so would I!"

This time, Greylock let her go without another word. For a few moments, he remained behind, oblivious to the death and the cold. Then, suddenly, the walls seemed to close in on him, claiming him. He left the deathroom quickly.

CHAPTER THREE

The throne room was cold and bare, redeemed only partly by the massive fireplace that filled the wall. The flames were stoked to a comfortable, cheerful temperature, but the double thrones were centered against the opposite side of the room as far away from the warmth as possible, Greylock thought miserably.

He sat shivering on the largest of the high-backed thrones and listened impatiently to another complaint by one of his subjects. The Tyrant wished that the man would finish, for there were only a few citizens left to be heard. The huge room was almost empty.

As the man told the familiar story of being cheated by the shrewd traders of Bordertown, Greylock's eyes wandered longingly to the chair set next to the fire, and he wished that he could sit by the roaring flames with a goblet of warm cider. Only the outer walls of Castle Tyrant were actually made of snow, but the inner quarters, constructed largely of porous black lava, seemed no warmer.

He was surprised when the wide doors swung open and Slimspear hurried in. The steward appeared worried, Greylock saw quickly. Seconds later, he saw the reason for his distress.

The Lady Silverfrost swept into the room as if accustomed to interrupting the business of the realm, Greylock reflected, as she undoubtedly had when her father was Tyrant.

She wore a gown embroidered in silver and gold, which her hair matched in brilliance. Her long, luminous hair was unbound, yet not one strand strayed free of her design. On her forehead was a tiara of glyden, which marked her, if her clothing and manner already had not, as nobility.

The citizen addressing Greylock stuttered and fell silent. Without being told, the man joined the other supplicants scuttling from the throne room. Her cold gray eyes followed them out; even the guards left at her glance.

Slimspear stood before her gaze defiantly for a few moments, and then reluctantly retired, drawing the doors closed behind him.

When she finally turned and smiled at him, Greylock found himself flushed with embarrassment. He could not take his eyes off her, and he was a little ashamed that she could have the same unsettling effect on him as she had had when they were small children, when she was the favorite daughter of the Tyrant and he the forgotten nephew.

"Good morning, Greylock!" she said pleasantly. "Or should I call you Tyrant Greylock?"

"What do you want, Silverfrost?" he asked. Her accent on his title made him wonder briefly if she had come to mock him. He had not seen her since the day he had motioned Mara and not her to the other throne. He wondered if he had made the right choice. Silverfrost was not the kind of woman one could dismiss easily. Her father, the Tyrant Ironclasp, had brought her up to believe that she would someday sit beside the next Tyrant. That an Underworld woman had taken her place only made her anger more dangerous.

"You never came to see me, Greylock," she replied. "So I thought it was time to come to you."

Greylock could not keep himself from comparing her beauty to that of Mara. Silverfrost was like the grandeur of the mountain, he thought, and as cold. Mara's beauty was simple and natural; and she was warm, like the green valleys of the Underworld.

Silverfrost seemed to guess what he was thinking.

"Are you still in love with the witch girl?"

"Why have you come, Silverfrost?" The thought of Mara was almost too painful to endure.

"I have come to see if there is anything left in your heart for me," she said, and as she came close to him, he felt himself drawn to her. "Remember how it was, Greylock? It can be so again!"

He did not answer, not trusting himself to refuse her offer. The memory of the love he had once held for her was strong.

The smile left her face. "No, I can see that there is nothing left of that love," she said, almost sadly.

"I am sorry that you came, Silverfrost," he said. He waited for her temper to appear; the Lady Silverfrost had never been one to hold back on her anger. He was amazed when her smile returned.

"No matter," she said lightly. "I wished to speak with you anyway. Mayor Tarelton has invited me to visit Bordertown and I have accepted his offer."

Greylock was not surprised that she had chosen to leave, her position on the High Plateau must have been miserable.

The ancient barriers to the Underworld had been opened for months, and the path of the Gateway was being cleared of its dangerous rubble. Few citizens of the mountain had yet found the courage to make the venture. The fear of the Underworld, ingrained by a belief in demons, was too strong for the ordinary man or woman to surmount.

Silverfrost, Greylock reminded himself dryly, was not an ordinary woman. For the first time he allowed himself to answer her smile.

"I hope you will be an example to others," he said. "When will you return?"

"I do not know yet," she answered. "Perhaps I will stay, if the lodgings are suitable. If I decide to return, you will know of it."

She swept from the room, and Greylock was left to wonder if he had misjudged her. She had not made a hostile gesture toward him in over a year. Perhaps she had found it within her to forgive him, he thought. He hoped so. She would be a formidable, if beautiful, enemy.

He rose from his throne and crossed the empty chamber. As he stared into the flames morosely, he heard Slimspear enter softly behind him. The Tyrant looked up with a smile, but saw that it was duty, not companionship, that had brought the steward. The staff of office came down once, softly, signifying that someone was about to be announced.

The fat shape of Gartlett, the servant of the Lady Silverfrost, waddled into the room and bowed.

"My lady has left the High Plateau, Tyrant Greylock," he announced, nervously. "But she forgot to leave her parting gift. She sent me back."

He produced a bottle of wine, which he set and poured with great ceremony.

Greylock was surprised by the princely gift. The citizens of the High Plateau had discovered the wines of the Underworld with delight. The Tyrant himself was one of the few who did not like the new beverage, feeling that its price in glyden was too high, and disliking the effects it had on him. Too many of his subjects had purchased the wine .at exorbitant prices. Still, he thought, an occasional glass was a treat.

He reached out casually, but awkwardly, from his warm chair and jostled the table with his elbow. The goblet of wine overturned.

With surprising agility, Gartlett moved to catch the first drops of wine before the red spill could reach of the edge of the table.

Greylock at first attributed this astonishing reaction to the rarity of the wine. The vineyards of Far Valley produced few grapes, and the wine was of great value.

A servant girl hurried into the room at the brisk commands of the guards. She took the damp cloth from Gartlett impatiently, and efficiently caught the drippings in the palms of her hands. She walked from the room slowly, unwilling, it seemed, to let a single drop reach the floor.

"I'm sorry, Gartlett," Greylock said, still wondering at the agitation of his visitor.

"You must be more careful, Greylock!" the man cried. "This is the rarest of all vintages, a treasure from Far Valley." The fat servant poured another measure of wine, this time without fanfare.

"Will you not have some with me?" Greylock asked, apologetically. The man was so upset, he observed, that he dared scold even a Tyrant.

Gartlett seemed horrified at the suggestion. "Thank you, no, Tyrant! I would very much like to taste it, of course, but I must decline. If my lady ever found out that I had drank of her gift!"

Greylock raised the goblet to his lips, eyeing the visitor speculatively.

A crashing of dishes, a painful scream, made him lower the goblet from his mouth without drinking. Seconds later, Slimspear rushed into the room.

"Do not drink the wine, Greylock!"

The Tyrant set the goblet down hastily, finally surmising what had happened. The servant girl had been unable to resist the temptation of tasting the liquid, and had strained the cloth rather than throw it away. She had died for her curiosity.

Poison was seldom used on the High Plateau. Such a cowardly means of assassination was repugnant to most citizens of the High Plateau.

Greylock's eyes turned to Gartlett, who stood beside him as though frozen, his face pale and frightened.

Before Greylock could stop him, the servant had swooped up the goblet into his beefy hand and gulped down its deadly contents.

"No!" Greylock cried. "I will not harm you!"

But he was too late. Gartlett collapsed. The Tyrant lunged from his chair, and caught the man's head before he had crashed to the stone floor. He wondered what terror the Lady Silverfrost had induced in her servant to make him do this. Gartlett, in horrid contradiction, seemed suddenly at peace.

"Beware of the Lady Silverfrost, Tyrant," he gasped. "Her hate is great. She conspires with Carrell Redfrock to murder you."

"Redfrock!" Greylock exclaimed. The name explained Gartlett's fear, as well as the means of assassination. Only Redfrock would use poison to destroy his enemy, for he had nothing to lose. It seemed that the old forms were dying away after all, Greylock thought bitterly. But it was only the traditions that preserved their land that were broken with impunity, while the traditions that held back progress clung tenaciously.

"They will not give up, Tyrant!" The servant choked. "I have overheard them plotting, late into the night. They are going to approach King Kasid of Trold. They will tell him of the Room of Glyden."

Gartlett's head fell away in his hands, and Greylock laid him carefully on the cold stone floor.

The screeching caw of a mountain crow came from over his head. He turned to see a huge black bird peering back at him from the high, narrow casements of the throne room, its stance cocky and arrogant.

Greylock's hands closed around the goblet, and he tossed it violently at the bird, the deadly wine splashing against the white walls. The crow easily evaded the cup, and noisily flew away.

The Tyrant knew that it was no ordinary crow, and that Carrell Redfrock would soon know everything that had happened in the throne room from his familiar.

Greylock berated himself for not suspecting that Redfrock would hide in Silverfrost's snowcastle. By this time they would have had all the time they needed, he thought angrily, to complete their plots against him. This attempt had only been a warning. The full wrath of Redfrock and the scorned Lady Silverfrost was only beginning to be bent in his direction.

CHAPTER FOUR

The priests of the Gateway had been adamant from the beginning in their objections to any kind of trafficking with demons. But Greylock had dared to override their protests against the opening the Gateway, and the Gatekeepers had withdrawn to Castle Priest with fervent vows not to emerge until the Underworlders were once again banished from the High Plateau.

After the failed attempts on his life, Greylock had reluctantly come to the conclusion that he would have to ask for the help of the Gatekeepers in the coming struggle. He was even willing to apologize and face their smug satisfaction.

The priests had a snowcastle of their own, of course, from which they would not normally emerge except on rare occasions to tutor the royal families, or at the death of a Tyrant. It was a snowcastle set at the very highest elevations of the High Plateau, so that they might better contemplate the three peaks of Godshome.

Before dawn, Greylock had donned his talons, those extensions of hands which every mountain climber used to grasp the ice, and had begun to climb leisurely toward Castle Priest. In the silence of the dark, with only the sounds of his own labored breathing and the crunch of the spring snow crust to accompany him, Greylock wondered why he had waited so long to make this journey. He had been too long within Castle Tyrant, he thought, too long surrounded by guards. This was what he had always loved most, to be alone on the white snows of the glacier on a clear, crisp morning.

The sun rose over the glacier while he was still more than halfway from his destination. The mountain plateau looked eternal on such a morning, but the Tyrant knew that it had been destroyed many times by the forces of nature, and that new castles had been rebuilt over the ruins of the old.

The High Plateau could easily be destroyed by the hands of man, he thought, and such a destruction might not be overcome. He had many questions to ask Keyholder and the other Gatekeepers.

Greylock avoided the other snowcastles, and tried to remain at equal distances from each of the white walls. He hoped he was only a small dot on the snows, and indistinguishable from the battlements. There were many who would try to take advantage of his vulnerability if they were to see him unescorted. It was safter to stay away, and much more private.

He was enjoying his solitude. He had disdained to use the much quicker and less tiring route of the lava tunnels so that he could be alone. Stopping briefly to rest, he looked back down the gentle slopes of the glacier until the snows dropped off into the Underworld. No other people were visible at this point. He felt alone in a sea of snow.

When witnessing such a vista, Greylock could almost understand the theology of the Gatekeepers. The inspiration of their Holy Hierarchy of Tiers was very evident on this morning, though Greylock thought it nonsense. Below the ever-present cloud layer were the hot, humid valleys of the First Tier, with its bewildering array of colors—and its demons. Above was the Third Tier, which the Gatekeepers said was the home of the gods.

Greylock turned to resume his climb with a sigh, but out of the corner of his eye he saw two small figures struggling against the snows far below. Their progress was slow and awkward, and Greylock guessed that they were not his own people. He debated whether or not to go on, for he still wanted to be alone. But he decided finally to wait and see who the curious figures were. As a precaution, he camouflaged himself in the snows, though he did not believe he was in any danger.

It was obvious that he could easily overcome these two clumsy pursuers, or if need be, escape.

Their progress seemed agonizingly slow, though Greylock knew that this was misleading. Against the backdrop of Godshome, any movement appeared lethargic. One could seem to be crawling yet be moving at a good pace.

This knowledge did nothing to help him restrain his impatience. One thing was clear, these two would very much like to hurry, if the snows would only let them.

The longer he waited, the more concerned he became. He was not frightened of any two people in the Three Tiers, but he realized that these two must have an important, even desperate, purpose for their pursuit.

He finally recognized the bent shape of the wizard Moag and the slim figure of Mara, bundled and constricted by heavy layers of clothing. The two were struggling against the snow, their clothes, and their own unfamiliarity with the thin air. Mara was helping her grandfather, but Moag was still having difficulty negotiating the crusted snow.

The sight of the two Underworlders made the Tyrant even more concerned. Not only would they not ordinarily seek him out, he thought, but things had to be desperate indeed for them to brave the cold and the snow. He turned and hurried toward them, his long strides barely breaking the crust of the snow.

The two laboring figures stopped when they saw him coming, and as he neared he saw that they were breathing heavily. Moag was bent over a cane and did not even raise his head. Mara rested lightly against the hump of his back. She tried to smile at the sight of the Tyrant.

Greylock did not wait for them to catch their breath.

"What's happened?" he demanded. Their expressions were distorted by more than their efforts and the snows, he thought.

Mara caught her breath first. "There is fighting," she managed to say before gasping for another breath.

Greylock could only stare at her in disbelief while she rested further. He had expected an attack from the Underworlders ever since the Room of Glyden had been unearthed; Gartlett had warned him of as much. But he had not expected an assault so soon after Redfrock and Silverfrost had left the High Plateau. The two conspirators had not been idle in the time they had shared a snowcastle, Greylock thought in alarm.

"But how did they get past Castle Guardian?" he demanded. The wizard and Mara had recently moved out of Castle Tyrant as threatened, and into the ancient snowcastle overlooking the only entrance into the High Plateau from the Gateway.

"Mayor Tarelton!" the wizard managed to spit out in his fury. The wizard and the mayor had been enemies from the day they had met. He had warned Greylock many times of Tarelton's treachery, but until now the Tyrant had thought the mayor was safely under the restraint of his own people. "He was at our castle last night!"

"Early this morning, while we slept, the guards were overwhelmed by the soldiers of Bordertown," Mara explained. "Tarelton must have let them in."

"But why would the people of Bordertown attack us?" Greylock asked in dismay. He had been certain that the two peoples would remain allies, that the tensions would not reach conflict. How had Tarelton escaped the control of the farmers?

"They are not alone, Greylock," Moag said grimly. "They have help from Trold."

"You must try to escape, Greylock!" Mara said. "You cannot fight the armies of King Kasid. Even if you defeat them, he will only send more. There is no end to his might!"

"A Tyrant must fight demons no matter how hopeless it may seem," Greylock said with a boldness he did not feel. Besides, he thought to himself, there was no escape. There was no way off the High Plateau except by the Gateway, and Castle Guardian overlooked that route. The only other possible route of escape was to go over the fhountain, and none who had dared that had returned.

"Where is Slimspear?" he asked. Only the steward had known where he was headed, he remembered with a shock.

"The surprise was complete," Moag said, shaking his head. "Only we escaped, and not by natural means. By the time we reached Castle Steward it was already under assault. Slimspear remained behind to hold them as long as possible. By now he must be a prisoner. They have even taken Castle Tyrant, Greylock! If you had been there—"

"They will not find it so easy to conquer the High Plateau!" Greylock vowed, angry at himself for not anticipating the attack. Yet, the old man was right. If he had been there, the victory would have been complete.

But since he was not their prisoner, any victory would be costly. The people of the High Plateau would not welcome the demons invading their homeland, he thought, and even now, most of the citizens of the High Plateau were certain that all Underworlders were demons. They would rally behind their Tyrant rather than let someone else rule the High Plateau with the aid of demons. Carrell Redfrock would be forced to lay siege to each and every snowcastle.

"Are you going to fight?" Mara asked.

"The other snowcastles must be warned," he said in answer. "I must not go myself. Above all, I must not be caught or all resistance will cease."

Greylock knew that despite their hatred of the demons, his people would not fight without the Tyrant. If Carrell Redfrock succeeded in defeating him, he would become the next Tyrant, no matter how distasteful that might be to the people.

"I think I can reach the nearest of the snowcastles, Greylock," the wizard volunteered. "From there messengers can be sent to the others. But where will you be?"

"I will be at Castle Priest. Since the ice tunnels do not extend all the way, the Underworlders will have to fight their way over the snows to reach it. Tell my people what I have said, Moag."

Greylock knew that he did not hold the love of his people any more than any Tyrant. But the citizens of the High Plateau were accustomed to following their Tyrant's orders, until that Tyrant was replaced by another. They would fight for him as long as he stayed free and alive.

"Tell them to harry the Underworlders," he continued. "But not to fight to the last man. Have them retreat slowly to Castle Priest."

The two of them immediately turned to leave at his orders, but he called Mara back.

"Stay with me a while, Mara," he said. When she still hesitated, he realized that she had misunderstood him and added hurriedly, "I need your powers as a wind witch, Mara. You may be able to save my people from a great deal of bloodshed."

"My grandfather has difficulty traversing the snow," she said doubtfully.

"I will be fine, Mara," the wizard assured her. "I can make it to the nearest snowcastle. It is not far, and I shall be going downhill."

Reluctantly, she agreed, and the trio split apart, traveling in opposite directions. Mara watched anxiously over her shoulders until the black speck that was her grandfather disappeared into the white expanse. The old man appeared to be moving much faster than they were, but again Greylock knew this was an illusion.

The slope became progressively steeper beneath Castle Priest, for the snowcastle was set against the very walls of Godshome. Terraces of snow were piled under the castle, making access difficult, which was exactly what the priests wanted.

Greylock intently examined the terraces of snow. The ice was piled high in huge blocks behind the barriers of rock and wood, and the snow pack was wet and heavy. The embankments had been erected in Greylock's youth to hold back the constant avalanches that had plagued earlier generations. It had been the sole innovation of Tyrant Ironclasp's reign, and the idea had come from a young nephew with a lock of gray hair. The stone barrier had worked beyond his expectations, and there had not been a major avalanche since.

Greylock had been worried that the recent tremors might have weakened the barriers, and it was the excuse of inspecting them that he had intended to use when he dropped in on Castle Priest. He saw now that the barriers were secure, though the snows had accumulated to unprecedented and frightening heights.

"Would you be able to send those snows down the slope?" he asked Mara, pointing to the crests.

"I have told you before, Greylock," she answered, when she saw what he meant to do. "I do not wish to use my powers of magic. Besides, I am not a water witch. Only the winds will respond to my urgings."

Greylock frowned impatiently. "But if I were to have some of the barriers weakened, could you summon a wind strong enough to start an avalanche?"

"That might be possible," she said, thoughtfully. "But I would not be able to stop it once it had started."

"We have rebuilt before," Greylock shrugged. "The demons must not be allowed to win."

Even as he said it, Greylock wondered if he was right, and that it was concern for his people and not for himself that made him risk the snowcastles. But he was strangely certain that Carrell Redfrock would be a worse calamity than any the High Plateau had yet faced.

Greylock watched the developing battle from the turret of Castle Priest's icetower. At first the Gatekeepers had objected strenuously to having their snowcastle made into a fortress, but when Greylock had explained that it was the Underworlders—the demons—who were attacking the High Plateau, the Gatekeepers had been transformed from his greatest obstacles to his most avid helpers. He did not need to point out that if the demons should succeed in conquering the mountain it was doubtful that the Gatekeepers would be allowed to continue practicing their religion.

Surely the gods would not stand for such a sacrilege! they had protested loudly. Why that would be as unthinkable as the people of the High Plateau seeking to storm Godshome!

Greylock had never seen the old Gatekeepers so energetic, or more willing to contribute their ideas and wisdom.

The Underworlders were having difficulty moving through the snows, as Greylock had hoped, and the more mobile and experienced mountain climbers from the plateau were harassing them from a distance.

But numbers were beginning to tell, and the Underworld army was slowly advancing. Somehow the demons had discovered where Greylock was waiting, and they were moving unswervingly toward Castle Priest. The black column was surrounded by the disordered specks of the defenders, who darted in occasionally to engage the enemy. Other dots, from both armies, were left behind in the snow, unmoving.

A few of the younger priests had agreed to serve as messengers, and now Greylock turned to one and barked, "Have them fall away! We need men up here working at the barriers. Tell the commanders to leave only enough men to slow the enemies' advance."

He caught Keyholder looking at him speculatively from the corner of his eyes. His old teacher never seemed to approve of any of Greylock's actions, and this had not changed with time. The tall, fragile man with bright eyes set in a wrinkled face maintained a demeanor that was slightly disapproving. Greylock suspected that the attitude was meant to keep the younger priests working hard, and his students self-conscious.

"Do you approve, Keyholder?"

"Approve?" The old priest raised his eyebrows quizzically.

"I mean the tearing down of the barriers."

"What if the snows should bury the icemelts? It. could be months before it all melts away." The question sounded merely curious, as if he were only testing his former student to see if he had thought of all the consequences.

"We will just have to hope that the old walls hold," Greylock replied. "There is no other choice, Keyholder! At worst, some of the snowcastles will survive. But if the demons should win, nothing of our life will endure."

Keyholder raised his eyebrows again, and for a few moments Greylock was sure that the old man would question the logic of his statement, or would rebuke him. But the old man said nothing. Sometimes, Greylock thought, it was difficult to remember that he was no longer the rebellious student when he was with Keyholder, but rather Tyrant of the High Plateau and answerable to no one.

Suddenly, he noticed that Mara was not standing beside him in the icetower, and he realized that he had not seen her in some time. He called out sharply for one of the messenger priests.

But before he could send the Gatekeepers hurrying after her, Keyholder volunteered the information.

"The girl is looking for her grandfather. She was afraid that he had not been told, and that he would be caught in the flow of the avalanche."

The young priest was still standing at his side. "Find her," he directed. "There is not much time. If she is worried about her grandfather, remind her that he is a fire wizard and can take care of himself."

The Underworld army was coming dangerously close to the last redoubts, he noticed. As they waited, he paced the parapet of the icetower, while Keyholder calmly watched him.

Greylock wished irritably that his old teacher would go away, but he dared not insult Keyholder. The Gatekeepers of the High Plateau had been known to defy even Tyrants if it was in their own best interests. Keyholder, with his influence over the priests, was his most valuable ally at this moment.

The young Gatekeeper, still resisting halfheartedly, finally rushed Mara into the room. She was out of breath, and angry with Greylock for not letting her warn her grandfather.

"I can't find him, Greylock! He told one of the soldiers that he was going to stay where he was, in one of the lower snowcastles. He said he was too old for fighting. What if he is buried? What if my magic were to kill him?"

Greylock grabbed her harshly by her shoulders. "We have no more time to look for him, Mara! If you do not summon the wind now, we will all perish. It is time that you thought of yourself, Mara. You cannot spend your youth looking after an old man."

When she still hesitated, he added, with as cold a tone as he could muster, "I will destroy the barriers, Mara, even if you do not help us. But it will mean sacrificing many of my own men beneath the snows. I do not want anyone under that avalanche when it goes, but I will order it if I have to."

She did not answer, but stared down at the glacier with a pale, strained expression.

The barriers were constructed of stone pillars at intervals along the face of the slope, lined by logs. The lumber had been awkwardly knocked away, with just enough of the timber left to hold the snows. There was no way in the short time given to them to pull out the last of the logs without sacrificing men. This is the reason why he had wanted her to add the force of her magic.

144

"Are you ready, Mara?" he asked softly, guiding her gently toward the balcony. "Do you need to be closer?"

He saw that she was yielding to his words. As she moved forward compliantly in his arms, Greylock whispered to the young priest over his shoulder, trying not to disturb her resolve.

"Tell the remaining soldiers to retreat behind the barriers! Quickly! There is no turning back!"

The last man had barely scrambled behind the terraces before Greylock whispered softly to Mara. The concentration in her pale face grew intense, and a lock of hair fell over her forehead unnoticed. At first there did not seem to be any change in the air currents, only a puzzled silence from the Underworld army. Greylock began to grow fearful that the demons would surmount this last defense before it came down on them. The Underworld army seemed to be startled by the sudden retreat. But finally, fatally mistaking the type of trap that was in store for them, they began to advance.

Mara's eyebrows curved downward severely, her green eyes became vacant, her jaw fell slack. Softly at first, and then more noticeably, Greylock began to feel a wind on his cheeks, a cold breeze coming from the frigid heights of Godshome. Then the wind became gusty, kicking up particles of ice, which were sent painfully into the faces of the Underworlders.

Belatedly, Greylock realized that this blinding storm alone might have been enough to turn the tide of battle. But it was too late for second thoughts. The brief gale was just a warning of the storm that was gathering above.

When the storm finally engulfed the High Plateau, it was as if one of the mighty storms of Godshome had descended full force upon the lower reaches of the mountain, to remind them that the mountain possessed the power to destroy them. As a child, Greylock had watched the tempests on the peaks of Godshome with a frightened and fascinated imagination. It had seemed to him that the gods were fighting among themselves, or playing with bolts of lightning. The storms of the High Plateau were just hints of those winds.

Now one of those storms had come down from the mountain with devastating force. The mild afternoon wind turned into a gale that had the men of both armies grabbing anything that seemed more bulky and secure than themselves. Some were sent rolling over the terraces, and down onto the crusty ice of the glacier.

The Underworlders could advance no further. Greylock could barely make them out in the blizzard, futilely holding their hands over their faces, drawing their cloaks over their heads. Many had turned around, but none had started back down.

And then it was too late. The white walls had been eaten away rapidly by the swirling winds, and now the first of the barriers buckled, bringing down the others with it.

Greylock could hear a few forlorn cries, and then a roar that seemed to shake the very core of the mountain drowned them out. Some of the demons tried to escape by running, but they made little progress before the snows covered them. Others seemed to be facing the approaching tide defiantly.

Then a billowing cloud of powder obscured the plateau. The spray of snow reached toward the balcony as if it wished to add them to its deadly toll. The rumble of the wave drowned out even the victorious cheers of the men standing in the icetower.

The clouds continued to rise, but Greylock knew that the avalanche had already surged beyond them. Judging from the sound of the roar, which was receding rapidly into the distance, Greylock feared that the avalanche had flowed far down the glacier.

The sound subsided at last, leaving in its wake a stunned silence. The cloud of powder fell on them softly, sounding like the spray of an ocean wave.

Greylock shuddered when he thought of that deadly mass perched above his land all this time, held back by a few pillars and logs that now seemed pitifully inadequate.

The victorious army of the High Plateau was now silent, not daring to even whisper their awe. Yet the one most shaken by the destructiveness of the avalanche was Mara.

She stared in disbelief at the devastation that was slowly being revealed, and then turned to hide her face. Greylock went to her and took her in his arms.

"There was no choice, Mara. It had to be done."

She turned her gaze up to his, and he was startled by the anger he saw there.

"I will never again use my magic to harm another!" he heard her whisper. "It has been twisted, made evil!"

He could find no answer to the accusation he saw reflected in her green eyes, and he turned, embarrassed.

There was no sign of the enemy, no trace of an invading army, just a jumbled layer of iceblocks. The mountain was deceptively peaceful. The nearest snowcastle was wedged in by huge drifts of snow, piled against its ancient walls. Where he knew other snowcastles to lie, there was nothing, no sign that their gardens, their spires, their icetowers, had ever existed.

He had won a victory, he thought, but he had destroyed much of his own land in winning.

Mayor Tarelton would pay for this destruction, he vowed. Instead of a victorious army returning from the mountain, the mayor would find a delegation from the High Plateau. And if Redfrock and the Lady Silverfrost should be caught waiting in anticipation, he thought, so much the better.

CHAPTER FIVE

The preparations for the expedition to Bordertown were at last completed, but Greylock found himself reluctant at the last moment to give the orders to march. Until now he had been anxious to hurry his confident army down into the Underworld, and he was not even sure himself what was causing his hesitation.

It was not that he was afraid of resistance, he thought, for the army of Far Valley had been utterly destroyed. Not one soldier of their once powerful invading army would have returned to tell of their doom. Greylock remembered Gartlett's warnings about King Kasid, the wizard's stories of the unending might of the fiefdoms of Trold, but he was not concerned. He expected the Underworlders to be completely demoralized by the sight of the men from the High Plateau. The people of Bordertown would be expecting a conquering army, instead they would find an angry and vengeful enemy host.

No, what was bothering him, he had to admit at last, was that by going into the Underworld he would once again have to cross the Twilight Dells, to face the Wyrrs.

If his sister Ardra had not interrupted at that moment, the Tyrant would have convinced himself that the trip was unnecessary. But Ardra reminded him of his most compelling motive for going to Bordertown: revenge.

He turned from the sight of the jumbled glacier at the sound of her soft voice, and his bitter expression softened at the sad look in his sister's round face.

Ardra and Slimspear had been a perfect match, he thought. She was plump, as Slimspear had been, and, once, she had been as cheerful. They had seemed to have the same thoughts, the same feelings, he thought, especially in their devotion to him. Now, Ardra seemed only half as strong, if even more brave.

They had found Slimspear alone in Castle Steward, and Greylock had known from his visage that they had tortured the steward to discover his whereabouts. Though the steward had been captured soon after Moag and Mara's escape, he had kept his silence until their mission to warn the Tyrant was complete.

Slimspear's mutilated body was the real reason Greylock had rushed to form a punitive expedition. The Tyrant had immediately recognized the handiwork of the torturer, for he had seen it used many times in the service of his uncle.

Only Carrell Redfrock would be so ruthless in acquiring his information, Greylock thought, so deadly in his results. Mayor Tarelton was a mere pawn in the schemes of Redfrock and Silverfrost. It was that heartless pair that the Tyrant hoped to catch in his trap. He could not be certain that both of them had escaped the destruction of Mara's wind-witchery, but he doubted that they would have exposed themselves to danger.

"You must not go to Bordertown for my sake," Ardra said softly, somehow sensing his hesitation.

"They will pay for his death," he vowed. Her words only seemed to make him more determined to make the journey. "They will learn that it is for Steward Slimspear, husband of my sister Ardra, that they are being punished."

"You must not let hate guide you, Greylock. You are leaving those who love you behind."

"Am I?" he asked bitterly.

"You must not doubt that she still loves you, Greylock."

"No?" he laughed shortly. "Why does she run from me? Why does she hide her face when I pass?"

Mara had fallen into a deep gloom at the destruction of her wind magic. Greylock feared that on top of his refusal to release her grandfather, that she would never forgive him for the annihilation of the demon army. She never blamed him out loud, but only because she never seemed to stay in his presence for more than a few moments before fleeing.

"It is because she loves you, Greylock. She runs because she is afraid that her emotions will come to the surface." When Greylock looked as though he were about to laugh, she insisted, "I know because she has told me."

Before Greylock could fully appreciate what she had said, she dampened his hopes with an admonition.

"Why don't you let the old wizard go? She would come to you if you did."

He turned from her, disbelieving. It seemed to him that the campaign to free the old man had become a conspiracy. He knew that it was his own stubborn refusal to let Moag go that was in the way of their happiness; but the mountain continued to shake, the Wyrrs continued to haunt him, King Kasid of Trold had only begun his assault on the High Plateau. Such problems never seemed to go away. Indeed, they seemed to be multiplying.

"I will free him when I have no more need of him," he said, stubbornly.

"How can you be so blind?" she said in disgust. "Don't you see that it is your own obstinance that is making you unhappy? Well, I will try no more to convince you. You will not see me again until you have come to your senses, Greylock!"

With that, she turned her back on him and marched from the icetower.

Greylock descended deep into the lower passages of Castle Tyrant until he had reached the network of caves that riddled the lava and formed a highway beneath the snows.

Unconsciously Greylock chose the same route he had used to lead his Underworld army in their conquest of the High Plateau. There were such a variety of tunnels that no one ever bothered to remove the fallen stones or drifts of dust. Every citizen had his own favorite paths, and these paths might not be used by anyone else. Even the Tyrant occasionally came across a fork in the caverns he did not recognize, and it was not unusual for men to become lost in tunnels they had traveled through since childhood.

Greylock kept his head slightly bent, both in thought and in anticipation of the sudden dives of the craggy roof. At the turn to Castle Guardian, Greylock was surprised to be met by Moag.

"Did you want to see me, Moag?" he asked uncomfortably.

"I have not come out of courtesy, you can be sure," Moag said sourly. "I have a few questions about the construction of your snowcastles. They are the only interesting feature in your land, Tyrant, your one truly unique art form. And since there is no telling when you will return—or if you will return—I had thought I better ask now."

"What is to keep me from coming back?" Greylock said, impatiently.

"You are not dealing with Mayor Tarelton now, Greylock," the old man replied sternly. "King Kasid is more evil and powerful than you can imagine. If he has learned of your Room of Glyden, then he will not give up with one battle. Your victory was no more than a skirmish. Next time he won't trust the men of Bordertown. He will send his own mercenaries."

"But you wanted me to go to King Kasid in the first place, Moag!" Greylock objected. "Why do you warn me of him now?"

"Then the Vault of Glyden was only a legend," the old man said uneasily. "And King Kasid was not our enemy. If you had chosen him instead of Mayor Tarelton, he would not be our enemy now."

"No," Greylock said sardonically. "He would have had our glyden without a fight!"

The Tyrant realized that he was getting into another argument with the querulous wizard, and changed the subject to business.

"What did you want to know about the architecture of the snowcastles?"

In the two weeks since the battle for the High Plateau, Moag had proven to be of invaluable help in the resettlement of the displaced, the clearing of the avalanche from the icemelts, and the rebuilding of the snowcastles and icetowers. Despite his grumbling, the fire wizard had used his magic in surprising ways to reform or melt away the massive piles of ice and to form new walls. Greylock suspected that the old man even enjoyed his new tasks.

Most of the dwellings had survived. The old, abandoned barrier walls had held better than anyone had expected. But all the snowcastles had sustained some damage, and a few had been completely destroyed.

The Tyrant knew it was necessary to answer Moag's last minute questions. In these latter days there were few craftsmen left who knew the ancient art of ice architecture. The Tyrant's training under the Gatekeepers had included what little knowledge was left, though he felt himself a poor source at best.

The wizard had already improved on some of the designs, and had substituted and implemented new techniques. Greylock wished he could convince Keyholder or one of the other priests to help the wizard, but, predictably, they had objected to Moag's innovations.

The Tyrant did not want to leave while the rebuilding efforts were still underway, but it was time to leave the High Plateau and teach the townsmen a final lesson in loyalty. Moag had proven to be an unexpectedly able engineer to leave behind in charge of the rebuilding.

"I wish to leave you in command while I am gone, Moag," he said, after obliging the wizard with as much information as he possessed. For some time he had been wondering who he could trust. He had his eye on a young nobleman named Kalwyn, but he had not yet named his new steward. Moag was the best he had. "Don't worry," he continued. "My people will follow you. You happen to be a hero at the moment. You may not even have to worry about assassination."

"Very well, if I must," the wizard grimaced.

"I wish you would let me reward you for your - help," he said. "Let me give you some of the glyden."

At first Greylock did not think the wizard would even acknowledge this attempt at friendship. Then finally, the old man grumbled, "My help these last few weeks has not been for you, Greylock, but for myself. But since you mention a reward, I had hoped that in the end you would feel that you must grant me what I desire."

Both knew what the reward he was asking for was, his freedom.

152

Greylock was once again torn by his nameless fears. They centered on the mountain. Someday soon he would need the wizard's fire magic, and he would need it desperately. He felt the danger stronger than ever.

Yet, there was no longer any real threat he could point to. Just his formless fears of the rumblings of Godshome, the spilling of steam that seemed to harmlessly shroud the mountain peaks.

Standing in the choking dust and darkness of the cavern, he admitted to himself at last that what he wanted most from the old man was friendship, and it was obvious that friendship would not be forthcoming as long as the wizard was held against his will.

"I will free you when I return, Moag," he said, softly, giving in at last.

"What!"

Greylock had to repeat himself several times before the excited wizard would believe him. But to the Tyrant, at that moment, the words seemed to echo off the close dark walls of the tunnel in warning.

The army of the High Plateau cautiously marched down the mountain trail of Gateway, with scouts fanned out far ahead, and others climbing far above the main force with their talons. The men of the plateau were actually more comfortable on the narrow animal trails and sheer precipices, Greylock thought, than they were on the newly carved highway.

Greylock was made forcefully aware that the mayor had not been exaggerating his complaints of obstructionism. Ironically, Greylock realized that the Underworlders knew the trail much better than did the natives of the mountain. He even had trouble finding guides to lead them over the new trail. Apparently, his people had refused almost to a man to work on the project, and it had been left almost entirely in the hands of the townsmen.

Greylock kept his eyes open warily for an ambush, for it was common practice when building any new construction to include a few secret pitfalls and hideaways. It was the first time he had seen the handiwork of the townsmen, for he had been as hesitant as any of his people to descend from Godshome, though he had admonished them. But where others feared the Underworld as a haven for demons,

Greylock feared it because of the Wyrr's mysterious power over him. Perhaps it amounted to the same thing, he thought. The Wyrrs were his demons.

Greylock did not like the look of the new Gateway, built over the massive and intricate stones of the old.

The trail was smooth and broad, but it had lost the aura of ancient culture that the old pathway had possessed. This especially saddened Greylock because he had once hoped to find in Gateway the evidence of where it might have originally led. He was sure that the pathway led to more than the snows of the High Plateau and the sweltering heat of the Underworld. Greylock suspected, as well that the new path would lack the permanence of the old.

He could not really complain, though seeing the new road was a shock. The new Gateway had been one of his modernizations. It had always been his ambition to unite the lands between Far Valley and the High Plateau by a network of roads, so that the traveler could pass through without an armed escort.

He had to smile at this thought when he looked about him. A larger escort could not be found! Many of his men were grasping their talons suspiciously, sure that at any, moment the unusually warm soil beneath their feet would drop away into a pool of firestone. Only molten rock could account for such widespread warmth; in their experience.

Greylock had to remind himself that he was one of the few men of the High Plateau who had actually descended down into the Underworld. The old fears of demons would not vanish overnight, he told himself. The people of Bordertown had had the advantage of knowing both winter and summer, and many would have visited the foothills. All would have felt the cold touch of snow falling on their bare skin. Snow and cold were a part of their reasons, something that occurred regularly every year.

But the warmth of the High Plateau was confined mostly to the few spots of volcanic warmth called the icemelts.

No, Greylock told himself ruefully, he could not show impatience with his people for displaying the fear of demons that he himself had displayed on his first journey to the Underworld. Indeed, traces of that fear were coming back now to plague him, but he attributed this reaction to his reluctance to meet the Wyrrs.

At last they completed the descent of Godshome, and the road leveled into the easy slopes of the foothills. There had been no sign of opposition, but as they neared the Twilight Dells, Greylock almost wished that something, even an enemy attack, would stop them before they could proceed into that mysterious land.

He stood at the borders of the Dells, and the maze of green valleys beneath a haze of fog greeted his sight like an imploring pauper. The land seemed to be pleading to him for his help. They called him Deliverer here, he thought miserably.

He wished now that he had completed his interrupted journey to the library of Castle Priest. More than ever, he wished that he could have had a chance to examine the ancient books. He had nothing he could tell the Wyrrs if they should confront him. Yet, strangely, once his decision to go down into the Underworld had been made, the nightmares had stopped.

Greylock felt a strong urge to turn back, to return to the High Plateau. As he stood and debated with himself, his men whispered uncertainly behind him, mistaking his hesitation as a fear of demons instead of what it really was, a repugnance of the land itself.

The soil radiated a malignant sickness, an air of stillbirth, an aura of dusty death. It was even worse than Greylock remembered, this land of the Wyrrs. Yet nothing happened, no Wyrr appeared to point an accursing hand. At last he moved forward, without looking back, as though nothing unusual had happened, and he had not been standing in the drizzling mists for many minutes. His men, who had been asking worried questions with no reply from him, gradually overcame their fear and followed.

Once he was committed, Greylock wanted nothing more than to cross the cursed land as soon as possible. The light snow that had been falling in the foothills turned to rain, and the valleys had never seemed so miserable and forsaken. As they trudged down the muddy road, which true to the mayor's word squarely intersected the Dells, he began to hope that the Wyrrs were unaware of his trespass.

But he had known from the start that they would sense his presence, and he was not surprised when he began to experience the familiar dreamy sensation that signaled another visitation of the Wyrrs.

Midway through the dells, deep within one of its steep valleys, with dead pines threatening on both sides, a single Wyrr approached them.

Though Greylock knew what to expect, the vision seemed to shimmer disconcertingly, like a waking dream. The illusion of a beautiful figure greeted him with a raised hand, crying out with the valiant tones of a message of celebration. Moments later the Wyrr flickered into his real form, and the visage of a hollow- eyed Wyrr, muttering pathetically, stared at them instead.

Greylock had no need of translation, as he had on his first journey to the Underworld. His transformation to Deliverer was as complete as the graying of his hair.

"I cannot help you!" he cried. He had almost convinced himself that he had imagined their pleas, that they had been only nightmares. After all, he had reasoned, none but the wizard and his granddaughter had ever seen what he had seen.

But he had known it would come to this.

"I cannot help you!" he repeated. How could he have dared come down from Godshome? he asked himself savagely. How could he have believed that he would not be confronted?

The denial seemed to have no effect on the Wyrr. The vision would not go away, but waited patiently. At one moment he would appear in his beautiful form and seem to be one of Greylock's own kindred from the High Plateau, as it had been under the gods, Greylock thought. The Wyrr had a proud, demanding face, strong and dark.

Moments later, the vision was changed back to what the others saw. The Wyrr stared out of deep set and feverish black eyes, his pale brow beaded with sweat and grime, his tattered garments hanging loosely and obscenely from his limbs. Greylock could hear the nervous questions of his men at his back.

But finally the pleading became so strong that Greylock took pity on the Wyrr. He promised something that he had never intended to promise, and did not know if he could fulfill.

"I can do nothing for you now," he said helplessly. "I do not know how to free you. But I promise that I will return with the answer. The next time you see me, the next time I come down from Godshome, I will be your Deliverer in truth."

This seemed to satisfy the apparition. The proud face smiled gratefully; the dirty face pathetically. The Wyrrs will wait a while longer, he seemed to say. They had waited many centuries for the Deliverer. A few days, or weeks, or even months were a small matter if it was what the Deliverer required.

The Wyrr turned to go, and vanished as though he had never been anything but an illusion. But Greylock knew from the stunned expressions in his men's faces that the visitation had been real. They stared at him curiously, and from their frightened banter, he knew that his men were now convinced that demons existed. He could not blame them. Though human, the Wyrrs looked extraordinarily like the images of demons that the Gatekeepers drew to frighten children.

They continued on to Far Valley, nervously expecting another visit by the disturbing inhabitants of the Twilight Dells. But they were not approached again.

CHAPTER SIX

The army neared Far Valley with a relaxed vigilance. The Tyrant knew that they were safe from attack. The Wyrrs were pitifully weak in the daylight hours, it was in the dark of the night that they were at their strongest. And there was no sign of the men of Bordertown.

The road, with the earth of its construction piled loosely on both sides, had turned into a muddy river. Apparently, Greylock thought, the road builders had neglected to create drainage canals for the runoffs of the spring floods. It was appropriate that the rains should wash away the last traces of the alliance between the two lands.

The farmlands surrounding Bordertown were unfurrowed and overgrown with weeds, in contrast to the lush but carefully tended farmlands he had observed on his first trip to the Underworld. The Tyrant knew when he saw this that they would encounter no serious resistance.

The fertile and abundant land, so different from the Twilight Dells, was obviously in chaos, its people in danger of starvation. Greylock stepped gratefully onto the muddy fields, feeling the taint of the Dells on his boots ground away by the clean earth of Far Valley.

Bordertown itself appeared deserted. The thatch houses, which were placed randomly in a field of cropped grass, showed no plumes of smoke from their hearths, and the well-worn paths were uncharacteristically choked by encroaching weeds.

As they marched down the one wide road at the center of the town, no one stepped forward to bar their way, or to welcome them. The road led to a gabled building that had once been the Lord High Mayor's Palace and was now the town hall. Greylock saw that the huge seal of glyden was once again over the entrance to the building. It hung crookedly, as if knocked askance by its owner's hasty departure.

Greylock no longer had any hope of finding his quarry within the town. While still mired in the mud of the Twilight Dells, they had seen the form of a black crow circling high above them, out of reach of their weapons. For a few seconds, Greylock had questioned whether the crow was the familiar of Carrell Redfrock, but when it had cawed at them with an unnatural, mocking cry, all doubt had disappeared. As the black bird had flown scornfully to the east, Greylock knew that the chance of surprise had been lost.

His men were uneasy at the silence, even at the swiftness of their conquering advance. They had expected at least a token of resistance, and this abandonment was disconcerting. They fell silent in turn, and nervously compared the pitiful abodes to their own magnificent snowcastles, the tangled greenery with the efficient gardens of their icemelts. Greylock knew without asking that they were offended by the lack of walls, the wasteful use of fertile earth.

They stood uneasily in the town square, and at last Greylock caught a glimpse of faces peering from behind closed curtains. They were gaunt faces, defeated, not the plump satisfied faces Greylock remembered.

He ascended the steps of the town hall and motioned for his men to search the building. A few moments later two of his men dragged Mayor Tarelton from his once luxurious and gilded palace.

The Tyrant found that his anger had left him, now that he was actually facing his prey. The mayor looked pitifully lean, his red hair was straggled and clotted as if the tall man had been tearing at it in frustration. The once brilliant emerald hue of his frock was almost obscured by the oil and grime of imprisonment.

"We found him locked in his room," one of the soldiers announced.

Greylock smiled at the mayor in pity. "So Redfrock has abandoned you to answer for his deeds again, Tarelton?" he said. "When will you learn what kind of person you are allied with?"

"I have no choice who I serve," Tarelton answered in a low voice. He stared at the ground, glancing up to glare at Greylock every few seconds.

"Then you admit that you serve Carrell Redfrock? That you have been in league with him from the start?"

"We both serve the same master," the mayor repeated dully. "I have no choice."

"You had a choice once, Tarelton," Greylock said without sympathy. "Perhaps you still have." He suddenly noticed that something was missing.

"Where is your rat, Tarelton? Has it abandoned you as well?"

A crafty look briefly crossed the mayor's smudged face, but he did not answer the Tyrant's question. Instead, his high voice cried out across the square, and Greylock realized that it was the people in the houses he wanted to hear him.

"Why have you come, Tyrant Greylock? Have you not killed enough of our people? Have you come to take our food as well?"

"It is for you, Mayor Tarelton, and those you serve, that I have come," Greylock answered, also raising his voice. "You have held glyden to be more important than the welfare of your people. They have suffered enough. I have come for neither glyden or revenge."

"Am I not innocent for following the wishes of my master?" Tarelton said quietly, not bothering to hide the bitter guile in his voice.

"Once you made your choice, Tarelton, your destiny was your own," Greylock snapped. He raised his voice to the surrounding houses.

"Come out, people of Bordertown!" he cried. "We will not harm you! You are not to blame for the treachery of your mayor!"

Greylock had thought that there would be many in Bordertown who would welcome him. The yeoman Harrkor and his farmer brethren would know him to be no worse a ruler than their mayor. It was for them that he had wanted to make this journey, as much as for his own people. He suspected that most of his old friends in

Bordertown, those who had helped him fight for the throne, would be imprisoned, perhaps dead.

At first there was no response to his call. Then one of the doors opened, and a young man stepped out. One by one the other houses emptied, and the people silently surrounded the steps of the town hall and filled the square.

Most of the surviving residents of Bordertown were either too young or too old to fight, Greylock noticed. The men of the town must have been conscripted into the army of Trold, he thought, to be used as shock troops.

The friendly, staunch face of Harrkor was missing, as he had feared. The broad-shouldered, heavy-set farmers of the outlying areas of Far Valley were nowhere to be seen. From the look of the untended fields, abandoned long before the battle of the High Plateau, the farmers had been absent from tilling for much longer than two weeks. There was a look of incipient famine in the town.

Apparently, the mayor had slipped away from their control long ago. Greylock berated himself for not noticing that the guards surrounding Tarelton on his last visit had been a sham.

It was like Tarelton in his avarice, to sacrifice the men who cultivated the town's food. Only now was the mayor discovering what Greylock had known from his first survey, that Harrkor and his like were the true strength and power of Far Valley.

"Where is Harrkor?" he demanded. "Where are your farmers?"

Tarelton paled and seemed in fear of his life for the first time.

".They are alive," he said hastily. "They are well—"

"Are they imprisoned?" Greylock asked in relief. "Give me the keys to their prison!"

"They are not here," the mayor said reluctantly. "They have been taken to the fiefdoms of Trold to be, ah, servants of King Kasid. It was the price of his aid to Redfrock."

Greylock drew Thunderer and took a step toward the taller man with his sword raised. It flashed in the sunlight as if it knew that it was at last to be used for the purpose it had been forged.

"It was not my idea, Greylock!" the mayor screamed, as the blade stopped only inches from the matt of red hair. "I protested. After all, they are my people too! It was the silver lady who thought of it. I swear!"

"I don't believe you, Tarelton. Harrkor would never become the slave of another. He would die first!"

"It is true, Tyrant," he heard an unfamiliar voice from behind him.

He turned to see the tall youth who had emerged first from the dwellings. The young man continued to speak, as if embarrassed before such a crowd, in front of such important personages. But there was no fear in his voice, and there was no doubting the truth of his statement.

"Harrkor himself told the others to submit. We were ready to fight, but he forbade us. Only I was allowed to escape in the confusion. I was to tell you this."

"But how did he know I would come?" Greylock asked, dismayed. "How can I free him?" On closer examination, the youth obviously came from the farms. His blond hair was bleached by the sun, his face reddened.

"He told me you would come," the youth shrugged. "He said that you would free him and the others."

Greylock's relief that Harrkor and the farmers of Far Valley were alive was dampened by the thought of yet another burden laid on his shoulders.

"What shall I do with you, Tarelton?" he asked, a little surprised at his own question. It had been his intention all along, though he had never voiced it, to put a swift end to the life of the treacherous mayor. But now he found that he did not have the stomach to kill the man. It would have been a mercy, perhaps, but Greylock realized that this pitiful man was the least of his enemies, a servant of others more evil and powerful. His death would serve no purpose.

"What shall I do with you?" he repeated in a louder voice, so that all could hear. The mayor looked forlorn without his familiar, he thought. It was the first time he had ever seen Tarelton without the rat on his shoulders, and he wondered again where it had gone.

"Shall I ask your people, Tarelton?" he said. "Shall we leave it up to them? The first time you betrayed them, they asked that you simply serve them."

A look of terror filled the mayor's face and he said, faintly, "Why do you taunt me? Kill me now, for I do not wish to be a slave to them again."

Greylock realized that he had indeed been taunting the mayor, and he suddenly realized what his judgment must be.

"I will not kill you, Tarelton," he said solemnly. "Though you may deserve death. You are henceforth banished from Far Valley, and all lands west of its borders. If you should return from your exile, your death will be permitted, nay, desired."

If he had hoped that in this dismissal the mayor would leave his sight and thoughts forever, he was very wrong. Tarelton had one last trick to play, one last desperate attempt to recover all he had lost.

Tarelton's own eagerness betrayed him, and the anxiety that the Tyrant would escape the trap by moving. His blue eyes darted upward, and Greylock instinctively followed his look even as he was in the act of turning away.

The glyden seal of the Lord High Mayor swung once before it toppled over, giving Greylock the time to dive free of its fall. He heard it land solidly behind him, and the ground shook with the impact of the heavy metal. He rolled to his feet, and saw that the seal landed where he had been standing only moments before. The yellow metal had shattered the steps, and had bent into a shapeless, battered lump.

Greylock looked up to the roof where the enormous shield had been hanging by thick ropes. The cords hung dangling, gnawed through neatly. The shape of the assassin was outlined briefly against the window, then vanished, but not before Greylock had caught a glimpse of a thin, filthy rat.

Several soldiers rushed the mayor with an angry shout and pinioned him against the doors of the town hall.

"Shall we kill him?" one of them demanded.

"No." Greylock's voice quavered slightly and he realized that he was more shaken by the near miss than he had thought. "It does not change anything. Get him out of my sight. But if you see his familiar, I want it killed!"

Greylock knew that he was being a fool to let the mayor go, but he could not bring himself to condone a coldblooded execution. As Tyrant

163

of the High Plateau he understood the grasp for power. In his land, if one could survive an attempt to overthrow the Tryant, there was a good chance that one might live; for whoever attempted but failed to assassinate the Tyrant was prohibited by tradition from trying again. In fact, Greylock had been considering appointing the young man who had tried to kill him—Kalwyn—as steward. Executions, the Tyrants had found, were a waste of good, ambitious men.

But Greylock knew this was different. Mayor Tarelton was not likely to play by the same rules.

His fears seemed justified by the last words of Tarelton, as he was dragged away.

"Redfrock will return, Greylock!" Tarelton shrieked. "He is already on his way to the fiefdoms of Trold. The King is a proud man. When he learns that you have destroyed his army, you are doomed!"

CHAPTER SEVEN

The wizard Moag met the returning army where Castle Guardian spanned the Gateway's entrance into the High Plateau. Though Greylock was exhausted by the campaign, the old wizard insisted on immediately showing off the latest of the rebuilt snowcastles. He was excited by the changes he had wrought in the construction of snowcastles, changes he said would make the structures stronger and safer.

Greylock smiled at the sight of the old man once more active and happy, now that his freedom had at last been granted. He knew then that he had done the right thing in letting the old man go.

"I am almost tempted to stay," Moag said smiling, "now that I am no longer forced to stay. These marvelous structures you call snowcastles, I wish I knew who first thought of them. The basic designs have not changed; I am certain, for many centuries. They are ingenious structures, really, to allow an entire people to survive the freezing cold of the mountain, to use the very material that threatens you to protect you instead. I am probably the first to make innovations in many years, though not many changes are needed."

"The gods themselves gave us the design for our snowcastles and icetowers," Greylock said, only half in jest.

"Of course, of course," the wizard agreed, obviously not believing him. "But I would like to know who built the first one."

Greylock sighed in exasperation, and followed the wizard.

165

When he saw what Moag had accomplished, he marveled at the beauty and strength that had been created out of the ice. The wizard had evidently succeeded in strengthening the structures by using a purer, heavier ice.

"It took many days of experimenting with my fire to find the right kind of ice," Moag explained. "Your people have never had access to such heat before, but I have taught them new methods of lighting fires."

This harder ice, he continued, melted and frozen again and again, gave the snowcastles new dimensions. The icetowers could be higher and narrower, and the snowcastles possessed a fragile grace the old walls had not.

Moag directed a final block of ice as it was lowered onto the topmost level of the icetower. When it was finally set into place, he stepped back to survey his handiwork. Greylock waited respectfully for the inspection to be completed.

"Will they hold in a storm, Moag?" Greylock finally said, doubtfully. "It would be a shame if these graceful towers should come tumbling down in the first quake or gust of wind."

"They have been tested by the full force of Mara's wind-witchery, which is more powerful than even 1 ever believed."

"Mara's magic!"

The wizard smiled at Greylock's surprise. "Yes, she is using her magic now. I believe she may have even forgiven you, now that you have freed me. But then, she was always yours if you'd only had sense enough to see."

"You have done wonders, Moag," Greylock said, wishing that he dared slap the old wizard on his hunched back. His tiredness had completely left him. Mara's quarters could be reached by dark, he thought, if the old wizard would only let him go. "I want you to have this snowcastle as your own. We will call it Castle Wizard."

Moag suddenly scowled, as if he thought the enthusiasm he had shown earlier unseemly.

"Mara may have forgiven you," he growled. "But I can never trust you again. I will be leaving soon, and I hope that Mara will go with me."

"But where will you go?"

"There are many lands I have not seen. I think perhaps I will see if I can find a pass through these mountains. Even your people do not seem to know what lies on the other side of Godshome."

Greylock shuddered, and quickly reminded himself that it was he who had always professed not to believe in the frightening legends. He had proven that there were no demons in the Underworld. Why should he be frightened of the unknown? Still, he had often wondered why his people could give no account of the lands beyond Godshome, and had never endeavored to reach them.

"You are free to go, of course," he said, sadly. He had begun to like this new Moag, as well as need him. But the wizard was slipping back to his old resentful self. "You are welcome to stay. You will always be honored by my people for what you have done."

The rest of the short tour of the snowcastles was conducted with less enthusiasm on Moag's part, but the joy continued to grow in Greylock.

Before he had left there had been no assurance that Mara forgave him, much less loved him. But Greylock was suddenly certain that the love between them had not vanished, but had only been hidden by his refusal to give the old wizard his freedom. He had been a fool!

Only Moag's decision to leave dampened his happiness. Despite everything, he had hoped the wizard would stay. And there was the old man's threat to take Mara with him.

Surely Mara would not give in to the wizard's obstinacy!

"Help me back to Castle Guardian," Moag said gruffly, interrupting his thoughts. "These old legs cannot fight the snows as they once could."

They began to move slowly down the mountains, both lost in thought.

"You do not look well, Greylock," the old man said suddenly.

The Tyrant was surprised that he had noticed. "I have not been sleeping well, that is all."

Despite his promise to the Wyrrs, the dreams of the demons had kept him tossing night after night, until he preferred not to sleep at all.

He was hollow-eyed and pale, and it was becoming difficult to concentrate.

"It's the Wyrrs, isn't it?" the wizard said, suddenly. When Greylock looked at him in surprise, he continued. "I owe you, no favor, but I would advise you if I may. My advice is this; it must be done. You cannot put it off any longer. They will not leave you alone until you have freed them of their curse."

"But what can I do?" He wondered how the wizard had known of his absorption with the Wyrrs.

"I am not the one to ask such a question. I do not know your legends, your religion. If I were you, I would go to the Gatekeepers."

Despite his distaste for the priests, Greylock had to admit that the old man was right. He had known it all along, even if he had not liked it. Once he had even set out for Castle Priest, and in the back of his mind had been the questions about the Wyrrs. Then had come the battle, and he had been relieved to forget their plight, if only for a little while.

The two had reached Castle Guardian again at last, and Greylock let go of the old man's arm when they reached the warm stones of the courtyard. He hesitated before leaving. It was Mara's home as well, but he was not sure he could venture any further into the snowcastle without invitation.

The old man continued up the walk without looking back, and Greylock feared that it would be the last time he would see the wizard. But at the last moment, the old man turned and motioned for him.

Greylock smiled hopefully, and hurried toward him.

"I wish to return your knife," the old man growled. "1 won't need it anymore."

The wizard produced the glyden-hilted knife, the price of his services to the Tyrant, and handed it back to Greylock. As soon as Greylock had taken it, reluctantly, the old man pulled out a single nugget of glyden. "Now I will be able to wield my magic for myself!"

"You can have more than that, Moag!" Greylock offered. "You can have all you want!"

The wizard smiled and rubbed the nugget in his fingers. "This is all I need." He paused. "My granddaughter wished me to ask you to have dinner with us tonight, Greylock. Will you come?"

"Of course I will come!" Greylock exclaimed.

The wizard nodded unhappily, and turned to climb up the steep steps of the snowcastle. The massive doors shut behind him without a sound.

Greylock walked back to Castle Tyrant with a spring in his step. Despite the old man's gruff ness, Greylock knew that Mara still loved him. And now that he had made up his mind to see the Gatekeepers about the Wyrrs, he knew that the nightmares would leave him. The High Plateau seemed at peace.

Greylock arrived at Castle Guardian that night without guards and over the snows, an unheard of honor and risk for the Tyrant of the High Plateau. But he did not feel that anyone could threaten him with danger on such an evening. With his suddenly revived spirit, he felt ready to confront any danger.

Mara greeted him with a smile, and Greylock felt himself relax. He had told himself it did not matter what she said. He dared not hope. Now, despite himself, his hopes soared.

He was enthralled at the sight of her. She was radiant in a gown the red of snowflowers, and the vivid colors of her eyes and dress contrasted with the shimmering shades Silverfrost had always chosen. In their year of separation she had blossomed into a beautiful and mature woman. The frown lines between her eyebrows, formed by a natural skepticism, now made her look thoughtful. Her unruly blond hair flowed freely down her back. Greylock knew that he had not been wrong to love her, though it had seemed foolish until this night.

Moag was still frowning, his mottled face seemingly unchanged from that afternoon. He did not rise. The meal passed without any serious discussion, and later Greylock could not remember what had been said, or what he had eaten—if he had eaten.

Mara broached the subject of Moag's leaving first, and the Tyrant saw that the wizard was as anxious for her decision as he was.

"Have you truly released my grandfather, Greylock?" she asked.

"He is free now," Greylock said, holding his breath. "He has already returned my knife of glyden. I have asked him to stay, but..."

She turned to the wizard.

"Are you determined to leave the High Plateau?"

Moag nodded. Greylock felt his heart sink at the question, certain that the matter had been decided against him.

"I will not be going with you, Moag," she announced softly, and Greylock cried out in relief. The old man sank back with a sigh.

"I know I should still be angry at Greylock," she said. "I know that he has broken the laws of magic by holding you against your will. But I love him, Moag! I have loved him from the first moment I saw him, descending from the clouds like a god, his lock of silver hair catching the sun."

"I had once thought that we could serve each other," Moag said in a resigned voice, and to Greylock it seemed as if both of them had forgotten his presence. "That is why I searched so long and hard for glyden, Mara. Not for the wealth it would have brought us, but because it was needed to free our powers. We needed glyden to be free. So I reasoned—"

"Grandfather, please!"

"No, I can see that I was a fool. You are too much like your mother, Mara. You never did like my wanderings, and a wizard must wander. Stay, Mara. I understand.

"But do not expect me to forgive him!" he pointed a long finger at Greylock. "I trusted him and he twisted that trust to his purposes. I warned him once that when he became Tyrant he would find his power difficult to deny. He had broken the edicts of the gods, though he lives at their feet and at their mercy. He will be punished, Mara!"

She did not answer, but stared back at him with an unblinking sorrow.

Moag rose from his chair. "I will be leaving in the morning."

"Please, Moag," Greylock stopped him, grabbing his arm. "Stay until the wedding."

"No," the old man shrugged off his arm. "I have been here too long already."

The wizard left the room slowly, bent almost to the floor. For the first time since Greylock had known him, Moag seemed to act his years.

Mara and Greylock were left alone at last, but they could only look at each other in sadness. She came to him, but it was not as he had envisioned. The old wizard had managed to cast a pall over their love. Greylock hoped angrily that the wizard would leave soon.

The procession worked its way slowly over the unblemished snows of the High Plateau. As they neared the slippery and jumbled iceblocks below Castle Priest, the Gatekeeper's careful steps gave an air of stateliness to the wedding party. Leading the procession was Keyholder, enrobed in ceremonial blue regalia, which despite the festive occasion, still managed to seem solemn, severe. Following him, surrounded by the other priests in the subdued accouterments of their calling, came Greylock, marching stiffly alone, and just behind him, Mara, accompanied by Ardra.

Mara wore the same dress she had worn to welcome Greylock back from the Underworld, and its scarlet hue and embroidered blue seemed even more colorful on the white snows, amid the drab, brown robes of the Gatekeepers. Her unruly blond hair was staying in place for once, held by a tiara of glyden. In contrast, Greylock had chosen to wear his customary black, with fittings of silver and red.

As the procession passed each of the snowcastles, the inhabitants joined at a respectful distance. Jostling among themselves for a place just behind the Tyrant were the members of the royal families, bedecked in their finest clothing. In an even more disorderly mass came the common citizens of the High Plateau, dressed in their cleanest and most colorful robes. None wished to miss the wedding of their Tyrant, and especially the feast that would follow.

In the courtyard of Castle Priest, Greylock and Mara were joined in marriage. The day was clear and warm. The whole of the High Plateau was revealed to those in the courtyard. The vista was breathtaking, but the Tyrant's eyes were drawn to the swirling mists far above, and Mara's eyes seemed fixed to the chanting figure of Keyholder.

When it was done, the celebrants quickly removed their ceremonial robes and donned festive trappings. The courtyard was given way to the feast, and music and dancing. The wine of the Underworld flowed, and the solemn priests retreated from the sight.

But Mara and Greylock did not eat, did not join in the dancing. They sat on twin thrones, holding hands slightly, and smiling. To observers the royal couple appeared unaccountably solemn. When the music suddenly stopped, and the dancers parted to reveal the form of a Wyrr, they did not seem surprised.

There was no doubt this time that the Wyrr was real. The demon's demeanor was unusually confident and vigorous. His wan, pale face was twisted into a grimace, what Greylock realized was meant to be a smile. The Wyrr was making no attempt to wield his magic to make his form attractive, and the celebrants drew away instinctively. When he spoke, all could understand his words, though few understood their meaning.

"It is time, Deliverer!"

"You must wait!" Greylock answered, knowing it was hopeless. "I do not know how to lift the curse! There is nothing I can do." His voice trailed off as he realized that he was trying to delay the inevitable. "You must wait," he finished as firmly as he could.

"You hesitate to do what you have promised?"

Greylock felt ashamed at the despair in the Wyrr's voice. "I must ask the Gatekeepers," he said simply. "If they do not know the answer, I cannot help you."

"You must not wait longer!" the Wyrr cried, and his commanding tone shocked the celebrants. "Godshome awakes!"

At his words a small tremor passed through the mountain, and Greylock realized that he had begun to ignore the insistent quakes. The Wyrr reminded him of the danger.

"I will come," he sighed, and beside him, Mara gasped. He dared not turn to look at her, afraid that her eyes would weaken his resolve.

The Wyrr nodded, satisfied, and turned away. But a young man stepped from the crowd and into his path. Greylock recognized the thin, elegant figure of Kalwyn, the young man who had tried to kill him.

"What does this being want of you?" the young nobleman demanded.

"Let him go, Kalwyn," Greylock commanded. "This is none of your concern. I have made a pact with his people that must not be broken."

Reluctantly, Kalwyn stepped from the Wyrr's path, and all eyes watched the emaciated figure march from the courtyard.

The Tyrant smiled, relieved. He had been uncertain until now who to name as the new steward. Kalwyn was the pampered son of one of the royal families. Greylock had no reason to trust or distrust him. Indeed, he hardly knew him. But Slimspear had thought him an able young man, he remembered, and Kalwyn was prohibited by custom from trying to assassinate him again. And he had just proven his reliability.

The Tyrant turned to the puzzled crowd. "All is well!" he cried. "Begin the music! Go back to your dancing!"

The music began again at his orders, though at first the musicians played without enthusiasm. But, inevitably, the music and wine blurred the memory of the Wyrr's visit, and dancing was soon at a pitch that drowned out even his worried thoughts.

CHAPTER EIGHT

Greylock maneuvered his way between the giant blocks of ice below Castle Priest that were still left over from the avalanche. They had not yet been able to clear away all the snow, or to rebuild the terraces. There had been more important constructions to complete first. After the snowcastles and icetowers there had been the fortifications to build, frost fortresses Moag had called them. They were set across the Gateway, which was now once again closed to the Underworld. Greylock knew he should be paying more attention to the problems of King Kasid, and the threat he posed to the High Plateau, but the Wyrrs would not leave him alone. Unfortunately, Moag was no longer there to help him; as threatened, the wizard had left shortly before the wedding.

On the Tyrant's wedding night he had had the nightmare of the Wyrrs, as he had every night since his return from the Twilight Dells. The silent cries seemed to be growing stronger and more disturbing with each visitation. The message was always the same, a soundless, wordless pleading with him to come to them. Greylock hardly dared close his eyes for fear of the terrifying visions.

Castle Priest towered over the choppy expanse of white rubble, the oldest and grandest of snowcastles. The dark ice rimmed the top of the glacier like a fringe of blue hair.

One of the younger priests greeted him solemnly as he neared the top of the jumbled slope. They must have observed him struggling against the snows from their icetower, Greylock thought. He wondered if they had been expecting him. All had heard his words to the Wyrr at the wedding feast.

The Gatekeeper guided him through the hidden trails behind what was left of the barriers, and they reached the snowcastle without further delay.

Keyholder met him in a small room that Greylock remembered well from his brief days as a student. The library was furnished with a single long table, lined with chairs. Along the walls were every book and manuscript that still existed on the High Plateau, the wisdoms of centuries past, all that was important enough to be committed to the sparse parchment.

The old priest watched his former student walk about the room with an amused glint in his sharp blue eyes. He sat at the head of the table passively, and waited for the Tyrant to announce the purpose of his visit. Greylock paced down each of the four walls once, his eyes running over the piled books, until he had circled the table.

"Welcome to Castle Priest, Tyrant Greylock," the priest said finally, when it seemed that his former student was reluctant to speak. "Have you finally come back to learn?"

Greylock knew that he had been one of Keyholder's worst students, for he had refused to listen to the Gatekeeper's dogma. Yet, though he did not know it, his inquiring mind had also made him one of the old priest's favorite students. Keyholder had tried subtly to encourage his freedom of thought.

"Tell me of the Wyrrs," Greylock said suddenly.

"The Wyrrs?" The lined forehead of the priest wrinkled even more in puzzlement. "You would know more of the Wyrrs than I."

"You know what I mean," Greylock said, impatiently. "Tell me what the books say about the demons."

"Ah, the demons," Keyholder sighed. The old Gatekeeper seemed deeply satisfied by the question, as though it was what he had expected to hear, the fulfillment of some private prophecy.

"We have been expecting you to come to us for some time, Greylock," he said. "Even before the Wyrr came to the feast. All that we have been able to learn from the books concerning the demons has been collected and is ready for you. Now, if you will just cease pacing and sit down beside me ..."

Greylock hesitated, and then plopped restlessly on the narrow chair.

The young Gatekeeper who had brought him to the library had been waiting quietly by the door. Now he came forward at Keyholder's motion and laid a tall stack of parchment on the table before Greylock, who was astounded by the amount of new parchment the stingy priests has apparently invested in this research.

"Remember, Greylock," Keyholder said, smiling, when the Tyrant seemed hesitant to dig into the pile. "We are believers in the old legends. We have not questioned the religion of our forebears, unlike some of our more headstrong students. Our beliefs told us that no one could descend to the Underworld and return as mortal unless he be a demon. Yet you were undeniably mortal and unchanged. Finally, we remembered the one prophecy, which would account for this paradox. The one story that deals with a mortal's obligation to the demons ..."

"The prophecy of the Deliverer," Greylock finished for him in a whisper. "So the Wyrrs have called me, but I dared not tell you, for I was certain that you would accuse me of blasphemy."

"On the contrary, only the idea that you are the Deliverer could answer all the puzzles," Keyholder said. "And yet, we were still unsure until the Wyrr came to you on your wedding day and demanded his freedom. This convinced the last of us. You are the Deliverer!"

"The Wyrrs think so anyway," Greylock said, unhappily.

"Yes, we have seen how you stop and stare into space, as though you are communicating with someone no one else can see. I must admit, I did not expect the demons to be such as the Wyrrs, and yet they call to you. And they do indeed seem to be imprisoned in their own land, not quite dead, but not quite alive either."

"But I do not know what is wrong with them, Keyholder! I do now know what causes the sickness in their land. Why do they not just leave it? What can I do?"

"You should have studied them more carefully when you were with us!" Keyholder sniffed, as if he was insulted that such a poor student could have become the fulfillment of a prophecy.

Greylock remembered how he had disdained the Gatekeeper's teachings. He had defied the Tyrant Ironclasp by descending into the Underworld because he had wished to find answers to the questions that had disturbed him. If there were demons in the Underworld, he had reasoned, then the way to prove or disprove this was to journey to the Underworld and see for himself. And if he could not be satisfied with the Gatekeeper's answers to his questions about the source of the Gateway, then the answer lay in exploring the rubbled remains of the path himself. Until this minute he had been unable to admit that he might have been wrong.

"Please, Keyholder," he pleaded. "I can see now that I was wrong about the demons."

"No," Keyholder answered, surprisingly. "You were not altogether wrong, Greylock, though I dared not encourage your blasphemy. There are many things we Gatekeepers do not understand, knowledge that must have been lost to the snows and the firestone. We can only guess at the meanings of some of the passages."

"But you always said I was wrong!" Greylock said, amazed by the old priest's admission. "You told me not to question!"

"We could not encourage you, or others might have started questioning our authority as well. We could not allow that. But things have changed. Your return from the Underworld, and the discovery of the Room of Aurim, has changed things a great deal."

"The Gateway leads into the mountain," Greylock stated, watching his former teacher intently. "It enters into Godshome."

"Yes, it is as we have always guessed," Keyholder agreed. "It is on the far side of the mountain that we will find the gods, if they exist."

"If they exist?" Greylock said, surprised at the sound of doubt in Keyholder's voice. This was the greatest of heresies!

"It has been such a long time," Keyholder said, looking old and tired. The many lines in his face, instead of being tools of his expression now appeared to be what they were, signs of age and worry. "We have had no sign of their existence. They may have left the Homeland by now. They may be gone from the Three Tiers of Existence entirely. I do not know. It is so hard to believe when there are no signs!"

"The Homeland?" Greylock asked. It was a new term to him. "What is the Homeland, Keyholder?"

"There are some things we did not teach you when you were here," Keyholder said. "There are some things known only to the Gatekeepers."

"Tell me!" Greylock commanded.

Now it was the priest's turn to get up and pace, and Greylock slowly turned in his chair to follow him.

"You know that the priests of the High Plateau are called the Gatekeepers," the old man began. "But you do not know why. The truth is that our entire civilization is descended from the keepers of the Gateway. Once, that road led through Godshome, as you suspected, to the Homeland. It was a magnificent roadway, and required the services of many men to keep it in repair, to rebuild, and to guard. We are the descendants of those men.

"On the far side of Godshome dwelt a people of grace and beauty; they were like gods to us. They were on this world long before us, and had achieved the heights of civilization while we were no more than barbarians. But they welcomed us, and taught us, and in exchange we became the Gatekeepers. Someday, they promised us, we would join them in the Homeland, if we did our duties well. It was from the gods 104 that we learned how to survive on the High Plateau so that we might be near the Gateway. They gave us the designs for our snowcastles and icetowers.

"You see, we ourselves once came from the Underworld, from far to the east."

"But what happened?" Greylock asked. "Why was the Gateway closed? Where are the gods?"

"I am telling you," Keyholder said. "If you will only listen!"

"Out of the east came others after us, barbarians in search of the fabled country of the Homeland, or Godshome. The gods welcomed them, as they had welcomed us. In return, they vowed to protect the Gateway. Like us they were not allowed to enter the Homeland, and were promised entrance someday. Unlike us, they resented being left outside. These people settled in the lands which are now known as the

Twilight Dells." Keyholder raised his hand when Greylock was about to object. "Let me finish, Greylock.

"Then came a final invasion of barbarians, out of what are now known as the fiefdoms of Trold, and these invaders refused to be left on this side of Godshome. They demanded entrance into the Homeland.

"The gods called on their sentinels to protect the Gateway. But, instead, they joined the invaders. Then the gods called on our descendants to close the Gateway, and using powers over the earth that we no longer possess, they brought down the walls of the Gateway by calling forth the firestone. The Gateway was closed forever."

"But what happened to the Wyrrs?" Greylock interrupted.

"The gods cursed the people of the Twilight Dells and named them demons. They were to be imprisoned in that land, a land that was cursed to grow only enough food to keep them alive. There they were to remain until a Deliverer shall come forth, to open the Gateway and lead the demons to the Homeland.

"We were given the duty of watching over them, to keep the memory of the Homeland alive. But before long our people began to forget what they had once been, and for this the priesthood was formed." Keyholder collapsed into a chair with a sigh. "And now you know all that the priests know or guess."

"Why was I not told this before?" Greylock demanded. The story explained much. Godshome was not just a frigid legend but the giant gate to another land. The Gateway did not end at the snows of the High Plateau but journeyed through the rock of the mountain. It explained the purpose of a civilization perched in the lap of a glacier.

"As Tyrant, you have always had a right to this information, Greylock."

"But you did not wish to tell me of this right until it suited your purpose?"

Keyholder looked hurt at the accusation. "We wanted to be sure that you were truly the Deliverer, and needed to know."

"Why was I chosen, Keyholder? And by whom?"

"By the gods, and because you are the Deliverer," Keyholder shrugged, and the Tyrant saw that his old teacher was lapsing back into a cryptic way of answering questions. He would not get much more information from the old man, he knew, from his experiences as a student. The Gatekeeper had told him all he intended to tell.

"If what you have told me is true, then I must find a way through Godshome," Greylock mused unhappily. "I have already tried to trace a route. It is impossible. The way is blocked."

"I would help you if I could, Greylock, but I do not have the answer. Study the ancient books. Perhaps you will find something that we could not."

Greylock sighed and pulled the stack of parchment over the table towards him. He was so fascinated by the new knowledge that he did not look up until Keyholder coughed at his ear. It could have been only minutes, or it could have been hours later.

The old priest seemed unsure of himself, even to be fighting the urge to speak.

"What is it, Keyholder? I have to know."

"I hesitate to tell you, Greylock, because it may mean your death."

"Tell me!"

"The prophecy of the Deliverer details two journeys into the Holy Hierarchy of Tiers," Keyholder said, reluctantly. "Just as the Deliverer was to descend into the Underworld and return alive, so too was he to ascend Godshome. Thus would the Deliverer know and save all the Three Tiers of Existence and lead their peoples to the Homeland."

CHAPTER NINE

Greylock scrambled up the narrow ledge and looked back down the mountain. Already he had climbed higher up the face of Godshome than he had ever attempted before. The snowcastles and icetowers of the High Plateau were completely obscured by the clouds, and the vista seemed deserted in all directions. Mists drifted under him and above him, and he was exhilarated by the danger of the climb and an anticipation of what he might find.

He decided to rest for a few moments on this secure ledge, for he doubted he would find another further up the mountain. He put his talons, the two claws of horn he used to clutch the cliff, into his belt.

Soon he would have to choose which of the three peaks to attempt first, for he thought it possible that he might have to try all three. If he found nothing on one, he would have to try the other.

Such a climb as he was contemplating, even the climb he had so far completed, would have been nearly impossible for any other man, but Greylock was confident of his ability. Besides, he thought, every other man who had come up here had been old or sick. Greylock could not recall any young fit men attempting the climb, only those forced by their age or health to seek the comfort of the gods. Of course none had returned! How could anyone survive if one did not try?

Greylock considered the higher summits of the mountain to be easier to scale than the ones he had just covered. But there remained the troubling clouds that obscured the very summit of the mountain, and which had never parted for the eyes of man. The Tyrant guessed them to be bare, windswept rock, like those upper reaches that could be seen.

Greylock was confident on bare rock. On the face of a cliff his climbing skills and feel for the lay of the stone came into play. He knew instinctively where the holds lay and which rocks would give way to his weight.

No, the sheer rock of the peaks did not frighten him. But the treacherous snows did, and they would continue to be a danger at these lower elevations. At any point, snow could come cascading down on top of him, jarring him from his ever tenuous hold on the cliff.

Greylock's one boon was that ever since he had decided that this pilgrimage was necessary, the nightmares and headaches had left him. He sensed that as long as he followed this course he would sleep soundly.

His greatest bane was his worry over Mara. Since they had married, and since her grandfather had left the High Plateau, she had objected to his every absence. Every journey to Castle Priest had caused arguments to erupt between them. And now he was leaving her with no assurance that he would ever return. It had been almost too much for her to endure.

Mara had insisted on coming along, but Greylock had told her that this was impossible. He alone had very little chance of making the climb, but he knew that with her along there would be no chance. When he was honest with himself, he knew that he was the best climber of his generation, in a land where that skill was highly valued. But he doubted he would survive.

The Tyrant knew that Mara would be honored, no matter what happened, for her role in the battle on the glacier. She would not want while she lived, he thought, no matter who was Tyrant. Still, he carried her face in his mind as he faced the walls of Godshome, and her worried expression, as he imagined it, created a cautiousness in his movements that was not usual.

Her last words had been a threat to leave the High Plateau and search for old Moag. Then she had broken down and run from him crying. He knew that she would be waiting.

The new steward, Kalwyn, had also objected strenuously to his leaving.

"But what if the army of King Kasid comes?" he had cried in alarm. Greylock could not blame the young man for being concerned, but he had explained that nothing could stop him, and the steward had been forced to accept it.

"Make what preparations you can, Kalwyn," he had said. "I will return as soon as I can. Until then, you will have to do the best you can."

The mountain trembled beneath him, and snow showered down on him, almost knocking him from the ledge. The tremors had resumed, he realized, after a short lull. "Godshome awakes!" the Wyrr had warned, and Greylock could not help but remember the many tales of catastrophe that had come down to them.

Greylock took a last mental picture of the High Plateau, burning the image in his mind. Then he began to slowly ascend into the clouds.

He saw the storm developing long before it reached him. Before he had started on his journey, he had estimated that he would not be able to finish his climb before at least one storm caught up with him. This had been his major worry, and he considered it his greatest danger.

Long before the first gales of the storm had reached him, he had found a narrow, deep crevice and had crawled into it to the rear. He forced his talons into the walls and made sure that they were tied securely to his arms. He tied his body to them as well, in case his grip on them should be lost. Then he settled back and waited for the storm, which looked to be a big one, to pass.

He woke the next morning to find himself still nestled comfortably in his little shelter. Despite the constriction, he had slept well, for the whistling winds had eventually lulled him. The entrance to the crevice was almost filled with new powder, he saw, but no flakes had reached him. The snow had effectively kept the heat from his body within the crevice, and Greylock was almost reluctant to stir.

He brushed the snowdrift away finally and peered out. The sky was clear, bluer than he could ever remember seeing it. But it was piercing cold, and he shivered uncontrollably for the first half-hour of his morning climb. The new snow made the threat of an avalanche even more dangerous, and he forced himself to climb slowly.

By evening, when Greylock looked up for a final survey of the mountain, it seemed to him that he had made little progress. The summit seemed no nearer than it had that morning. Already the air was growing rare, and yet he was not yet halfway up the stone face. Greylock wondered if it would be possible to breathe at all at such a height.

The snow and ice had crusted almost permanently to his hair and clothes, and he shook them off, cracking the ice where he could find some flexibility. As his eyes followed the lumps of snow as they flaked off into the air, he realized that he had indeed climbed far that day, for the High Plateau was now no more than a minor glacier, one of many covering the mountain.

He was too tired to find a secure place to sleep, and as night fell he chastised himself for letting himself be caught out in the open. Such a situation was exactly what he had admonished himself to avoid before he had started out. But he did not have the energy to search. If a storm happened along that night he was finished.

He was just beginning to realize that his thinking was becoming distorted by the height, the cold, the thin air, and his own exhaustion. But this recognition did not take on much significance because of that very distortion.

The next day's climb was like a dream, and he knew in the back of his mind that he was fortunate that the weather remained mild, that the one severe storm had occurred while he was still at a relatively low height. He moved sluggishly, his hands and feet automatically and instinctively finding their holds in the stone. By night, he did not think he could have covered more than a few hundred yards.

Still, his mind was at last beginning to learn how it could pierce the fog that was enveloping it, just as his view was being obscured by strangely warm mists. By concentrating solely on his next step, and his next thought, he managed to make some progress. He actually went further the next day than he had the day before, and over rougher terrain. Several times he slipped, and he realized dimly that he had barely avoided plunging to his death. But it had no significance to him.

All that filled his mind was the next step, and the larger determination to reach the top.

As his third night on Godshome neared, and the light grew treacherously flat, Greylock looked for another place to spend the dark, cold hours. In the late afternoon a pushing wind had threatened constantly to blow him off the cliff, and he knew that another storm approached.

He did not have far to go. As he surmounted another rocky, icy ledge he spotted the mouth of a cave, set at the very center of the cliff. Curious, he worked his way over to it. The cave had not become visible until he was almost level with it. From below, he knew, even from the base of the High Plateau, it could not be seen, nor had he ever heard anyone talk of it. Which meant he was already higher than anyone could see from below, he realized with a shock. For centuries this gaping split in the gray rock face of the middle peak had lain concealed by the snow, the clouds, and the rock ledges.

Greylock did not think this out. To do so would have required too much of his precious energy. Instead, he was moving gratefully toward it, vaguely amazed at the way he thought he would spend every bit of his energy on the next step, only to find still more reserves for the next step. Fortunately, the ledge he was already on continued straight toward the cave. He crawled into the black hold, and had barely stretched out before he was asleep.

When he once again began his upward journey, he was well rested, though the suffocating lack of oxygen—which he had almost convinced himself that he was used to—struck him with redoubled force. The wind soon froze his exposed flesh numb, and he began to fear that the feeling would not come back. There was no comfort in the lack of feeling, in the escape from the pain of cold. He grew accustomed to checking to see if, in fact, his fingers were clutching the crevice, and that his feet had found the purchase in the rock he meant them to. This constant distrust of his own movements slowed him down even further, though he also needed the brief stops to catch his breath.

He could see no further than a few feet away, for the constant snow flurries swirled around him and blinded him. He soon lost all measure of how far he had come or how far he still had to go. The immense drop he knew to be below him was obscured by the mists, and created in his mind a misleading sense of security. He did not dare stop even when it grew dark, and he continued on, by feel alone sometimes for the cloud cover suffused the light of the moon. He felt instead that he could have simply stepped through the carpet of clouds, to fall forever. He knew that if he stopped climbing for even a moment, he would not be able to gather the strength and resolve to start up again.

He reached the top of the cliff before he was really aware that the end was near. A gentle slope of snow continued upward, so he knew that he had not reached the summit. He hurried onto the ice flow in gratitude, happy to be away from the yawning drop at last, for the fall had been preying on his mind from the first moments of his climb. Only now did he feel safe, and though it was just as cold and windy as before, and the air was thinner, he found new energy to keep climbing.

Sometime during the night before he had decided that he would not attempt to try to go back down the mountain. He knew that in his present state, he would not make it very far. If there was not an answer on the top of Godshome, he was doomed.

He finally reached the summit and found himself stumbling almost imperceptibly downward. Unaccustomed muscles collapsed on him, and when he once again lifted his head, after lying there for many minutes, he saw that all four sides of the gentle knoll he was on went down. Unless he had surmounted only a finger of the top, this was the peak of his world! The clouds parted for just a few moments to reveal that he was indeed perched on top of Godshome.

He collapsed gratefully and did not move again.

CHAPTER TEN

Nothing really woke him for he was never really asleep. He hovered in a state of comfortable weariness, his limbs lulled by the soft caress of the powdery snow, a warm lassitude that seemed to belie the sounds of the screaming wind. Below, far below, it seemed to him that he could feel the earth's fires, the firestone that filled Godshome, the hearth of the gods. The glowing heat seemed to reach through the snows to fill his own body.

At the back of his mind, Greylock knew that this warmth was an illusion, a charitable illusion brought on by his own suffering body, and that he was dying. Even this did not stir him, for it seemed to him a kind way to die, that the gods were there watching over him and giving him a comfortable release. He could not return to the High Plateau or the Twilight Dells without an answer, he thought. He could not face the nightmares and sleepless nights, the haunted days. Better that it end here.

Alone among the men of the High Plateau he had investigated the Three Tiers of life and death. And he had found that there were neither demons nor gods on Godshome.

The mountain's bowels rumbled, stirring him briefly to open his eyes. All was white, and he realized dimly that the snow had blinded him. The hot lava was restive far below, and Greylock could feel it trying to find an exit, meeting blocked passages everywhere, going higher to find a release, an unplugged corridor. He felt it seeking, and he directed the heat to him.

The earth shook briefly beneath him, throwing him onto his back. Then he heard a hissing, as steam and firestone found a weak layer of earth only a few yards below him and began melting the snow even before it had reached the surface. Unlike the heat he had felt before, this heat was real. Unlike the illusory warmth, the misting dew that landed on his face stung. The mountainside ceased moving as the firestone found an escape, and squeezed through the last crack to erupt in a fountain of showering ash.

The fiery fountain was only a few yards away, and the once comfortable sensation of warmth was becoming unbearable, the gray ash threatening to bury him. The firestone began to pour out sluggishly and to flow down toward the cliffs he had just climbed.

Coughing bitterly, he rose to his knees and moved away from the heat. He could see nothing but a white blur in his snow blindness, lit occasionally by a falling firestone. He felt his way at first, and then ran stumbling as his feet snagged the crusts of snow. Any moment now, he thought, trying to still his panic, he would tumble over a cliff. But panic had seized him fully, and he could do nothing to stop his rolling retreat. He had to get away from the terrible pressure that was building beneath him, he thought. The fountain of firestone was doing little to assuage that pressure, holding it off but not relieving it.

When the snow suddenly reared up in front of him in a wedge, he was brought up short, and with that, he collapsed. He was amazed that he had had the energy to run so far. Despite his blindness, Greylock could guess where he had run. If he had run down the same slope he had climbed, he knew, he would have long since sprung into space. Therefore, he reasoned through his exhaustion, he had gone down the other side, the side of Godshome that no man had ever seen, and whose features could only be imagined.

Exploring this thought further, he discovered that he could sense the lay of the next few yards. Somehow, he could tell that from this point on lay a long, gentle incline off Godshome. Confident in his guess, he found the strength to continue. Exile, after all, seemed better to him now than death. Even his excruciating weariness and miserable cold were preferable to nothingness.

By nightfall he was already encountering dry patches of earth, warmed by the sun, and his eyesight was slowly returning. Unless this side of the mountain was much warmer than the High Plateau, he thought, he had already descended below the level of the glacier. He clutched the warm rocks of one of the western icemelts through the night, but they slowly grew cold with the temperature of the night skies, and by morning he was shivering violently.

He had misjudged the warmth, he realized. It was not due to the volcanic firestone running beneath the mountains, but was from the heat of the sun. That night he came his closest to dying, as the last of his body heat deserted him. But it was a clear morning, and the rays of the sun beat down unhindered by the clouds that wreathed the mountain and revived him.

His eyesight was almost normal by the time he left the snows, and as his blindness left him, his acute sense of the lay of the land also began to leave him, as he depended more heavily on visual clues.

It did not matter, he thought, for in the distance he could see green trees and blue water. Like a beckoning maiden, it drew him, and he staggered toward the reassuring light. The bare, gray rock of the foothills gave way to patches of hardy grass, then to shrubs. Finally, he was able to throw himself onto the soft matting of a field of high grass, and he soaked up the warmth from the chalky soil and the sharp sunshine.

Now that he had found the warmth to succor him, Greylock's attention immediately turned to the problem of finding food and water. Both turned out to be relatively easy to find, for the land was rich and bountiful. Orchards of fruit trees were as common as wild stands, and small clear creeks from the glacier provided all the water he wanted.

Only one thing bothered him as the lush morning drew on. He had yet to see any form of animal life. The land was clean and unspoiled, as if newly created and awaiting only his discovery. The rushing stream into which he dangled his feet was clean and cold, and the trees and bushes overflowed with ripening fruit and berries. But there was no sign of the wildlife, which could have been nourished by such abundance. He continued on into the forest in a dreamy state.

He was astonished when he came across the footprints of another man. The tracks were only a few days old, and there was no doubt that a man had made them.

Now the pleasant euphoria that the warmth and the landscape had induced dissipated, and he found that he resented the intrusion of another being into this paradise.

He scanned the horizon warily and realized that this was his normal way of approaching the world. It kept him alive but perpetually suspicious. He had been enjoying the brief respite from caution.

For a few moments, he hesitated, debating whether to continue on in search or to avoid the stranger. For he was oddly certain that there were only two of them in all the land.

He smelled the fire first, and glanced up to see the white smoke swirling like a white cloud over the tree tops. Summoning all his wariness and suspicion, he approached the clearing with a stealthy caution.

There was no one tending the campfire, but Greylock knew immediately who had set it. The flames had bluish tinge that told him that the fire was not entirely natural. Only a fire wizard could have set such a blaze, he thought.

Moments later, Moag entered the clearing carrying a load of firewood. He did not seem to sense Greylock's presence until he had reached the fire, then he dropped the wood with a shout and whirled as Greylock stepped from the shadows of the surrounding trees.

"Are you trying to frighten an old man to death?" the wizard shouted, annoyed by the surprise.

Greylock himself did not know whether to be annoyed or surprised that Moag had managed to cross the mountain before him and seemed no worse for wear.

"I'm sorry, Moag!" Greylock said, suppressing a laugh. "I was not trying to sneak up on you. I was surprised to find anyone here."

The wizard seemed mollified by this, more angry at himself for jumping than at Greylock for surprising him.

"There are no other people," he said. "I have been here for two weeks and I have seen no one." Suddenly, the old man's surprise seemed to wear off enough for him to wonder why Greylock was there.

"Have you been following me, Greylock?" he asked, worriedly. "Is there something wrong with Mara?"

"No, Moag," Greylock quickly reassured him. "She was fine when I left her. I did not follow you. I was looking for the people of this land. I was looking for the gods ..."

As night fell and the wizard built up the fire, Greylock told him the story of his ascent over Godshome and his search for the Gateway.

"But I failed," he concluded. "There are no gods, as Keyholder feared."

"Perhaps there never were any gods," Moag answered. "Or perhaps they have gone away to some other land, or some other existence."

"If there are no gods, how am I to lift the curse of the Wyrrs?" Greylock asked, miserably. "I have failed."

"Do not be so sure, Greylock," the old man said, frowning. "Have you not found a new land for the Wyrrs?"

Now it was Greylock's turn to frown. Bending down, he took up a handful of the dark earth while the old man was still talking. The land felt good, fertile, and it contrasted with the poisoned aura he had felt from the Twilight Dells.

It was the Wyrr's land that kept them in the throes of sickness and poverty, he remembered. And this was the answer to their curse, a new land. It was what he had sensed from the beginning but until now he had not been able to pinpoint the cause of his unease, or to express it in words. The land of the Wyrrs had long since been exhausted of all its nutrients. This was why they were so savagely possessive of their territory. This was what he had to deliver them from, gods or no gods.

But first he had to find some way to bring them to this fertile land, and he knew that he could not bring them over Godshome.

"How did you find your way here, Moag?" he asked, eagerly. "We must return immediately!"

"I came through a pass far to the north, Greylock." The old man looked at him curiously. "A land where the people are even more

191

suspicious than yours. But we cannot go back that way, Greylock! King Kasid annexed the land just before I passed through. That is why I was so surprised to see you, he was marching to the High Plateau."

"I have to get back to the Twilight Dells!" Greylock said, through clenched teeth. The haunted images of the Wyrrs came unbidden to his mind. It was frustrating to be only a few miles from the Dells, and yet the only way to reach them was a long, uncertain detour and the even more dangerous climb over Godshome. But he had already decided that he would make the attempt to scale the mountain again, though it would assuredly mean his death.

The Tyrant stared up the slopes of Godshome in despair. Without help, such a climb was hopeless. He had barely survived the first ascent through luck and ignorance. He would not survive a second assault, he knew. But what choice did he have? By now, the king of Trold would be marching on the High Plateau. If they took the time to go back by way of Moag's pass, even if they made it through, they would be too late.

Perhaps the easy slope on this side, and the descent on the other, would be easier this time. But even as he thought this, he knew that it was unlikely.

"I'm going back, Moag," he said, grimly. "I will not ask you to come with me. I am going over the top, not around."

"I understand," the wizard said. "I am too old to make such journeys, whatever I might tell my granddaughter. Especially such a journey as you now contemplate. Still, I do not think your quest is as hopeless as you seem to think, for it is obvious to me that you have the earth-power."

"Earth-power?" Greylock asked, confused.

"From what you have told me of your climb," the old man continued, nodding. "I would guess that you are an earth wizard. I should have known before. There have been little hints all along that you had the earth magic, but I disregarded it, for in my lands such power would not have been hidden and wasted. It was you who summoned the life-giving heat of the volcano, Greylock. There is no other explanation for the impossible feat of your climb."

Greylock did not answer, for now that the wizard had brought it to his attention, it was indeed obvious. Perhaps it came from his ancestors, who had had the power to close the Gateway. Or perhaps he had the power because he was the Deliverer.

"Trust this power, Greylock," the wizard continued. "Your earth magic is untrained, but it will lead you to where you want to go. Perhaps you will even find the entrance of the Gateway itself."

Despite his gloom, Greylock's eyes scanned the mountain, looking for some sign of a break in its white surface, for some kind of portal. But as far as he could see there was only an unbroken expanse of snow. It would be a miracle if he were to stumble on the mythical entrance — if there was such an entrance. In the morning, as the heat of the sun filled the Homeland, he would once again ascend the frigid heights of Godshome.

CHAPTER ELEVEN

Reluctantly, Greylock left the warmth of the Homeland and climbed into the cooler air of Godshome. Over the night he had come to realize that he had no choice on what he must do: he had to find the Gateway. He could not lead the Wyrrs on the long and dangerous journey that Moag had described, nor could he lead them over Godshome. Going back the way he had come made little sense.

He relaxed a little at this thought, for he had been dreading the challenge. Instead, his task would be to find a break in the seemingly featureless west side of the mountain.

The sun beat down on the shining ice, making it difficult for him to scan the snow for long even when he shielded his eyes. Through his watering eyes the snows looked unblemished. He knew this was an illusion, for under that flat white layer was the same lava that had built the High Plateau. But he feared that he would become snowblind before he could find an opening.

He climbed the huge glacier in a diagonal direction, hoping that he could return to the lower elevations if he did not spot anything by dark. He could do so every night, he thought, making his forays into the snows more thorough, if more lengthy.

With this comfortable thought, he began to pay less attention to his path. When he felt the snow give way under him, he knew immediately what had happened. He had made the first mistake of every mountain climber by not checking his footing. But it was too late to recover, despite his swift reflexes. He had no time to even brace himself before he struck bottom.

When he woke again, it was dark. So much for returning to the Homeland, he thought ruefully. He searched his body gingerly for injuries, but there were no broken bones, just a few painful bruises. The knock to his head was potentially the most dangerous, he knew, but it was too dark for him to tell if his vision had been affected. His head was ringing with pain.

Feeling beneath him cautiously, he moved off the layer of snow that had preceded him into the crevasse, saving him by breaking his fall. The cold rock at the bottom of the crevasse was a little warmer, and he perched on his heels, wrapping his arms around him, leaving as little of his body touching the stone surface as possible. More than anything he was angry with himself for falling so easily. No man of the High Plateau should be caught by surprise by a crevasse!

He decided not to waste a fire on this night, even if he could somehow light one of the small torches that he had, with the help of Moag, fashioned in the forests of the Homeland. The fire wizard had assured him that they were the best design possible with the materials at hand.

He might as well make the best of it, he thought, and try to sleep. At least he was protected from the worst of the cold, and his clothes were still dry. Curling up in the small space, he finally managed to fall asleep through his shivering.

When the day's light finally reached him by crossing the sky directly over the ceiling of the crevasse, Greylock woke to discover that an attempt to climb out would be futile.

Scaling the walls of the crevasse would not be difficult, he thought, but there was no possible way for him to reach from the stone of the walls to the narrow hole he had created by falling through the middle of the crevasse. The snow was several feet thick, he saw, and frozen solid, so that trying to cut through would be difficult and tiring, especially from the angle of the steep walls. Worse, it was dangerous. Even if he succeeded in loosening the snow pack, it could very easily come down on top of him, causing him to fall again, perhaps burying him. He couldn't take that chance.

The crevasse narrowed into darkness on both sides of him. From experience, Greylock knew that the ice caves could extend for great distances, while not always remaining level. There was a chance that the floor of the crevasse would angle upward in places almost to the surface, he thought, or at least to a safer level to attempt a climb.

But this tunnel only seemed to go deeper into the mountain, instead of up and away. He was about to turn back when he noticed that the ceiling turned from ice to-stone just ahead of him. Lighting the first of his tapers, he started forward. Was it possible he had stumbled upon one of the portals of the Gateway by chance?

He knew that at some time he would be forced to feel his way in the dark if he was to conserve his tapers for the long journey under the mountain, but after a moment of thought he decided to light the second of his tapers in hope that he would discover where the tunnel was heading, and if it went far.

Eventually, other passages opened off the main passage, but he ignored them, using his instincts to strike deeper into Godshome. Occasionally, dim light through the ice above him showed that he was within another crevasse, but he paid no attention to this either. Whenever he came to a dead end, he quickly backtracked to the nearest offshoot and tried again.

The entire mountainside was honeycombed with these narrow caves and crevasses, he realized after a while, existing unsuspected in a network just a few yards beneath the snowpack of the glacier.

But try as he might, he could penetrate no deeper into the mountain than this shallow depth. All he had really succeeded in doing, he realized with disgust, was to climb higher up the mountain, which he could have done much easier on the surface.

He stopped his search, frustrated, as night fell. He was determined to search every one of the myriad of caves until one of them opened into the Gateway. For he was certain that this was the avenue into the huge, legendary passage.

The dull, soft light of morning was just enough to wake him. He began his wandering search again, this time with enough foresight to mark the passages he had already explored. This day, as on the day before, he often came across likely exits from the glacier, but he was no longer interested in these. Time enough to find his way out of the maze, he thought, when his food and strength were exhausted.

From the distance he covered that morning, in contrast to the number of caves he found already marked, Greylock knew that these little tunnels, with their rivulets of glacier water running through them, were infinite.

It was growing steadily colder, and he knew that he was now much higher than the night before. As it began to darken through the ice, though still early afternoon, he decided to give up the futile search in favor of one night's rest in the warm valley of the Homeland. It was apparent to him now that his search for the Gateway would not be immediately successful, and though only two days had passed he could see enough of the enormity of the task ahead to consider going back to the High Plateau by way of the old man's detour after all. But he quickly discarded this idea; he had no intention of ever facing the Wyrrs without an answer again.

He came upon a likely looking upward turn in the maze, and began to follow the slight incline up toward the roof of ice. Taking out his talons again, he began to dig at the snow, making little progress before nightfall. He realized with disappointment that he would have to spend another night on the mountain.

Though his supplies were getting low, he decided to continue his search the next morning, and return in the afternoon to hack his way through the rest of the covering layer.

He had already taken the turn he was looking for before he was truly aware that he was descending in a seemingly straight line into the bowels of the mountain. Retracing his steps, and marking each twist and turn carefully, he returned to the exit of the night before. With the energy of his excitement, he quickly chopped his way through the same barrier he had made so little progress against just a few hours before.

He was blinded by the intense glare of the sun. Finally, after many long minutes of adjustment, he dared open his eyes to squint out.

He was far up the mountain, perhaps near the top of the glacier, though he could not tell for sure from this point. There was absolutely nothing to mark the spot he had emerged from, and he knew that he would lose sight of the small hole in the glacier after only a few yards.

Though he was anxious to start his exploration of the new cave, he patiently dragged every bit of loose rubble he could find on the floor of the crevasse, until he had built a large shelter on the snows above. Even then he realized that it would be hard to find, but he was confident that he knew its approximate location on the mountain.

The dim light of the sun, trying to make its way through the thick ice of the glacier, was left quickly behind, and at the entrance to the inner cave Greylock chose to light one of the remaining torches. He needed the light, he thought, at least until he had fathomed the general direction and condition of this new tunnel.

Though the corridor continued to lead into the mountain, it was a disappointing avenue. It twisted constantly, narrowing in places so much that Greylock was forced to inch his way through on his hands and knees; once, he was even compelled to squeeze his way under a swooping, craggy roof on his belly. Often he had to clear away dirt and rubble to enlarge the passage.

It would be difficult, if not impossible, he realized, to lead the Wyrrs along this route. Certainly, there was no sign of man's markings in this tunnel, either in its making or its design. He guessed that no man had ever traveled its length, and that it was not the Gateway.

He quickly lost all sense of time, and when the last torch went out Greylock was totally disoriented. His only comfort was that he could no longer see the roof flickering, seeming to come down on top of him.

He had overestimated his ability to proceed by touch alone, he quickly discovered, and the effect that darkness would have on him. Only the knowledge that he had already traveled a great distance into the mountain kept him moving forward. The sense of panic crept up on him so slowly that when he jumped at the sound of a falling rock and hit his head on the roof of the tunnel, he was surprised at his own tenseness. It was the fear of being buried alive, he realized. The custom of his people was to face death alone, outside, on the bright surface of the mountain, not within its dark, dank interior. Now that ingrained instinct was rebelling against his goal to reach the center of Godshome.

After hours of this steadily mounting pressure, Greylock abandoned his careful touching of the path and began to move down the tunnel in panic, hoping desperately for an end to the darkness.

He was able to avoid the worst of the sudden dives of the roof by reaching with his outstretched arms, but when the path abruptly ended under his feet, he was unable to stop his fall.

He imagined that he could hear the sounds of a crackling fire and the words of the wizard Moag.

"Why do you not listen to my advice?" the old man seemed to demand, querulously. "Why do you not trust your earth magic? Let it guide you and protect you, Greylock. No light will keep you as safe. Let the earth magic work through you."

Greylock did not answer, for the thought of a fire dominated his thoughts. Why did the fire not warm him? he wondered angrily. Why did the fire not light the cave?

Suddenly, the sounds of sparks turned to their elemental opposite, into the cold spray of water. Then the flow of the water expanded around him, threatening to engulf him. It seemed to lift him and toss him headlong down into a rushing whirlpool.

Finally, when the fright grew intolerable, Greylock's eyes popped open.

He was awake, he realized, but the sound of falling water, sounding deceptively like the roar of a fire, did not go away with his consciousness. His brow was wet from the steadily dripping spray. He blinked as his eyes were filled with water, and sat up coughing.

He moved away from the small, but irritating flow of water hastily. It was only then that he realized the extent of his injuries.

Once again his legs had been saved from injury only because he had instead landed awkwardly on his upper torso. This time his left arm was made useless, hanging limply down at his side, sending stabs of pain if he moved it. But motion was unavoidable, he quickly discovered, for when he walked it seemed to flap against his side. He clenched his teeth, and allowed himself to moan.

Now was the time, he thought, to light the last small sliver of a torch he possessed. Working painfully with one arm, dreading to drop it onto the wet surface of the cave's floor, he managed to finally light the taper. It sputtered in the mists, threatening to go out at any moment.

Raising the pitiful light over his head, and moving away from the small falls of icy water, he desperately scanned his surroundings. The faint light slowly illuminated a giant cavern.

The floor of the cavern was a jumble of boulders, which had fallen from a roof far above, lost from view. The slabs sent shadows stretching across the cave. The walls were honeycombed with many small tunnels, much like the one he had emerged from a few yards overhead.

Though Greylock tried to memorize every feature of the huge cave, the taper quickly flickered out in his hand, burning his fingers. But just before the light faded from his eyes, Greylock saw a large tunnel about halfway up the surface of the walls, an unnaturally square portal. As the taper sputtered into darkness, Greylock realized that he had found the Gateway at last.

Climbing over and around the huge blocks of stone with one hand and in the dark required all his skills and power. He could only guess at the location of the portal that he had glimpsed so tantalizingly in the last few moments of light. In that brief second Greylock had judged that one of the boulders, an almost square block, reached very near the mouth of the Gateway. But the stone, which he had readily recognized by its shape far across the cavern, became featureless and impossible to find by touch alone.

He forced himself to climb each likely boulder of the same size and height, which quickly consumed most of his remaining energy. Accustomed to judging his own needs for food and rest on the cycles of the sun, he had no idea how long he had gone without sustenance.

It could have been hours, or days, he thought. He could no longer tell.

When he finally found the Gateway, he cursed himself for wasting time on lesser caves. He had wanted to be sure that he would not miss it, and by so doing he had lingered much too long over unlikely caves. When he touched the Gateway, he recognized it for what it was at once.

The floor of the corridor was smooth and carved, the stone cut at right angles and crafted with precision. There was no mistaking its features for the haphazard lines of a natural cave.

He crawled onto the wet surface of the floor gratefully, and curled up. He told himself that it was important that he eat something, but sleep was already overtaking him; to stir was too difficult, even if it meant never waking up.

When he awoke, he knew that he would have to finish the journey this day—or he never would. His clothes were soiled, damp, and uncomfortable, and after one last meager meal, his pack was empty. He started to toss away the bag, but at the last moment he held onto it.

He moved down the broad corridor, strangely confident that nothing more could happen to him now that he had found the Gateway. He walked with assurance, certain that he could tell by the echoes of his footsteps that the path was solid. The echoes promised an unbroken and unhindered path.

Perhaps because the uncertainty and fear were gone, he realized that he trusted his own instincts, that which the wizard Moag had called earth magic.

As he trailed his right hand along the wall, his fingers stuttered across a series of grooves. Stopping to investigate further, he found that the wall was carved with reliefs. He could not tell with his untutored sense of touch what the carvings revealed, but he was certain that they were manmade, kept unnaturally sharp by the protection of the earth.

Suddenly he stopped, stamping his foot on the surface of the tunnel, and listened intently. The returning echoes did not sound right, he thought, as though somehow muted and muffled.

As he proceeded cautiously, he began to feel a soft warm mist falling over his head and arms. As the mist became thicker, he realized that it was this fluid barrier that had strangled the sound of his echoes.

The mist soon soaked him to the bone, and though it was warm, he dreaded its touch, for later, he knew, this warm, caressing liquid could as easily turn icy cold.

After a while he realized that he could see through the clinging mists. A soft red glow was illuminating the droplets of water; the sound of the spray began to turn into the rushing of steam.

The tunnel suddenly opened up over an enormous pit, apparently created long after the Gateway had been built. A waterfall tumbled from its walls far above, forming a veil of steam when it struck the hot lava that filled the pit.

The upward-reaching flames proved more powerful than the water, clearing the air of mists, sending them reeling into the Gateway. Both of these elements had proven more powerful than the surface of the Gateway.

The tunnel continued on the other side, but the melting force of the firestone sheared it cleanly. It was too far for him to reach by jumping, he realized with a sinking feeling.

It was only then that the Tyrant knew that he had been deluding himself. He had hoped that the Gateway was still unchanged beneath the mountain, and he had ignored the signs. In the back of his mind he had hoped that they could rebuild where necessary. He realized now that this was beyond the skills of his people, perhaps even beyond the skills of the gods. The elements worked against them: the cold rushing water, the hot firestone, the dank, stuffy air. Too much time had passed since the tunnel had been abandoned, a long time even by the measure of the earth. The active volcano that was Godshome had swallowed up the Gateway, and had left only fragments for Greylock to find.

The lava of the pit was flowing downward, he saw, sending only the heat of its flames upward. Somewhere under the surface of the lava must be an opening, he reflected. If that exit were to be blocked, the lava would quickly rise to fill the chamber.

As he thought this, the level seemed to rise imperceptibly. When he looked more closely, the lava shot upward a few more inches, and then started to rise steadily. The steam began to sting his bare skin. Hiding his face, gasping in the mist, he reeled backward into the relative safety of the Gateway.

The water touching the firestone turned instantly into a scalding steam. But at the same moment, Greylock noticed, the water briefly blackened the red flow. It seemed to him that the volume of water was growing as well—and then he was sure of it.

The threatening lava ceased to rise at last, only inches from the lip of the Gateway. As the mountain water continued to cascade down it in increased flow, Greylock suddenly saw a way to reach the other side. The lava began to move sluggishly, even congealing.

He ripped his empty pack into strips and tied them around his feet. He would have to choose his moment carefully, for at any time the lava could begin flowing again, or the waterfall could subside. Either occurrence would destroy his already slim chances.

The searing heat threatened to destroy his lungs, but holding his breath, he started to move across the hardening lava. He tried not to put his weight too much on either foot, but this proved impossible. Skating across, rather than punching down with his weight, seemed to help. It was almost like walking across crusted snow barely thick enough to hold him, he thought. Only this time his leg would be burned if he fell through. Several times a sickening crunch revealed that he had put too much pressure on the crust, but he did not dare stop.

Then he was on the other side. He fell to his knees. His stomach heaved in relief. The dull ache of his feet slowly came to him, the pungent odor of burned flesh. Would he be forced to end his journey on his hands and knees? he wondered in anguish. How could he help the Wyrrs if he was a cripple? How would he defend the High Plateau from the mercenaries of King Kasid?

Somehow, he managed to rise to his feet, for the next thing he knew he was stumbling down the Gateway, his feet numbed and blistered. Later he would realize that he must have walked in a fog for many hours, for when he once more became aware of his surroundings he was very near the end of his journey.

He recognized the huge cavern below the High Plateau by its size and shape. But from the intensity of the heat, he guessed that he was much lower in the cavern than he had ever been before.

Tiredly, he peered upward and spotted a narrow ledge spiraling up around the sides of the pit. He ventured onto it, hugging the wall, and began to inch his way along it. Several times he was almost pitched into the cavern by the weakness in his knees. The last few yards were the hardest, as his legs felt ready to collapse at any moment, trembling under the effort to stay taut. Finally, there was only the crusted lava of the tunnel that led to Castle Tyrant to surmount. He pitched over it, falling safely to the floor of the cave.

Get up! some part of him screamed. He could not allow himself to stop so near his goal! He knew that if he stopped here, only a few hundred yards from the snows of the High Plateau, he would perish.

He staggered to his feet and let his earth magic guide him along the familiar twisting corridors. The air turned blessedly cool, and he gasped to breath in the soothing balm. Sunlight filtered down from the upper corridors, seeming unbearably bright.

Blind, limping, and half awake he emerged onto the white glacier, too far from any snowcastle to be seen, and collapsed into the cool snow. He could go no further.

Cool air continued to flow over his blistered skin, and ice froze the pain from his nerves. When he opened his eyes he found himself not on the glacier, but in the deathroom. The small, almost featureless room caught the cold winds, soothing his burns.

Beside him sat Mara, and he knew that it was her witch's power that was sending the soft breezes over him. About his body were loosely tied compresses of ice.

"I mustn't stay here!" he said, when he realized where he was. "I must go to the Wyrrs!"

The effort to speak hurt his throat. All that came out was a croak. His mouth had been burned raw, and the wracking cough that followed his effort to speak was excruciatingly painful. The room smelled vaguely of smoke, and he slowly became aware that the odor emanated from him and his clothing.

"You are not going anywhere, Greylock," Mara said. "You are badly hurt. You must heal. And it is better that you do not remain awake while your skin repairs itself. It will be very painful."

"There is no time!" he objected weakly. "I must speak to the steward, the Gatekeepers. King Kasid is coming."

It was no use. The cool breezes, created and controlled by her wishes, seemed to have a narcotic effect, and his voice trailed off.

Even the deep sleep into which he was cast could not quite protect him from all the pain as new tissue slowly formed and pulled tight. He struggled to awaken and confront the pain, but, unaware of his suffering, Mara kept him under her spell.

When she at last allowed him to regain consciousness, he saw to his relief that she had moved him from the deathroom. He must have been very ill indeed, he thought, for even Mara to accept it, and prepare for his death.

The pain that had filled his life for the last few weeks had subsided to a dull throb.

Mara came quickly to the side of his bed at his call.

"I must see Kalwyn!" he demanded, sitting up and getting ready to move off his bed. "Bring me the commander of the guard!"

She pushed him gently back into bed. "Rest for a few moments more, Greylock," she said, softly. "I have already called for your advisors. We know that King Kasid is coming. He is already here."

CHAPTER TWELVE

Greylock paced the earthen walls of the redoubt, waiting for the scouts to return. The long ramp spanning the trail was a hastily assembled bulwark, a small defense against the enormous force that was fast approaching the Gateway. The Tyrant was thankful now that he had had the foresight to order a succession of ramparts built across the mountain pass, one every few hundred yards, effectively sealing the Gateway again. He doubted that the walls could withstand a frontal assault by the large army the scouts were reporting separately, but he hoped that together they would prove a hindrance, and provide the defenders with a chance to recoup.

Greylock loosened his robe, wishing that he dared to remove his outer garments as completely as his soldiers had. From where he stood he could see the dead, tangled growth of the Twilight Dells. The dry wood and briars that choked that land were piled up in front of the walls as a further hindrance to the advance of the enemy, ready to be lit at the command of the Tyrant. The heat of the lower elevation was suffocating to the men of the mountains, but Greylock would not remove the robe with its royal markings.

He wanted to remain identifiable to his men.

It was not the approaching battle that he was thinking of at that moment. The Wyrrs had not given him a moment of peace since he had awakened from his convalescence. He was very close to the Twilight Dells now, and the power emanating from that sick land was reaching out to him. The earth seemed to send out tentacles of mists, which wrapped themselves around him and his thoughts.

The cry of the lookout startled him from his gloomy thoughts. Looking up he saw an orderly column of soldiers crossing the swift mountain stream that lay below the lowest bulwark, a dark line that stretched through the next valley, over a bridge, and into the next dell. But even the scattering of the enemy that he could see were far too many for the army of the High Plateau to repel for long, and according to the reports of the scouts, these were only a fraction of those who would come.

The advanced units of the enemy stopped a short distance away from the first rampart, just beyond the flight of an arrow. They began to set up camp in full view of the defenders. Tent after tent of canvas were erected in orderly rows. Fires were lit at equal distances between, all in anticipation of the vast host that followed. Other soldiers came very near the walls, and, with a contempt that was visible, began to build another rampart opposite them, which soon grew to be nearly as thick and broad.

The day was passed in waiting, both armies allowing the other side to prepare fully, each thinking this an advantage for themselves. Steward Kalwyn boasted that it showed that the enemy was afraid of them, but Greylock thought it more likely a simple professionalism. They would want to be in full force, he reflected, before they attacked. For their part, the enemy undoubtedly believed that the sight of such a vast army would frighten the men of the High Plateau, and were giving them a day to think what it would be like to confront such a host.

Greylock smiled to himself, for unwittingly the enemy was giving him the chance he needed to seek out the Wyrrs.

He turned away finally as darkness began to fall, and the shadows of the fortifications stretched across the land. As he began to move down the mountain path, soldiers at each of the barriers saw the face of their Tyrant and trembled.

At last, Steward Kalwyn caught up with him.

"Where are you going?" the steward panted. Greylock was walking with a firm gait and the tall gangling youth had to hurry to keep up.

"I will be back in the morning," Greylock said simply.

"But what of the enemy?" the young steward cried. "What if they should attack?"

"They will not advance further this day," Greylock said impatiently. "Darkness will fall soon. They will not take the chance of spending their first night without fortifications."

"But what if they do attack?" Kalwyn insisted.

"Then do what you can to delay them," Greylock snapped. "Surely you do not need me for that."

Kalwyn objected strenuously to this statement. "Tyrant Greylock! The men need to see that you are here! They need to see Thunderer!"

"Nevertheless, I must leave until morning," Greylock said. The fervor in his tone told the steward that he would not be able to talk his master out of it.

As the Tyrant strode away into the shadows, the young nobleman stared after him with his mouth open. Then, swallowing noticeably, he rushed to the first defense. As steward, it was his duty to command when the Tyrant was not available, but he wished he knew what was going to tell the soldiers!

Under the full moon, the Twilight Dells were a dark purple dotted with yellow points of light where the enemy had set his campfires. The valleys looked deceptively peaceful. The shadows of night had long ago crept over the land, but there was little sleep on either side of the ramparts. Greylock slipped past the High Plateau's defenses with little trouble, despite the watchfulness of the guards.

The Tyrant briefly admired the work his citizens had done under the direction of Moag. The frost fortresses had been built along the narrowest, steepest portions of the mountain pass. Only Greylock, with his formidable climbing skills and his knowledge of the mountain could have avoided being sighted by his nervous soldiers. He knew that he could have easily walked through the barriers, for he knew the passwords and once recognized was not likely to be challenged. But he did not want to have to answer the questions the guards would inevitably ask. He suspected that Kalwyn and some of his commanders would even try to stop him once they discovered just where it was he was going.

Leaving the earthworks behind, the raucous laughter of the guards fading slowly, the light of the moon glancing off the points of their spears, Greylock once again experienced a revulsion toward the land at his feet. It was a poisoned land, infertile, and lacking in the minerals needed to sustain healthy life. Curious now that he knew the cause of the Wyrrs' ill, Greylock bent to one knee and examined the dry, chalky earth between his fingers. The soil did not give back the vibrant tone he associated with healthy earth. Instead, he felt the curse of a depleted land.

Nodding slightly to himself, Greylock quickly rose and brushed the dust off his hands. He dismissed the taint from his mind, sure now what caused it, and certain that there was only one cure.

He kept to the cover of the sickly, but abundant growth, and, where he could, to the stands of pines. The moon was full and he did not want to be seen outlined against the light.

But the growth proved almost impossible to negotiate even in this light, and he more than once slammed into a fallen trunk hidden by a matt of shrubbery. He muffled his curses, for he was in danger from both sides now. Unless he was instantly recognized, any sighting would be fatal. His mission required all his stealth.

There seemed to be a great deal of activity in the enemy army, and Greylock was forced to take a twisting, turning course through the woods to avoid them. Unaccustomed to the greenery of the Underworld, he made little progress, and stopped constantly to listen above his panting breath for any sound of discovery. It seemed to him that he was making an unusual amount of noise. He hoped that it was just his heightened sensitivity and not his clumsiness.

There was a desperate need for speed as well as stealth, though he continued to make little headway against the tangled brush. He needed to complete his mission and return to the High Plateau by first light if he did not wish to be caught behind enemy lines.

Yet the Tyrant did not even know where to look for the Wyrrs. All he could do was probe further into the dreaded land, he thought, and hope that the Wyrrs would detect his presence.

In the end he did not have to go far. He was barely within the Twilight Dells before he was met. Just beyond the campfires of Trold, the form of a Wyrr suddenly filled the path.

The Wyrr seemed to hover, his feet somehow gliding over the land. It was the first time Greylock had seen one of the beings in the darkness. He remembered Moag's warning of their awesome powers in the night hours. The characteristic hollowed face and emaciated appearance was not as noticeable in the gloom. He could almost visualize what visage the Wyrr might have had but for the curse, the kind of handsome demeanor that Wyrrs could now only portray with the help of magic.

Without speaking, the Wyrr quickly made it clear that Greylock was not to move, that he was to be silent. At the same moment, he heard a patrol approaching, and he dropped to the ground. As he listened to the hushed voices of the enemy, grasping the hilt of Thunderer but not daring to draw it out in the undergrowth, he realized that he had just been saved from walking into their midst.

The Wyrr seemed to have disappeared, and there was no outcry as the patrol passed. Perhaps the soldiers of Trold had learned to disregard the scrawny inhabitants of this nightmare land, Greylock thought. From a once murderous rabble, the Wyrrs had become a strangely acquiescent race.

When Greylock finally dared to rise and look about, the ghostly Wyrr appeared immediately to beckon for him to follow. Greylock suppressed a shudder. Knowing the natural causes of the Wyrrs' emaciated appearance did not dispel the horror Greylock always felt when he saw them.

The Wyrr seemed to float above the arid soil, as if his feet scorned to touch the lifeless earth he was forced to till during the daylight, for so small a harvest. They passed an orchard of dead trees, a soft moss covering the branches, glowing in the moonlight, a singular and surprising sight in this land of evergreens. Apparently, Greylock thought, the land had once been able to nourish more cultivation than it now did.

Again, Greylock was soon lost among the identical valleys, and had to trust his guide to lead them. Yet, at last, they came to a dell he was surprised to recognize. It was the same dell that the Wyrrs had gathered within to meet him on his first journey to the Underworld, where they had proclaimed the startled young man with a lock of silver hair as the Deliverer. It was here that his hair had turned its silver hue, as if they marked him.

It was a larger valley than the others, treeless, and cleared of the persistent undergrowth that choked the other dells. It was filled with silent, waiting Wyrrs. Waiting for him, he realized. He sensed their welcome, their gratitude, and hated himself for what he was about to ask.

He hesitated as an overwhelming silence of anticipation radiated toward him. They would listen to every word he said, he knew, and would follow where he led. Did he have the right to ask them what he was about to ask? Did they have free will in the matter, or were they no more than slaves to his commands?'

Standing before this multitude of pale, hopeful faces he could still think of no alternative.

"I bring you the judgment of Deliverance!" he said, softly, knowing that all would hear and understand. The wave of gratitude that met his words was overpowering.

"But first, you must fulfill your vows to the gods of Godshome," he continued, and for the first time Greylock felt dismay coming from the Wyrrs. The single Wyrr who had guided him—Greylock was beginning to recognize him as the same Wyrr who had made the visitations—spoke for them all.

"From the day we were cast down to this land we have protected the Gateway!" the Wyrr cried.

"You must do so again," Greylock answered, firmly. The dismay replaced by a surging resolve, as thousands reacted as one.

"We will do what you ask," the Wyrr said.

"You know what the curse of your betrayal is," Greylock said, kneeling and taking up a handful of the porous, exhausted soil. "This land will destroy you if you do not leave soon. I have discovered a new land, a bountiful land that will feed you and your children and make you strong. But I must warn you now that there is great danger on the path to the Homeland."

"We will follow."

"I have found a passage to this land. But my own people are in danger, and I must help them first." He took a deep breath. "I do not know if I will survive this struggle."

At this a great swell of concern washed over him. Its force took him aback.

"If I do not return you must find the Homeland," he continued when he could speak again. "If I do not survive"—again the wave of concern met his words— "then you must make your own way."

He waved his hand toward the massive barrier of Godshome, its white snows glowing faintly within its looming shadow, all that was visible from where they stood. "Beyond Godshome is a land, a good land, waiting for you!" The distress of the Wyrrs grew as he spoke, until he realized that they were no longer listening to him.

"We will not go without you," their spokesman said firmly.

"But you must!" Greylock said. "If you do not go soon your people will die."

"We have always known where the Homeland lies. But we cannot go there without the Deliverer. This is the judgment of the gods."

Greylock knew then that no matter how much he pleaded with them they would not go without him. They would not so easily free him of this responsibility, it seemed. He felt a sudden impatience.

"We will not go," the Wyrr repeated, implacably, as if they could understand what Greylock was thinking.

All knew that the matter was settled. If anything happened to him, they would stay. They would die away slowly and inexorably to extinction.

The responsibility of this was frightening to Greylock. But he reminded himself that he was also Tyrant of the High Plateau. Though he may not survive the battle with the forces of King Kasid, he must absolve himself of that duty.

Greylock thought gloomily that it was very likely that he would die. And if he fell, the lands of the High Plateau, the Twilight Dells, and Bordertown would fall with him. The victory of the barbarians of Trold would be complete.

"We will help you," the Wyrr announced.

Greylock knew that their offer was boundless, that they would sacrifice everything for him. He felt ashamed for having expected it, for demanding it, for maneuvering a helpless people to do his bidding.

"It will not be an easy price," he warned one last time, not entirely succeeding in banishing the guilt from his mind.

A mental shrug, an awesome fatalism—Greylock could not describe it any other way—greeted his words.

"No matter what happens to me," he announced, not sure if it would do any good, "I proclaim you free of this land!"

"Now," he began. "This is what I ask ..."

The Wyrr, Greylock could not tell if it was the same one, led him surely but quickly toward his own lines. Boisterous and frightened laughter rose up all around them, from both sides of the battle lines, but the two were not seen. The Wyrr instinctively seemed to know where to go.

Not until Greylock had reached the barren space between the two armies, where it seemed safest, was he discovered and hailed. It was one of his own men, but for a few moments—until the guards had discerned his identity—the danger was as great as if it had been the enemy. His men were amazed to find their Tyrant emerging alone frm the moonlit wastes. The Wyrr had disappeared moments before he was accosted.

Shaking their heads and exchanging glances, the men of the High Plateau watched the Tyrant as he was escorted through each of the barricades. Whereas the day before his demeanor had caused the men to tremble, so now did his assurance on the eve of battle raise their spirits. The Tyrant had spied out the camps of the enemy, they whispered. He had listened to their councils of war. Victory was assured!

Greylock managed to have one last look at the defenses.

The frost fortresses certainly seemed adequate, he thought, but he had seen that the scout estimates of the enemy strength were, if anything, low. The enemy was composed of mercenaries who fought war after war for King Kasid, mercenaries for whom fighting was a way of life.

In contrast, the training and defenses of the men of the High Plateau, their small number, seemed wholly inadequate. Yet, Greylock thought grimly as morning broke, these men would have to hold off the finest army of the Underworld for one full day.

CHAPTER THIRTEEN

Greylock spent the final hours of morning unable to sleep, conferring with his commanders, and going over his strategy, finding many flaws, but no overwhelming ones.

The frost fortresses were constructed of the same materials that formed the mountain. Lava stone had been piled high across the pass, reaching from the steep cliffs which towered over one side of the Gateway to the abyss on the other side. The black lava boulders, of all shapes and sizes though always rough, slid apart easily at the first pressure, and any attacker would quickly find himself back at the bottom, with his feet and backside torn by sharp rock.

To remedy the treacherous footing on the side of the mounds they patrolled, and to provide walkways along their tops, Moag had ordered snow packed into the crevices. He had then melted the snows with his fire-wizardry and waited for the cold of night to freeze the stones solidly into place. On top of this, especially in the lower, warmer portions of the mountain, had been spread a layer of soil to insulate the ice. The Tyrant thought the frost fortresses permanent, unless the weather changed drastically.

Morning found him trying to rest at last, but when the horns sounded from the first barricade, he quickly rose and hurried to the rampart. He arrived just in time to meet the delegation of Trold.

At its head was a triumphantly grinning Carrell Redfrock. The man looked truly majestic, Greylock admitted to himself, in his scarlet cloak and ebony staff. On the broad tip of the staff, above his thin, manicured hand, was the sleek black crow. The man had become even more elegant in his sojourn to the fiefdoms of Trold, Greylock thought, than he had been before his exile. Tall and dark, with his white hair intricately curled, the traitor looked satisfied with himself.

At Redfrock's side, like a cur at the side of its brutal master, stooped Tarelton looking exceedingly unhappy. His once long, red hair was falling out in patches now, giving his rat nowhere to hide. The familiar was crouched under the collar of the mayor's filthy robe, once an emerald green, but now an indistinguishable brown.

"I told you I would return, Tyrant Greylock," Carrell Redfrock said in a pleasant voice. Greylock thought the former steward used the title less as a greeting than to show to his new allies his familiarity with the High Plateau. "It would have been better for all if you had never opposed me, young man."

"Better for me, perhaps," Greylock answered. "But I doubt that it would have been better for my people. Yet, it did not need to come to this, Redfrock. I had not intended to punish you."

"No?" Redfrock laughed bitterly. "Perhaps not. But we both know that I could never have sworn my loyalty to you. From a time long before you were even born, from the day I became aware of my hunger, I meant to be Tyrant!"

"What a pity you did not use your powers to eliminate that hunger instead," Greylock said, realizing too late that the old steward was as much a victim of the snows of Godshome as any of them.

Redfrock laughed at this sentiment. "Your uncle was too clever for me, but I will not be beaten by a mere boy."

Greylock ignored him, knowing this to be the best answer. If the old man wished to persist in believing him a boy, then it was his own mistake. But the Tyrant did not really think that Redfrock would continue to underestimate him. *

Instead of trading further insults with Redfrock, Greylock examined the soldiers of Trold.

The men from the fiefdoms were small men compared to the farmers of Far Valley; light men compared to the dark-skinned men of the High Plateau. But they bore the scars of many battles, an air of stolid professionalism. They seemed to want to get the bickering and the formalities over with so that they could proceed with the battle. Greylock guessed that they would fight with the same kind of dispatch.

"What has the traitor Redfrock told you?" he addressed them, ignoring the old man. "There is nothing you could want here. This is a poor land, a bitterly poor land."

The commander of the party, a lean hard man with a few flakes of gray at his temples but otherwise tough and fit, merely shrugged.

"I am Marshal Derrion," he said, in a calm voice. "I speak for King Kasid of Trold!" The old soldier frowned at Redfrock, and Greylock realized suddenly that Derrion did not like the traitor.

Four mercenaries were arrayed behind their leader, each dressed alike, and yet each unique. All wore unadorned burnished helmets close over their heads, and had light chain mail and long spears. But there the similarities ended. Each spear had a unique blade, some jagged, some smooth. The helmets were also different in subtle ways, some with nose guards, others with flaps hanging loosely over the neck. All the armor looked battered and often used, though well cared for.

Marshal Derrion wore a thick leather gauntlet on one hand, but Greylock did not know its meaning until he heard the sudden beating of giant wings. The huge bird hovered over their heads, whipping the cloaks of the delegation about in the powerful wind of its wings. Then the eagle landed delicately on the marshal's gloved arm. The imperial beak of the eagle turned arrogantly toward its master.

Greylock knew with a sudden certainty that the eagle had scouted the mountain pass for Marshal Derrion, and was now reporting. A suspicion was confirmed in his mind, for if this soldier had received his pet from the same source that Tarelton and Redfrock had received their familiars it meant that they had been allies from the start; all serving under King Kasid of the fiefdoms of Trold.

"We know of your Room of Glyden," Marshal Derrion said without emotion. From the tone in his voice, Greylock knew that the soldier was merely repeating instructions. "King Kasid has ordered me to say that he is not a greedy man. He asks only that you recognize his authority and bequeath a small tithe of four hundred weight a year to the treasury of Trold."

Greylock was surprised at the offer of peace. He suddenly saw an opportunity to delay the inevitable. He did not really believe that the King of Trold would settle for four hundred weight of glyden, not when he learned how much glyden filled the vault and the weaknesses of the defenses. But Greylock decided to go through the motions of bargaining simply to take up more time. If he could hold off the battle through the morning, he thought with sudden hope, then the chances of lasting the full day were that much greater.

"We do not have such quantities of glyden!" he lied. "Your information is wrong, as it must be if it comes from him." He pointed at the frowning Carrell Redfrock. "We are not a rich people, as I told you."

"He lies!" Redfrock said, seeming upset that Greylock had contradicted him. "Tell him, Tarelton! Tell Marshal Derrion how you found the Room of Glyden."

The tall man turned to his servant, and though he did not raise his hand, Greylock thought of a master whipping his dog.

"I have seen it!" Tarelton cried. His fright raised his high voice even higher. "There is a Room of Glyden in the mountain, filled with bars of great wealth."

"There," Redfrock said, with a satisfied tone. "What did I tell you7"

Marshal Derrion did not seem to care if the glyden actually existed or not. He had his orders.

"Enough of this bickering!" he commanded. "Do you refuse to grant us the glyden?"

"I would be very happy to recognize the sovereignty of King Kasid," Greylock volunteered. "If he will leave us in peace. But we cannot give him such a tithe. There is not so much glyden in all the High Plateau! Surely you can see that the man is mad."

Tarelton did indeed look demented at that moment. A tall man, he was so stooped that he seemed smaller than the others.

But Marshal Derrion was not convinced.

"If you will not pay," he said impassively, "then I must warn you to prepare for battle. The king will accept no less. However, as a last gesture of his respect he has authorized me to offer you the freedom of some of our slaves."

"Slaves?" Greylock repeated, confused.

"King Kasid thought their lives might be of some importance to you." The marshal raised his hand a few inches, and the eagle stirred its wings uneasily.

The gates of the hastily erected walls around the enemy camp opened and about one hundred men emerged. Greylock could hear his men muttering nervously on the ramparts above him, and he motioned for silence.

Only a few men looked dangerous from a distance, those who prodded at the others with long spears. But not until the prisoners were a few hundred feet away did Greylock finally recognize them.

It was quickly apparent why he had not recognized them sooner. The farmers of Bordertown were shockingly changed. The once muscular men had been starved until their skin and clothes hung from them.

But the Tyrant could see that their will had not been broken. They glared back at their guards, and Harkkor even summoned a smile at the sight of Greylock.

"What is your answer?" Marshal Derrion demanded.

When Greylock did not answer immediately, the soldier began to turn away, motioning away the guards with their prisoners. Redfrock gave him a triumphant stare.

"Wait!" Greylock shouted. The sight of the huge vein of glyden filled his head like an unwanted nightmare, and despite his instinct that conflict was inevitable, he began to hope that the glyden would satisfy them. After all, he thought, it meant nothing to him, little to his people. Let the covetous Underworlders have it if it would buy the High Plateau peace. He could at least buy the freedom of the men of Bordertown.

"Will you leave my people in peace if I give you four hundred weight?"

Carrell Redfrock seemed surprised by the offer. Obviously he had not thought that Greylock would give in. For the first time Greylock began to think that the deal was genuine, and that the soldiers would go away with the glyden and not return until it was time to collect the next tithe. Marshal Derrion seemed an honorable man.

The soldier was all business at these words and did not seem at all surprised by the sudden surrender. He smiled grimly as if he sympathized with the Tyrant.

And indeed, if Greylock but knew it, Derrion was thinking that subjects always protested that they would not pay the tithe. Sometimes they managed to pay. It did not matter to him. There was always work for him and his soldiers. No land was ever conquered peacefully, his experience told him. In the end, there was always a battle. Sometimes, however, it was more profitable if the other side gave in at first.

"Do you accept King Kasid as your overlord?" he asked.

"Yes," Greylock nodded. "What of my authority as Tyrant?"

"You may keep your title, and where it does not affect the business of the fiefdoms, you may keep your authority."

Again it was the experience of the Marshal that what affected the business of Trold sooner or later included all the business of the realm. But it was not for him to tell this young man the hard reality of Underworld politics. Sooner or later the Tyrant would rebel against this interference, and when this happened it would be his duty to crush the rebellion. It was not the way he would have done things. He would have fought the battles in the first place. But King Kasid thought it better to take them over piecemeal.

"It is a trick!" Redfrock protested. "He would never give you so much glyden, Marshal. Do not believe him!"

"Quiet!" Derrion turned cold eyes on the old man. "We are here to discover if it is true or not.

"Show me!" he directed Greylock, showing a willingness to leave at that moment.

"Now?" Greylock asked, surprised that the commander would endanger himself.

"If it is a trick, then little will be lost by my King," Derrion replied. "There are many men to take my place. If it should be a trick, you will gain little."

And if it was a trick, the soldier told himself, the Tyrant would pay with his life. Derrion was sure that he could slay Greylock at this distance guards or no guards.

"It is a long, dangerous trip," Greylock warned. He wondered at the discipline that would make a soldier accept such an uncertain fate. "We will not be back before noon."

"Lead on," the Marshal said, turning to bark an order to one of his men. The man started back toward the camps of Trold. "You have until noon. If we are not back by then ..." His voice trailed off warningly.

"You do not need me," Redfrock said. "I will send Mayor Tarelton in my place."

"No," the soldier commanded, freezing the steward from leaving. "You are coming with us. It was the king's wish that you share in any danger. How else can he be sure of your loyalty?"

Greylock wondered if he saw a smile in Derrion's face. At the same time, he noticed the grimace in Tarelton's. The mayor looked near the breaking point, he thought, and more dangerous than he had ever been.

He turned to give the same orders to his men. "No harm is to come to these men," he said. "If I am not back by this afternoon they will attack! Be ready for them!"

CHAPTER FOURTEEN

The small party of enemy soldiers led by the Tyrant created a stir in the camps of the High Plateau. Soldiers gathered around the ramparts and lined the trail as the grim, silent delegation marched toward Godshome. All but Greylock were blindfolded, and it was left to the Tyrant to lead them carefully over the thin ramps set out from the barricades, allowing them to pass over the jagged lava stone. The three soldiers and their leader fingered their swords nervously, but had left the spears behind as too threatening.

At the narrow door of Castle Guardian, the only entrance to the High Plateau, they were met by Steward Kalwyn, who at first refused to admit them.

Greylock frowned at the nervous steward, who peered through the peephole, and ordered him sharply to open the door. Reluctantly, the young man unbarred the door.

Castle Guardian spanned the trail, its icetower perched on the very edge of the abyss, its massive white outer walls set against the cliffs of Godshome. The snowy bulwarks converged at the door, and on all sides of the narrow enclosure Greylock could see the weapons of the defenders. It was the last, perhaps most formidable defense of his land, ever surmounted.

He led the delegation carefully up the icy steps and into the broad courtyard beyond. Mara and Ardra were waiting within the inner stone buildings. The Tyrant had sent word ahead of him for them to wait, to serve as guides to the Room of Glyden.

As the party waited shivering still blindfolded, Greylock told the two women his plans.

The vault of glyden was no longer a secret, but few people knew the way to the secret room. Greylock had ordered the opening closed when it was first revealed, and Moag had built one of the massive frost fortresses up against it after Greylock had explored the lava caves and found a route underground. Now only he and a few others close to him, such as Ardra and Mara, knew the path to the Room of Glyden.

The Underworlders shivered uncontrollably as he gave his instructions to the two women. Finally, he relented and led them out of the freezing court. The main hall of the inner castle contained a stairway that led to the top of the icetower, where it overlooked the Gateway. It also went down into the network of caverns beneath the High Plateau.

They descended the twisting staircase into the darkness of the cellars, where Greylock lit the torches and unfastened the heavy locks to the tunnels. The Tyrant allowed his charges to remove their blindfolds while he prepared the way. It had been the defenses of the mountain trail that he had wanted to keep from Marshal Demon's experienced eyes. Let him learn the hard way, Greylock thought grimly. If they thought there was just one frost fortress instead of a dozen it might delay them just a little longer and let them come upon the walls of Castle Guardian unprepared.

He was certain that they could gain no useful information from the cellars. Redfrock, of course, would recognize it as Castle Guardian, but once they were within the caverns he planned to blindfold the old man again, at least part of the way. The soldiers, he was confident, would never be able to retrace their steps through the maze of caverns. They would be depending on him entirely, which was exactly what he wanted; it was his safest insurance against treachery.

When Marshal Derrion removed his blindfold and saw where they were headed, he blanched. It was the first time Greylock had seen the commander show any trace of fear, and he realized from the nervous whispers of the other soldiers that they were thoroughly frightened.

The marshal took a single step toward the yawning black hole of the cavern, and the eagle let out a screech that echoed off the close walls of the cellar, deafening them. The huge wings spread, knocking several of the soldiers aside, and fluttered dangerously.

"Tordra will not enter," the soldier said, after quieting the bird.

"Perhaps if you hooded it?" Greylock suggested.

"No," Derrion answered fatalistically. "She would never allow that.

"I was told once by an old witch woman, soon after King Kasid granted me my familiar, that if I ever dared to enter the bowels of the earth without Tordra I would not come back. I dismissed the prophecy as nonsense, of course," he finished wryly, "for I saw no possibility that I would ever do so."

"It's a trap!" Redfrock said, hoping to play on his allies' fear. "He is going to lead us in and abandon us!"

"I told you to keep quiet," the marshal growled, scowling. "There would be no purpose."

"He wants to kill me!" Redfrock said, angrily, losing his polished, charming manner. "This is his revenge!"

Derrion and Greylock locked eyes, understanding each other.

"I doubt he would throw away his kingdom, the lives of his people, for you," Derrion said.

"You are wrong!" Redfrock cried, panic edging into his voice. "Can't you see that!"

In reaction to the old man's fear, Tarelton shied away, as a dog would from a master who showed fear. The mayor had been watching them with shining eyes, and Greylock wondered what the scheming man was thinking.

"If you will let me return to the courtyard," the marshal said, turning his back on Redfrock, "I will free her to wait for my return."

Greylock motioned for Ardra to lead the marshal to the courtyard, and as he watched the strong back of the soldier recede up into the shadows of the stairway, he could not help but think that he was more concerned about the prophecy of the old witch woman than the marshal. From a once rather skeptical youth, Greylock had come to respect the ancient legends and prophecies.

The tunnels felt cool and dusty at first. But slowly the ground seemed less traveled, the air warmer. Greylock led staight into the mountain, holding a torch and leading Derrion, Redfrock and Tarelton. Ardra and Mara followed, leading the other three soldiers.

Their progress was unimpeded until they reach what Greylock thought of as the core of the volcano. Long ago the forces within the mountain had built up an enormous cavern, at the bottom of which lay a pit brimming with molten firestone. All the lava tunnels eventually led to this central core. Other balconies, built up by the shooting shards of liquid rock, branched off the walls of the cavern above and below them.

Greylock could not help but flinch at the sight of the firestone, memories of his nightmare journey up the side of the pit coming back to him all at once. The men of Trold seemed stunned by the flames shooting high into the air, as if the firestone was straining to reach them. Before they could change their minds he gestured at the ledge of rock which spiraled around the core of the pit.

"You don't expect us to go down that!" Marshal Derrion said. "You ask too much, Tyrant! Let us go back to the surface and fight our battle. This is no way for a man to die!"

"I warned you," Redfrock said, hurriedly. "He is going to kill us!"

Fortunately, the traitor's importuning had the opposite effect than he may have wished.

"Lead on, Tyrant. The witch said that I would die in a fire under the ground and I can see now that she was right."

"It is possible to traverse," Greylock said, quickly, sensing the mayor could eventually sway the steady commander. "Even Mara and Ardra have done so," he said, pointing to the two women, hoping that it would shame the soldier.

"I said lead on, didn't I?" Derrion growled.

The path was not as treacherous and demanding as Greylock remembered. He found the climb an easy challenge. But the men of Trold found the climb almost impossible. They clutched the sides of the walls and stared down into the pit, and did everything they could, it seemed, to frighten themselves into a fall. Only Greylock's great skill, the patience of the two women, made the climb successful. By leading the way, marking and widening the trail as he went along, and shouting out the hazards well in advance, Greylock insured that they made it to the lower chambers without losing anyone.

He overheard Mara, leading the men directly behind Redfrock, questioning the former steward about the Lady Silverfrost. He smiled at the jealousy he detected in the question. He too had wondered where the silver lady had gone.

"Has she abandoned you as well, Redfrock?" she asked. Her steady voice was somehow threatening. That, coupled with the traitor's nervousness at the height and the precarious footing, was an effective assurance of the truth. If the old steward lied, her voice implied, he would find himself falling into the pit.

"She is the guest of King Kasid," Redfrock said, uneasily.

"So she has found a more powerful suitor than you?" she laughed. "Is that what has happened, Redfrock?"

"King Kasid has found favor in the lady," the old man said, conceding that what she said was true. This seemed to reassure Mara, for she asked no more questions.

They needed to descend only a few hundred feet into the pit before turning aside, but it was far enough for a few of the globules of firestone to ascend over their heads, hanging there threateningly. None of the firestone rained down on them before Greylock turned into a new cavern and away from the fire. Despite their exhaustion, none of them wished to stop until they were well away from the heat of the central core and into the blessedly cool passages a few hundred yards away.

However, once inside the new cave, Greylock was not certain of his way. He had traveled over this portion of the path a few times; the tunnels could play funny tricks on the unwary. Sometimes it seemed that whole caverns had disappeared, or had shifted into entirely opposite directions. The closer he came to the vault of glyden, the less certain he became. But with the help of Mara and Ardra, who each remembered important fragments of the path, they reached the corridors that Greylock had marked.

Thankful now that he had had the foresight to mark the more complicated portions, Greylock Jed them quickly toward their goal.

Every few yards, at every turn in the path, he had faithfully scratched directions into the walls. If the others could find their way this far, he thought, they would have little trouble finding the rest of the way. But he doubted they would ever make it this far. And if they tried, they would wander the endless, twisting corridors until they dropped from exhaustion.

An evil red shimmer slowly filled the corridor, until all could see without the torches. At last, they turned into a smooth and broadly curved hallway, and there, reflected on the polished walls like a mirage, was the Room of Glyden. The soldiers rushed forward without him, and the image of the glyden sprinted along the walls ahead of them, like a beckoning pool of water to a thirsty man. At the end of the broadly curving walls, the vision promised, they would find more glyden than they had ever dreamed could exist.

By the time Greylock had caught up with the men of Trold, several of them were already fondling the heavy bars of metal that lined the walls of the vault. Even Marshal Derrion was moved to curiously scratch a few nuggets from the naked vein that ran along one side of the room.

On the far side of the room, stone walls had been melted away by an intense heat, leaving a shattered, lumpy appearance to the rock. The source of the glydens' glow was revealed to be a river of firestone cutting across one wall of the room. Fortunately, the river of firestone had missed the vein of glyden itself and had receded to the bottom of the fissure that had been burned into the rock. It flowed slowly several hundred feet below. The room was sweltering, and glowed eerily with the blood-red color of the magma.

To Greylock it was one more proof of the renewed activity of Godshome; for the fissure of firestone had not existed the last time he had visited the chamber.

Redfrock, with Tarelton forgotten at his side, stood at the center of the vault, faintly contemptuous and aloof from the greed of the Underworlders. The three citizens of the High Plateau stood watching in amazement from the door.

Having given into his greed enough to fill one pocket, Marshal Derrion was suddenly all business. He directed the loading of bars into the heavy canvas bags the soldiers had brought folded in their uniforms. There seemed to be no way of measuring the glyden exactly, but Greylock and Derrion arrived at an estimation of each bar which satisfied them both.

Incredibly, the full tithe was reached before even a quarter of the bars were depleted. The three soldiers were already heavily weighted down. They would not find it easy to negotiate the spiraling ledge over the pit of firestone, Greylock reflected. But he doubted the excited soldiers had thought of this yet, so blinded were they by the precious metal.

Marshal Derrion unhesitatingly began to load more glyden into the makeshift bags for Redfrock and Tarelton to carry, and then removed his own armor in preparation of carrying the remainder himself. The marshal had evidently decided to trust him, Greylock thought.

The soldiers began digging at the vein to fill their own pockets further, gouging the soft metal awkwardly with their knives. Greylock did not try to stop them. Instead of depleting the glyden, the further they dug into the wall the wider and deeper the vein proved to be. It was apparent to all that there were many more tithes left in the Room of Glyden.

When Greylock and Derrion agreed that some four hundred weight of glyden had been mined, the marshal gave orders to pack up and leave. There was no discussion of taking more than the agreed upon amount. They were all suddenly aware that it was fast approaching noon, and they remembered the difficult climb that had brought them there. They knew the climb back would be even worse.

Mayor Tarelton had not taken his eyes off the glyden since they had entered, but he had not dared to leave the side of Redfrock. Now he darted forward as they were about to leave and began to feverishly line his pockets with nuggets. Redfrock took two steps forward and brought his ebony staff down hard on the back of the mayor, who howled and retreated to the corner of the vault.

"Is that all you are going to take?" Redfrock demanded, turning to confront the marshal. His once elegantly curled hair had straightened about his shoulders, and his red cloak was stained with sweat. On his shoulder drooped the familiar. The crow had chosen to stay with its master, but it seemed unhappy at the heat and constriction of the caves.

"King Kasid ordered me to take four hundred weight, and I have done so," the marshal snapped. "I will not change the agreement now."

"There is ten times that much glyden here!" Redfrock protested. "A hundred times! Don't you understand? The amount of the levy was imposed on my advice. I had no idea there was so much."

"I'm sure not," Derrion commented. "I suspect, rather, that you purposely made the amount of the tithe far more than you thought could be filled. Nevertheless, I do not have the authority to change the king's orders!"

"Fool!" Redfrock said, angrily. "You will answer for this. When King Kasid learns how much glyden was left behind—"

"I told you to be quiet!" Derrion commanded, and Redfrock was shocked into silence.

Picking up one of the heavier bags of glyden, Derrion tossed it into the arms of Redfrock, who staggered back against the wall from the weight.

"If I decide to take more out," he snapped, "you will carry it!" Then he made the mistake the witch woman had predicted. He turned his back on Carrell Redfrock.

The old man threw the bag to the floor and lunged for the retreating soldier, catching him at the small of the back. Derrion tried desperately to stop his fall, and his soldier's trained sense of balance almost saved him. But the weighted bags of glyden toppled him inexorably forward to the fissure of firestone. He crashed against the edge, and then the metal dragged him head first over the side. The molten lava claimed him without a sound.

There was stunned silence for a few moments, and then chaos as Redfrock began to shout orders at the soldiers.

"Kill him!" he screamed, pointing at Greylock. "Kill him and the glyden is yours!"

The soldiers of King Kasid hesitated, glancing from the gestating mayor to Greylock. Carrell Redfrock had traveled far with the mercenaries of Trold. They had seen him walking and conferring with the king. And though it had been obvious that Marshal Derrion had held him in contempt, assassination was common in the mercenary army. Most important, there was the glyden. Let King Kasid keep the four hundred weight, they reasoned as one, without speaking, and they would take the rest.

"Nothing has changed!" Greylock cried, too late. "Do not listen to Redfrock. Take the glyden and go!"

The Tyrant saw that they were not listening, and reluctantly drew Thunderer. He could immediately sense the respect with which the battle-hardened soldiers held the long blade. He saw them eye his stance and grip. When the first soldier lunged at him, he sensed from the practiced fluidity of his movement that it was a well-used gambit.

Mara and Ardra stood at the door of the vault, uncertain whether or not to join the fight.

"Run!" he shouted without turning. "I will find you!"

Then Greylock did the unexpected. Before the three men could fully develop their ploy, he attacked. With a flurry of two-handed blows, he scattered them. With a rapidity that astonished even himself, he found himself on the far side of the soldiers, near the door and out of the trap.

Too late, the soldiers realized their mistake. Greylock could easily escape into the tunnels and they would never find him or their own way out.

But Greylock did not leave them there. Before he could turn to follow Ardra and Mara, he noticed Redfrock. Out of them all, he thought angrily, Redfrock deserved to die. And he did not trust the caves to finish him. The cunning traitor had spent most of his life on the High Plateau, and it was possible he might be able to find his way out.

An anger filled him, and Greylock once again did the unexpected and attacked. The blinding rage he had been building up for so long against the treacherous Redfrock seemed to shake the very earth. Suddenly he realized that the trembling was not an illusion. Godshome was once more awakening, as if to his summons.

The frightened look in Redfrock's eyes showed that he thought Greylock had caused the earthquake, and the Tyrant took advantage of momentary amazement of the soldiers to break through.

But he was too late to take out his revenge on Redfrock. Tarelton was there before him.

The mayor had remained cowering in the corner after the beating. Now he sprang forward with a cry, his mad eyes glinting, and buried his knife into the back of his master. Redfrock dropped without a sound and rolled over the edge of the fissure.

Before either Greylock or the soldiers could react, the mayor had fled the Room of Aurim. Greylock quickly followed, though he had no intention of chasing him. His anger had left. It was a better fate for Tarelton, he thought, for him to wander the caverns lost and alone.

As Greylock left them behind, the cries of the soldiers echoed off the walls, pleading with him to come back. As their shouts became more and more frantic, he hesitated in the darkness of the tunnel. But he no longer trusted them. The lure of glyden was too strong.

When he was sure he had left them far behind, he stopped to light a torch. From this point Greylock did not intend to leave any traces for others to follow, should they make it this far. He began to brush his tracks from the heavy dust of the floor.

But he underestimated the determination the panic of being left in the darkness had instilled in the men of Trold. He heard their footsteps moments before they entered the light of his torch. He debated briefly whether to extinguish the light and lose himself in the dark, but realized it was too late. They could find him by touch and sound alone now.

He barely had time to draw Thunderer before they burst into the light and were upon him. He thrust the torch into the face of the first soldier, who howled and went to one knee. The torch burned fitfully on the floor of the cavern. The other two men were more careful. They stopped at a respectful distance from the tip of Thunderer, and waited for their companion to get to his feet. Then they began to put into action what Greylock knew was another well-used gambit. Apparently, he thought, they had decided that if they were to be left behind they would make sure he was left too. He had no hope that he could outfight all three men.

The point man of the battle triad came in on him with the long narrow blade of his Underworld sword. Greylock swung Thunderer

231

and the lighter weapon of his opponent shattered, but, by then, the other two men had penetrated his defenses on both sides.

Suddenly, Mara and Ardra burst into the middle of the fight. Ardra engaged one man, and Greylock turned to engage the other with the point of his sword. The soldier seemed to be trying to look behind him as well as ward off Greylock's attack. He went down with Thunderer penetrating his body.

There were still two men standing, one of them with a shattered weapon but still dangerous. The other man was trying to deal with Ardra's savage attacks. As the weaponless man stooped to pick up the sword of his slain comrade, the Tyrant knew that he would not make the same mistake. The man would know that Thunderer was the stronger, though slower blade and would fight accordingly.

If he knew how to use the thin rapier-like sword he was holding, Greylock thought, he would inevitably win in the close quarters of the tunnel. Thunderer was meant to be swung two-handed, bowling over its opponents. With the narrow walls of the cave he was forced to handle it as a weapon that could thrust and parry.

He knew that not far away Mara was concentrating on summoning her magic wind. Throughout the fight, he had felt a few brief gusts of wind blowing over his neck, but the wind was unnatural so far beneath the earth, and took a long time to gather strength.

Finally, as both Ardra and Greylock were pressed by the attacks of the soldiers, the wind blasted toward them. It seemed to part for the shapes of Ardra and Greylock and to strike the soldiers at full force. Ironically, the bags of glyden saved them for a few moments. They stood against the blast, and even advanced a few feet toward them. Mara frowned, grew pale, and redoubled the winds. The soldiers fell before the sudden gust, landing solidly on their backs. As they struggled to rise, Greylock and the two women fled into the darkness of the tunnel.

Later, Greylock realized that it was a miracle that they stayed together, with only the sounds of their footsteps to keep them in touch. Greylock took turn after turn in the darkness, unsure of where he was going, but hoping that they were leaving the men of Trold behind. At last, deep within the mountain, Greylock stopped and collapsed against the wall. He heard Ardra breathing heavily beside him, and Mara found his arms.

After resting and listening for pursuit, they dared to light a fire. It was necessary for only a few hundred yards, for they emerged miraculously on the shelf of the fiery pit. They climbed the spiraling ledge at a pace they would not have dared earlier, quickly reaching to top.

CHAPTER FIFTEEN

Greylock watched helplessly as the forces of war gathered. The sun neared its zenith, and the last few minutes to the deadline passed in stillness, both sides knowing that it could not be met.

On his return, Greylock had immediately sent a regretful explanation of Marshal Derrion's death, and had reasserted his willingness to give up four hundred weight of glyden. But he had known that the offer would be refused. The new envoy had nervously approached the ramparts, no doubt certain, Greylock thought, that he too would be sacrificed to the treachery of the High Plateau. He had given a flat rejection. There was to be war.

Now the Tyrant could see the full might of the fiefdoms of Trold, and his heart despaired. The king's commanders would be unable to utilize the full force of their numbers on the narrow mountain pass, he thought, but they would have an endless supply of fresh reinforcements to fling against the frost fortresses. Eventually, exhaustion and attrition would dwindle the army of the High Plateau. Greylock meant to retreat slowly against the tide of Underworlders, hoping that night would fall before the last redoubt had been breached.

At his side stood Mara, radiant and happy on this day, despite the approaching battle. Only she knew that she was carrying Greylock's child. Her long blond hair flew in the wind, and her green eyes glittered above the reddened cheeks of her marble skin. She seemed to have confidence that the High Plateau would prevail against the enemy. The defenders, looking upon her expression, took heart. Many remembered her wind-witchery and were encouraged.

"If all else fails," Greylock vowed grimly, "I will bring down the mountain over them." He had already prepared places for rockslides that would take months to remove.

"Why do you not close the pass now?" Kalwyn objected. "Why risk the lives of our people?"

"If we do not fight them now," Greylock sighed, "we will just have to fight them another day."

"No army can climb the cliffs of Godshome if we do not want them to!" Kalwyn insisted. "Only the Gateway can give them entrance."

Greylock felt his anger rising, but did not answer. Once before his people had slammed the gates shut, he thought, but never again. He would not be the one to close the Gateway.

Thankfully, Keyholder answered the steward for him.

"King Kasid will not give up his efforts to conquer the High Plateau if we close the Gateway," the old Gatekeeper said. "He would find another way to reach our land. Not long ago fiefdoms were separate countries, Trold one land among many. Kasid has molded them into an empire. He is a proud man. Even if we did not possess the Room of Aurim, he would seek to vanquish us, for we have shamed him. No one can ignore his lust for power. We shall learn today if he can be stopped."

A roar that seemed to shake the earth was hurled at them from the ranks of the demon army, and the thunder of their war cries grew as they emerged from the earthworks of their camp. It ended only with their charge. Then there was deadly silence as the wave of men rushed toward the defenders.

Greylock raised his arms and the brush piles that had been placed between the armies were ignited. For a few moments the conflagration promised to sweep toward the enemy unopposed and engulf the army, but suddenly the flames subsided back to the original fires. There they sputtered fitfully, and Greylock knew that the fire wizards of Trold had negated the fires.

The invaders had hesitated only momentarily at the sight of the fire, and now surged forward again. The men of the plateau waited helplessly for their assault.

Now Mara raised her arms, and black clouds that until then had been lingering far to the north began to blow across the skies, obscuring the sun. The skies above the battlefield grew dark, as though the day had chosen to retreat from the sight of so much blood. The clouds remained, despite the opposing wizards, which aided the men of the plateau, who knew the mountain much better than their enemy.

In the eerie light of flaming trees, and a darkened, eclipsed sun, the dark mass that rushed toward them up the long, gentle slope were at first only dark shadows, and then became individuals with pale, determined faces.

Greylock motioned with a short chopping signal, and thousands of small, cruel missiles, whistling with a trembling deadliness, swept into the air. The first rows of the charging enemy fell beneath the deadly hailstorm, and a second wave dropped beneath another flight of arrows.

The armies met, not in the great clash Greylock had been expecting, but with the rolling percussion of thousands of swords striking metal. The rumbling did not die away, though at times it would seem to subside for a few moments only to become louder with the next surge of battle. The cries of dying men rose above the clatter of swords, and like some horrible song began to develop an eerie rhythm, a melody that rose and fell like a wailing cry.

If Greylock had dared close his eyes, he would have imagined himself surrounded by demons. He had placed himself at the head of his army, to show his presence and that of Thunderer, the sword that had never been defeated in battle.

He swung the sword over his head and down over the wall like a pendulum, its glyden hilt catching the light of the fires and glowing brightly. The enemy was scaling the loose lava of the frost fortresses more easily than he had expected.

One man scrambled up the slopes toward him, and as Greylock swung the sword at the invader, the man lost his footing. As the enemy soldier fell under the sweep of his sword, Greylock saw the sharp tip of the other blade darting toward his legs. He tried desperately to dodge the thrust, but he knew he was going to be too late.

Then Kalwyn's sword was there, catching the enemy blade awkwardly but enough to deflect it.

This first charge was driven back by such efforts, but every surge after that proved disastrous for the army of the High Plateau. They quickly gave way to the overwhelming numbers of the Underworlders, abandoning the low, broad frost fortresses one by one.

Before the first hour had passed the defenders had retreated to the last frost fortress, far up on the narrow reaches of the Gateway. There the snows and height finally began to slow the enemy.

Greylock sent down the first of the rockslides before the pursuing army, using this last weapon much sooner than he had wished. But the rockslides had been carefully scouted and prepared, and with the help of Mara's wind magic they proved devastating.

The men of the High Plateau gathered wearily behind the last of the frost fortresses, as the army of Trold began to tenaciously remove the rockslides. Above them, Greylock could see the turret of Castle Guardian's icetower. The wounded stretched in a ragged line towards its white walls. He hoped that Ardra had succeeded in mustering the women of the High Plateau for a last desperate defense. The men around him lay in clusters, trying to catch a few moments of rest before the implacable mercenaries attacked them again. Greylock knew that their army had suffered far more casualties than his own, yet it hardly seemed to make a difference in the numbers of Underworlders.

Mara stood mute beside him, no longer really aware of her surroundings, so concentrated was she in wielding her magic against the enemy wizards. Keyholder and his attendant priest had thankfully taken on the duty of guiding and protecting her. Kalwyn stood bruised and bleeding. The young steward had proven to be a valiant ally, standing beside the Tyrant and conveying his orders. Now Greylock gave a last urgent command.

"We must hold until darkness!" he gasped, surprised that the thought came out aloud. "If we hold until darkness, we have won."

Kalwyn stared at him uncomprehendingly for a few moments, and then rushed away.

Normally, darkness would still have been hours away. But unwittingly Mara was bringing on the night much sooner with her magic wind. The skies were dark and threatening, the light barely perceptible.

When the two armies came face to face again at last, both sides were exhausted. The army of the Underworld seemed to stand off for a few moments in respect. Every soldier was aware that this was the final confrontation of the day, and probably of the battle.

The Underworlders attacked with silent and deadly purpose. The men of the High Plateau, their country almost overrun, put up a last desperate fight. Behind the high lava walls of the frost fortress, only a few hundred feet wide, the small number of defenders made less difference, and the strength of each man was more crucial. The plateau men staggered and wielded their swords clumsily, but their determination held off attack after attack.

When Greylock heard the men around him mutter, "Hold until night. Hold until night and we have won!" he knew that Kalwyn had spread his words. He hoped it was enough to strengthen them for one last stand.

The last frost fortress was overrun, and the defenders were barely able to escape to the white walls of Castle Guardian.

But before this last awesome fortress the Underworlders were at last forced to pull up short. As night fell, the men of the mountain still held the high ground.

The moans of the wounded, the low murmur of the commanders, the reassuring voices of the women, filled Castle Guardian. His army was collapsing around him, but Greylock would not retreat from the cold guardroom of the icetower to rest.

Mara entered the turret behind him, and he turned with an expressionless welcome. Mara seemed almost asleep on her feet, her white face even more pale than usual from holding the cloud cover over them all day. Now she was letting the winds blow the dark clouds where they willed, and was on the verge of collapse.

"Come, Greylock," she said, softly. "There is nothing more you can do. Tomorrow will decide." But she obviously thought that the morrow would bring defeat. The white walls would have to eventually succumb to superior numbers. And when Castle Guardian fell, the battle for the High Plateau would be ended.

Greylock still refused to leave the icetower, refused to even acknowledge her leaving when exhaustion at last claimed her. He stared into the dark with reddened eyes, as if he could see something in the murk that would save them.

The night grew quiet but for the moans of the wounded. The sounds of battle still seemed to ring in his ears, and when he closed his eyes, the sickening motion of his bloody sword came back to him, the slight, almost imperceptible impacts when the blade met bone and sliced through. The cries and moans of the wounded accompanied these nightmares, as he lay with his head against the cold ice of the parapet.

New cries suddenly filled the air, of men freshly wounded, frightened of something more than death. Greylock jerked awake, and realized that he had not dreamed those new screams.

Another battle was occurring in the darkness beyond the frost fortresses, but a silent battle, a battle that was one-sided.

Now his own men were awakening, below in Castle Guardian, and one by one the soldiers were drawn morbidly to the ice walls, to look out into the night and wonder on the deadly battle that was being waged in the gloom, seemingly without weapons.

"Demons!" Greylock heard them mutter. Behind him, Mara came up beside him, and then Kalwyn. They listened in silence to the slaughter.

"You were waiting for this!" Kalwyn said. "You expected it!"

"Yes," Greylock said. "I expected it." But he had not expected it to be so horrible!

"What is killing them, Greylock?" Kalwyn said. "What would cause such horror in men?"

"It is the Wyrrs," Mara answered suddenly for Greylock. She turned to him sadly. "Yes, I have known of your powers over them and your obligation. I too have dreamed of the Wyrrs. Long before I knew I was to become your wife, they knew I would be so."

"Then you know what I must do," he answered simply.

When the Wyrr came to him, Greylock was not sure if the specter was corporeal or a dream. If the Wyrr was real, Greylock thought, he had passed through an army of sleepless men undetected. If he was a dream, he had a firmness that most dreams did not possess.

The Wyrr stood silently in the middle of the icetower, waiting for Greylock to awake and become aware of him. Then it stepped into the moonlight flowing through the casements, and his visage was one of triumph and anticipation.

"We have done what you asked of us," the Wyrr intoned. "We have fulfilled our vows to the gods."

"Yes," Greylock answered. "And now you must wait a little longer. I must rebuild the Gateway."

"No!" the Wyrr cried. "Godshome awakens a final time, Deliverer! Your land will soon be no more. You must lead us to the Homeland now!"

"You don't understand," Greylock said. "The path is too difficult."

"I will tell you this though my people owe you nothing more, Deliverer," the Wyrr said. "An army comes through our land out of the east."

"An army?" Greylock asked, confused. "But we have defeated them!"

"You have but defeated their vanguard, Deliverer," the Wyrr said calmly. "But they will find nothing here. Godshome will bury them."

Greylock shook his head, and when he looked up again the Wyrr was gone, as silently and mysteriously as he had come. The Tyrant could not tell if he had slipped through the narrow door of the icetower or had simply vanished.

CHAPTER SIXTEEN

True to his word, the Wyrr appeared the next morning at the gates of Castle Guardian. Behind him stretched the ragged remnants of his people, many more than Greylock would have believed possible. Kalwyn brought him the news, bursting into his room and exclaiming that the High Plateau was being attacked by demons.

The Tyrant quickly dressed. He had to reach the Wyrrs before they were massacred! Greylock thought in alarm. The frightened soldiers of the High Plateau had had all night to imagine what was destroying the enemy.

The enemy camp had disappeared; even the earthworks had been leveled, their tracks obliterated. In place of the mercenaries of Trold appeared the ghostly pale and emaciated shapes of the Wyrrs. It was difficult to believe that these people had defeated the greatest army of the Underworld, Greylock thought. But there was no other explanation.

The soldiers of the High Plateau lined the walls of the snowcastle when he arrived, clutching their weapons nervously. But the Wyrrs stood quietly and patiently, unarmed and seemingly peaceful. Greylock was thankful that none of his men had lost their composure, or there would have been an end to the Wyrrs that morning, he thought.

Now that they were here Greylock wondered what to do with them. He was certain that they would not turn around at his request and return to the Twilight Dells. The Wyrr the night before had made it clear that they would wait no longer. Nor could he invite them into the High Plateau, he realized, for the stores of food for his own people had fallen below safe levels. Nor, he thought in dismay, could he lead them into the Gateway. If that road had proven too dangerous for a single, skilled climber he knew that the Wyrrs would have no chance at all.

Two occurrences happening at almost the same moment quickly changed his mind.

The first was the most threatening. Though quakes had continued to rumble through the High Plateau, most of its citizens had learned to ignore them. Structural damage to the snowcastles was uncommon and easily repaired.

But the earthquake that struck at that moment was different, and they knew it immediately. Even Castle Guardian, the oldest and strongest of the snowcastles, cracked under the trembling. The white walls opened and spilled soldiers out onto the path of the Gateway, at the Wyrrs' feet. Greylock looked up in time to see the icetower crumble and fall over the edge of the cliff, rolling down the side of the mountain to land beneath the clouds in a pile of snow. It would quickly melt in the Underworld heat.

"Godshome awakes!" The words came unbidden to his mind, and Greylock was unsure if he was remembering them or if the Wyrrs had silently spoken into his mind again. He looked up, startled to find the Wyrrs gazing at him impassively.

The second occurrence would have decided for him if the first already had not. Out of the east appeared the sight of a vast new army, which seemed to fill the Twilight Dells, winding through the entire length of the road to Bordertown. Greylock knew then that King Kasid had come to finish his war against the High Plateau.

"Open the gates!" he cried, and when his men hesitated, the Tyrant turned to Steward Kalwyn impatiently.

"You heard the Tyrant!" the young man cried, swallowing. "Let the demons in!"

The quake had died away, the rumbling sound fading into the distance. But it was only a brief respite. Another, even stronger, quake struck before all the Wyrrs could make it through the gates. Greylock saw several of the beings buried beneath the rocklike ice. The other Wyrrs seemed to pay no attention to their loss. They seemed to be waiting for the Tyrant to lead them, and made no effort to find shelter or to save themselves.

A third quake, slightly less violent, traveled the length of the glacier, opening new fissures in the ice, crumbling the last of the icetowers. Then the mountain seemed to grow quiet.

But the Tyrant had at last had enough warning. He realized that the mountain had only begun its destructive process and that he had been a fool to ignore the Wyrrs and his own instincts. He hoped it wasn't already too late.

There was no choice but the lead the Wyrrs into the caverns, he thought. To leave them on the snows would be to leave them at the mercy of the mountain and King Kasid's army.

And not only the people of the Twilight Dells must go with him, he realized at last, but his own people as well. Yet, he saw little hope of leading his people through the firestone of Godshome unharmed.

Thankfully, most of his people, the women and children, as well as the soldiers, were gathered at Castle Guardian. He wondered if his authority as Tyrant would be enough to convince them to leave their homes for the seeming dead end of the mountain caverns.

Mara must have thought of this problem long before him, for she now showed up on the ramparts leading a sleepy Keyholder. Greylock smiled at her gratefully. If his subjects refused to listen to him, they would surely listen to the old Gatekeeper.

"We must leave the High Plateau," he told the priest as soon as the old man had reached them. "All of us, not just the Wyrrs. Godshome will destroy us if we do not leave now."

Keyholder searched his face intently, and then turned and extended his hands over the crowd. The fearful murmurings of the citizens of the High Plateau stopped abruptly at his gesture.

"The day of Deliverance is at hand!" he cried. "The Gateway has been opened and the home of the gods awaits us beyond the mountain. It is time to leave the cold and the ice for the Homeland!"

"Do you wish us to become demons?" one of the soldiers cried, the face hidden by the crowd. "Why should we leave our snowcastles? We have been through earthquakes and famines before. We have twice defeated the Underworlders. Why should we leave now?"

Greylock was surprised to hear anyone question the Gatekeeper's words, but he realized that what Keyholder was asking seemed too much for even the people of the High Plateau.

The priest's face flushed at the questioning of his command.

"Go to your homes and gather your families," he cried, ignoring the objection. "Bring out your most valuable possessions! For the mountain will surely destroy this land and all who remain!"

"But where will we go?" There was no longer mutiny in the unknown questioner's voice, just dismay and alarm. "Are we to look like demons?"

Though Greylock could not see where the questioner was indicating, he knew that he meant the Wyrrs. Keyholder turned to him helplessly, and the Tyrant realized it was up to him to convince his people to go with him.

"I have been to the land beyond Godshome," he said softly, and all eyes turned to him. "It is a land that is free of demons and yet still green with life. It is our land, if we want it. The Wyrrs will share this land with us for it is what the gods wish. But there is enough room for all." His voice trailed off as he realized from his men's skeptical faces that he was not convincing them. Once again, the mountain spoke more eloquently than he could.

Godshome gave a last awesome shake, throwing most of those standing from their feet. When order was at last restored there were no more objections to Greylock's orders.

The Tyrant took Kalwyn aside and instructed the steward to stay behind with a rear guard until the last of his people had entered the caverns.

"Do not try to fight the Underworlders," he said. "Let them know that the High Plateau is armed and ready for them. I doubt they will attack immediately. They will want to know what has happened to their vanguard first. As soon as the last civilians are in the tunnels, follow us."

Greylock started for the courtyard of the snowcastle, and behind him came the Wyrrs. The citizens of the High Plateau opened up before them uneasily. Greylock saw only a few of his people follow the last of the Wyrrs, and then he was at the head of the staircase down into the network of caverns. As he wound his way down into the hole, with Mara at his side, the Tyrant realized that he would be unable to see more than a few of those that followed him once he had entered the twisting corridors. He would have to trust that all his people would be frightened enough of the mountain's rumblings and the Underworld army to come with him. He would be unable as well, once started, to see how many of those following might be losing their way, and he was certain he would lose some, if not all.

The beginnings of this exodus were not encouraging. The heat of the tunnels had increased since the last time he had been below. As they reached the huge central core, he saw that the entire structure of the lava tubes had been changed radically by the volcanic activity. Instead of the many small tunnels snaking their way through the lava, there were a few great fissures leading straight and unhindered into the mountain.

He turned into the largest of these central caves, fully realizing that the earthquakes that had opened it up could just as easily close the passage shut while they were still inside.

A series of small quakes continued to shatter the rocks of the walls, raining small chips down on them. The Gateway gleamed before them where Greylock had never before seen it. He hurried his pace then, and the Wyrrs followed eagerly. They seemed unafraid, fully trusting in him to lead them to their new land. For the first time he could see hope glinting in their dark eyes. Greylock hoped he wasn't leading them to their destruction.

The unbroken stretch of the Gateway ended, as he had known it eventually would, but the smaller, natural corridors continued again toward the east, and he took them unhesitatingly.

Throughout this nightmare journey they had not needed to light torches, for a soft red glow had filled all the corridors, trickling through the many small rents and tears in the earth's fabric. But not until they were midway through Godshome did they catch sight of the firestone.

Greylock recognized the pit as the same one he had crossed on his journey back from the Homeland, but the lava had subsided to the bottom of the pit, and the waterfall had all but disappeared. In place of his temporary bridge of lava was a jumbled mass of boulders where the roof had caved in, creating a natural path over the fissure.

It was as if the gods were arranging their escape, Greylock thought, for the Gateway started up again on the far side.

They soon entered dark, cool passages that were strangely quiet. The mountain had ceased to tremble around them, and the Tyrant began to breathe a little easier. His memory of the path from this point on contained no special hazards, and he began to hope that they would reach their destination without casualties.

Danger arrived from an unexpected quarter. From far to the rear of the column, out of range of his view, came the sounds of fighting. Greylock knew then that he had guessed wrong, and that King Kasid had not waited to attack, and had even pursued them into the mountain. And this time it would not be so easy to lose pursuit, he thought. The pathway was open, it seemed, all the way through Godshome, his people vulnerable. Even if they managed to reach the Homeland, he realized with dismay, the mercenaries would simply follow them. The battle would continue, and inevitably the stronger, more numerous army of the Underworld would be victorious.

He almost despaired then, but the sight of the Wyrrs standing fearlessly behind him, waiting for him, trusting in him, spurred him to make the final effort.

The far side of the mountain was almost unrecognizable. It was as if it had been pryed open by the gods. The white light of the sun contrasted with the evil red glow of firestone, and Greylock hurried toward it. The sound of fighting followed, coming closer with every second.

When he emerged onto the western slopes of Godshome, he saw that the internal heat of the mountain had melted much of the snow. Small streams rushed down the craggy slopes of lava.

The Wyrrs followed him out onto the slope, protecting their weak eyes against the glare of the sun. The exodus of Wyrrs ended finally, and his own people began to emerge from the caves, looking behind them nervously. Only when he was sure that the last of his people had emerged into daylight did Greylock begin the descent into the Homeland. The sounds of fighting faded slowly behind them.

They reached the bare soil of the Homeland, and there the Wyrrs fell to their knees, digging into the earth with their hands. Greylock felt as though a great burden had been lifted from his shoulders.

But this concern was quickly replaced by the even greater worry over the battle above them. There were few men of fighting age among those who had reached the Homeland. The women and children stared anxiously back up the mountain, straining to see who would emerge onto the muddy slopes.

They did not have to wait long. The battered and beaten soldiers of the High Plateau came stumbling out of the Gateway. The cheers of those waiting died away as they saw that there were far fewer survivors than they had hoped. Greylock saw the tall, slender shape of Kalwyn emerge last, clutching his side, but motioning his men. They reeled down the slopes, in full retreat, defeated.

The men of the plateau had already staggered onto the level plains of the Homeland before the first soldiers of the Underworld appeared, lining the portals from the mountain with an imperious and arrogant assurance. They did not fear attack. The enemy soldiers continued to emerge from the mountain, filling the slopes with row upon row of ordered phalanxes.

The Tyrant watched helplessly from below. The Wyrrs had already vanished into the woodlands, and the men of the High Plateau had collapsed around him. There would be no further resistance to the awesome might of Trold.

When the last of the mercenaries had come to attention, facing the Homeland, there was silence. Greylock wondered what they were waiting for. Could they not see that they had won?

Suddenly, two small figures appeared between the soldiers guarding the mountain's exit. Greylock recognized them immediately. The luminous glow of Silverfrost's hair was unmistakable. Beside her stood a small man of imperial bearing, dressed in black. Greylock could tell by the subservient manner of the soldiers that this was King Kasid, but he could see nothing remarkable about the man. Silverfrost stood near the monarch possessively, and even from this distance Greylock could see the triumph in her gestures. With a wave of her arms the huge army began to descend the slopes in slow, measured steps.

Godshome gave no warning when it finally gave vent to the pressures that had been building up within its core. It exploded, tearing away the top of the peak. To those below it seemed as if the mountainside had dropped out from under the feet of the Underworld army, only to surge outward again, merging the stuff of the earth and that of life, fusing them together forever.

The last thing Greylock saw before the force of the eruption knocked him from his feet was the glowing hair of Silverfrost dropping into the cauldron, as she ripped frantically at the man in black, trying to climb over him to safety. But there was no escape from this holocaust, he thought at that moment, no one to plead with, or seduce, or betray. The forces of the earth gave no thought to her charms, but took her and mixed the strands of her hair with the granite of the earth.

When the Tyrant picked himself off the ground he saw that the entire side of the mountain had collapsed inward, exposing the huge caverns at the core. The top of the mountain was gone altogether, and with it, Greylock sensed with a mixture of awe and relief, had gone the vast powers of the fiefdoms of Trold. Soon, the subject countries on the far side of the mountain would come to realize the weakness of Trold, he thought, and would fight for their freedom. Bordertown would soon be free, and the farmers allowed to till their fields in peace.

But that was on the other side of Godshome, he thought with satisfaction, and thus no longer concerned him. A huge cloud was hovering over the remnant of Godshome, as if uncertain where to go. As Greylock watched, a wind came out of the west, blowing the dust and ash away from the Homeland.

He looked down suspiciously, but Mara gave no sign of wielding her wind-witchery. Instead, she looked radiant, and for the first time he noticed that her waist had widened. Only then did he fully realize that the destruction of Godshome and the High Plateau was not the end, but the beginning of a new life in the Homeland.

ABOUT THE AUTHOR

Duncan grew up and spent most of his life in Central Oregon, the dry side of the Cascades, and whose terrain is featured in many of his books. He wrote several books out of college, including the heroic fantasy novels *Star Axe*, *Snowcastles*, and *Icetowers*. In 1984, he and his wife Linda bought Pegasus Books in downtown Bend, Oregon, which they still own and operate. They also ran a used bookstore, the Bookmark, for 15 years.

In the last five years, he's been able to get back to writing again, and found that he has a lot of pent-up creative energy. He's written numerous books for several different publishers, mostly in the horror or dark fantasy genres, though recently has been branching out into fantasy again, as well as thrillers.

BIBLIOGRAPHY

The Tuskers Series
Tuskers I: Wild Pig Apocalypse
Tuskers II: Day of the Long Pig
Tuskers III: Omnivore Wars
Tuskers IV: Rise of the Cloven

The Vampire Evolution Trilogy
Book I: Death of an Immortal
Book II: Rule of Vampire
Book III: Blood of Gold

The Virginia Reed Adventures
Led to the Slaughter
The Dead Spend No Gold
The Darkness You Fear

Other books
Star Axe
Snowcastles & Icetowers

Blood of the Succubus
Castle La Magie
Deadfall Ridge
Eden's Return
Faerie Punk
Freedy Filkins
Gargoyle Dreams
I Live Among You
Shadows over Summer House
Snaked
Takeover